THE

LOST

JEWELS

Also by Kirsty Manning

The Song of the Jade Lily

THE
LOST
JEWELS

A
Novel

KIRSTY MANNING

wm
WILLIAM MORROW
An Imprint of HarperCollins*Publishers*

P.S.™ is a trademark of HarperCollins Publishers.

THE LOST JEWELS. Copyright © 2020 by Osetra Pty Ltd. All rights reserved. Printed in the United States of America. No part of this book may be used or reproduced in any manner whatsoever without written permission except in the case of brief quotations embodied in critical articles and reviews. For information, address HarperCollins Publishers, 195 Broadway, New York, NY 10007.

HarperCollins books may be purchased for educational, business, or sales promotional use. For information, please email the Special Markets Department at SPsales@harper collins.com.

Originally published as *The Lost Jewels* in Australia in 2020 by Allen & Unwin.

FIRST U.S. EDITION

Library of Congress Cataloging-in-Publication Data has been applied for.

ISBN 978-0-06-288202-8
ISBN 978-0-06-300714-7 (hardcover library edition)

20 21 22 23 24 LSC 10 9 8 7 6 5 4 3 2 1

For Henry, who showed me London anew.

Stay curious, adventurous, and true.

Beauty is truth, truth beauty—that is all
Ye know on earth, and all ye need to know.

John Keats
"Ode on a Grecian Urn"

Prologue

The smoke was so thick she had to draw her apron across her mouth. Her long braids were singed black from falling firedrops. They'd need to be chopped off; Mama would be furious. But she had made a promise to Papa—she had to see it through, even though the roar of flames raced through the narrow cobblestone streets.

No one would be missing her yet. Mama would be passing under London Bridge in the longboat with the baby, both wrapped in heavy woolen blankets to protect them from the embers raining down. The girl had begged, then pushed mother and baby into the overcrowded boat as barrels of oil and tallow exploded behind her, promising she would jump in the next boat behind.

"Think of the baby. Papa would—"

Her words had been whipped away by the searing easterly, and the boat was swallowed by the haze as it left the dock. Onshore was chaos as families unloaded trunks and leather buckets filled with their most precious goods. Horses snorted with terror and threw their heads back. Hooves clanged against cobblestones. The beasts' ears were pinned back with fear.

The girl was grateful her mama and little Samuel were gone. Safe.

The flustered captain had braced his leg against the timber wharf to steady the boat. He'd held out a hand to the girl, but she'd stepped backward into the smoke and shower of embers, turned on her heels and ran.

She'd kept running uphill—away from the Thames—until she could make out the line of St. Paul's steeple, tall and gray against the orange sky. The cathedral's stones exploded like gunpowder as she fought her way through the panicking crowds streaming toward the river.

Her steps slowed now as she trod carefully, looking down to avoid the rivulets of lead and shit flowing over the cobbles. She put a hand out to feel her way along the walls. Her fingers trailed across rough timber beams as her boots crunched over broken glass.

The girl had lived and played in these streets and lanes all her life, and she counted them as she passed. Ironmonger, King, Honey, Milk, Wood, Butter . . . then Foster Lane.

Almost home.

The two buildings flanking hers were engulfed in red flames. Men with rolled-up sleeves were trying to douse the fire with paltry buckets of water. The fire hissed and roared up the walls and across the wooden shingles, as if laughing at the people below.

"Get away—"

"It's too late—"

"—dray to Blackfriars—"

"—St. Paul's is afire—"

It was too late to turn back. Not when she was so close to home. Not when she'd promised Papa . . .

The frenzied chimes of St. Mary-le-Bow's church drew her closer, and she inched through the thick smoke. When she felt the familiar wrought-iron number beside her front door, she threw herself against the door and forced it open.

As horses cantered past and people scrambled to climb onto carts headed for the docks or beyond the city walls, nobody paid any attention as the girl slipped inside number thirty-two.

Her chest was burning, as if with each breath she was drawing the fire deep into her lungs. Tears formed, but she wiped them away with her filthy sleeve. Now was not the time for self-pity.

Instead, she fell to her knees and crawled over the blue Persian carpet in the entry hall and into the tiny room beyond—Papa's special workshop.

Quick as a lark, she removed the key tied to a ribbon around her neck. She kept it tucked under her clothes whenever he was away on one of his trips, like a talisman to sing him home.

The firestorm surged. Heat poured in through the smashed windows and the open front door. The thunk of timber beams and collapsing houses surrounded her. The shingles atop her own roof started to smolder and whistle. Time was running out.

The girl unlocked the door and hurried down the narrow stairs.

Stepping into the chilly cellar she felt a moment's relief; it was so calm, so quiet, after the tumult of the streets.

She squatted to find the telltale bump in the dirt. It was their secret, and she had to retrieve it; she knew Papa would understand. She'd promised him she would look after Mama and little Samuel, but the coins hastily wrapped in Mama's shawl wouldn't last long. She mumbled a quick prayer, then seized the shovel stowed in the corner and started to dig.

Chapter 1

DR. KATE KIRBY

BOSTON, PRESENT DAY

Luxury-magazine editor Jane Rivers had been the one to offer Kate the trip to London for the Cheapside story.

The call had come when Kate was sitting at her desk in the library of her unrenovated Boston brownstone, sipping hot chocolate sprinkled with cinnamon and shivering under a gray woolen blanket with a heater blasting at her feet. Technically, her parents still owned the house—it had been in the family for four generations—but no one wanted to live with the drafts and the damp, musty smells of yesteryear.

No one except Kate.

The study was her favorite room—and the only one she'd sealed and finished. It was grand, but comfortable, with floor-to-ceiling bookshelves lining three walls, her great-grandfather's desk, and a peacock-blue sofa that Kate slept on far more often than she cared to admit.

On the wall opposite her desk was a framed bill of sale for the first steamer her great-grandparents had bought back in 1915: the SS *Esther Rose*, named for her great-grandmother Essie. On the desk itself sat a framed photograph of her glorious four-year-old niece, Emma, squeezing her King Charles spaniel, Mercutio— terrible name for a dog, but Molly had insisted. (Kate's sister had very strong feelings about secondary characters in Shakespeare's plays.) Beside the photo was a journal Kate had begun four years before. She didn't write in the journal anymore; she hadn't, in fact, after the first nine months. But she couldn't bring herself to throw it away either, or to put it in a box with other keepsakes from that year.

Now this call. "Can you be in London next Monday for a huge investigative feature? We'd need you there for at least a week, I think. I realize it's short notice . . ." Jane's voice was all East Coast vowels and courtesy, but there was a hint of a plea.

"What's the job?"

"It's the Cheapside jewels."

Kate's skin started to tingle. "Finally! Who'd you bribe?"

"I promised the cover and both gatefolds in exchange for the exclusive. We want to cover this before *Time*, *Vogue*, or *Vanity Fair* get to it. The Museum of London just finished recataloging and some restoration of the jewels last week. It will be the final chance to access this collection before the museum relocates to West Smithfield in a year or so. Advertisers are already bidding. De Beers, Cartier . . . the whole lot." She paused, delicately it seemed. "There's, ah, a ton of interest and cash this side of the Atlantic—our competitors will be livid. The CEO and chairman are tripping over themselves—they're sure this series will bring people back to the print magazine. Gemstones look so much better in print than on-screen."

It was true. A beautifully lit photo printed on good-quality stock was the next best thing to actually touching the jewels. But the method of reproduction was only a secondary concern for Kate. It was the story itself that compelled her; the urge to deep-dive into history and pluck something original from all the facts that had been overlooked—or forgotten.

"Now, I'm about to go into a meeting, so is it a yes or no?" pushed Jane. "I have a big budget, and I don't need to tell you how rare that is these days. But for this series I've been authorized to cover any travel required."

"You mean in addition to London?"

"Well, I take it the jewels didn't start their life there. So diamond mines, for a start."

"I get it," said Kate. "I could really cover some ground."

Jane chuckled. "Thought you'd appreciate that."

"Thanks. And thank you for thinking of me."

There was an awkward pause.

"Well, the suits upstairs were actually pushing for the Smith-sonian's Jocelyn Cassidy, but the Museum of London weren't keen on that idea . . . and I understand you know the museum's current director, Professor Wright, from Oxford?"

"Of course."

"She tells me your research in this area is unparalleled. And the last piece you did for me—on Bulgari—was excellent. It was an unusual angle, but I liked that. It was quirky."

"The artistic director would only agree to be interviewed over lunch. Ridiculously long lunches. It was actually my duty to eat pasta and drink a carafe of Chianti every day for a week."

"Can't promise food this time, I'm afraid! Just priceless jewels. So, what do you say? We need to move quickly on this."

Priceless jewels . . . and the Museum of London, Kate thought to herself. "I have a few things on my plate at the moment," she hedged. "Let me take a look at my calendar and call you back." They finished the call, with Jane promising to forward what information she had on the collection.

Kate leaned back in her chair and gathered her curls into a ponytail, tugged the blanket tighter around her shoulders, and sipped the rest of her cocoa as she compiled a mental list of things that would have to be done before she left for London. There was an insurance report due in the next two weeks for her Swiss client. Scattered across her desk was a series of photos of some archival pieces Cartier was planning to show in Paris during Fashion Week. Underneath that was the synopsis for her postdoctoral fellowship at Harvard, due next month. Right at the bottom was a brown envelope stamped with a silver fern containing her divorce papers. She needed to sign the papers for Jonathan's lawyer, then move on. Everything had been settled—everything except her heart. Kate sighed and reached for the envelope, then withdrew her hand. *Later,* she promised.

Instead, she picked up the synopsis, screwing up her nose at the number of red annotations, each representing an error she needed to fix. After a moment, her eyes were drawn to some fine black-ink sketches she had stored in archival glassine envelopes to protect from air and dust until she moved them back into her filing cabinet.

The first was of two little girls with their heads together, laughing. They wore identical dresses and aprons, and they both had messy braids tumbling over their shoulders. The second sketch was of a cockerel standing proud, and the third was an exquisite jumble of roses, rings, necklaces, oranges, and grapes, all overlapping so there was hardly any white space on the page. On the flip side was some kind of herbal recipe written with a childlike scrawl:

2 spoons honey
pinch of thyme leaves
ground peppercorns
squeeze of lemon (fresh)
(Add to boiling tea, or water)

The last sketch was of a brooch, or perhaps a button, shaped like a rose. Gemstones were studded at the center and along the petals. Kate had no idea what kind of stones they were—without color there was no way to tell—but the design was similar to images of Elizabethan buttons she'd come across while doing research for her doctorate. Buttons that were in the Museum of London . . .

She turned over the first envelope and admired the lines of sinewy limbs and loose braids. Both girls had dimples and dark hair—like Essie, Kate, and all the Kirby kin. Would Noah have grown up with these same dimples pressed into chubby cheeks? Her bones ached for the baby boy who'd never drawn breath. She pressed away tears with her palms and studied the little girls.

Kate had found the drawings among Essie's private papers in the filing cabinets she'd inherited with the brownstone. Her parents had dismissed these sketches as little more than Essie's private doodles. After all, they were scratched across neat columns—as if hastily written in a bookkeeping ledger; Essie had insisted on doing the bookkeeping for the fledgling shipping company she had started with her husband. Her parents had thought they should be discarded, but Kate couldn't bear to part with them. She liked to imagine her youthful great-grandmother doodling in the margins in a quiet moment, wild curls wrestled behind her ears, a cup of steaming Irish breakfast tea beside her as she looked out across the busy shipyards.

Hearing the ping of an incoming email, Kate put down the sketches and clicked her computer screen on. The email was from Jane and, as promised, there were a number of attachments. Kate opened them one by one, scrolling through a series of newspaper clippings from 1914 heralding the launch of a jewelry exhibition at the newly minted Museum of London.

ANTIQUE JEWELRY ON DISPLAY AT THE
LONDON MUSEUM
*Secret Hoard of Elizabethan or Jacobean Jewels Added to
Priceless Collections*

MYSTERIOUS JEWELRY HOARD
Romance at Every Turn at London's Museum

SECRET UNEARTHED
London's Buried Treasures

TREASURE TROVE IN CENTER OF LONDON
Workmen's Extraordinary Discovery

She scanned the clippings, noting descriptions of the media frenzy and the crush of the crowds at the museum. She picked up her phone and called her editor.

"Hello, Jane. I'm looking at the articles about the 1914 exhibition now. Thanks for sending these through."

"Good! You can see details about the discovery were vague."

"Weren't the jewels found in 1912? I wonder why it took two years for the collection to be announced to the public."

"Who knows? I'm hoping you can find something new there."

Kate sat back in her chair and scrolled through the clippings once again, almost forgetting she was on the phone until she heard Jane ask, "So will you go to London? I need to know now . . ."

"Oh!" The chance to research the provenance of the mysterious Cheapside jewels was certainly tempting, and—she glanced once more at her great-grandmother's sketch of the brooch or button—perhaps she might have an opportunity to do a little personal research on the side. "Okay," she said. "I'm in."

"Great." Jane sounded relieved. "Professor Wright will be available to brief you and the photographer on Monday at nine a.m. Does that work for you?"

"Sure, thanks." Kate was about to ask who the photographer was, when Jane cut her off.

"Monday it is then—nine o'clock at the Museum of London. Email me your passport details, and I'll have my assistant book your flight and a hotel near the museum. Choose a handful of key pieces. Go tight. I want origins. You have a month to file."

"But, Jane, nobody knows the origins of—"

"Exactly. I want you to uncover the stories nobody else has."

Chapter 2

KATE

LONDON, PRESENT DAY

Why would someone bury a bucket of precious jewels and gemstones and never return?

It was all Kate could think about as she scrawled her signature on pages of disclaimers and security forms at the research desk of the Museum of London.

"Dr. Kirby, we expect you to wear this lanyard at all times," the receptionist informed her with the crisp efficiency of a prison warden. "This gives you access to our viewing room—accompanied by security guards, of course—for today only, after which the jewels will be returned to our storage vault. Does that give you enough time?"

"I hope so. If not, will you let me take them home?"

The receptionist chose to ignore Kate's lame attempt at a joke. "You'll have to take that up with the director. Take the service stairs down to the basement, please. Professor Wright is waiting for you."

"What about the photographer?" Kate asked.

"Your colleague will be joining you shortly. We are just trying to find somewhere to put his . . . gear."

The young woman tapped her pen on the desk in apparent irritation, but couldn't completely hide the whisper of a grin. Kate sighed. She knew instantly who the photographer assigned to this story was—she'd seen this look a hundred times.

"Mr. Brown?" The receptionist waved a security guard over. "Please escort Dr. Kirby downstairs."

The guard led Kate downstairs into the basement, each of them tapping their lanyards on locks in the stairwell to gain access to the next level.

The museum stairwell felt more prison than museum, and it took a few minutes for Kate's eyes to adjust to the dim lighting. With every step taking her deeper underground, she imagined murky layers of Viking tools and plague pits pressing up against the concrete foundations. Slicing through the middle would be red ash from when the furious Celtic queen Boadicea set the city ablaze. Debris from the Great Fire and the Blitz would be scattered among the top layers of soil.

Now it was all blanketed by the Museum of London, with its tunnels, pipes, and cables linking the museum to neighboring skyscrapers. You had to hand it to London: she was the queen of reinvention. For more than two thousand years, London had picked herself up and raised her fist—like the defiant Boadicea—at anyone who tried to quash her.

London also buried her secrets deep in the layers of damp bog.

Kate needed to uncover at least one of them.

"Here we are," said the guard as he keyed a code into a number pad on a steel door and shoved it open with his shoulder. "After you, Dr. Kirby."

Kate stepped through the door into a fluorescent-lit, low-ceilinged room that was part laundromat and part middle-school science lab. Rows of tables covered in leather and velvet dissected the room, and a pair of women in lab coats peered into microscopes or maneuvered pieces onto felt-backed mounts. Pieces Kate recognized from the articles Jane had sent.

"Dr. Kirby—Kate. At last! Welcome." The elegant museum director crossed the room with her arms outstretched. "I trust you had no problems signing in."

"It's great to see you, Lucia," Kate said, beaming as she stepped into the older woman's embrace.

Lucia Wright's dark hair had the faintest silver threads at the temples, and her body—toned and lithe from years of marathon running—seemed almost waiflike in her navy Chanel suit. Kate rested her head briefly on her mentor's shoulder and breathed in her jasmine perfume—a blast of summer in this sterile room.

When they drew apart, Lucia put a maternal hand to Kate's cheek.

"You look . . . well," she said softly, a strange alloy of pride and sympathy in her gaze.

Kate broke eye contact and glanced across at the security guard, who seemed a little bewildered by this familiar greeting.

Ten years ago, Professor Lucia Wright had supervised Kate for her PhD in medieval and Elizabethan history at Oxford, and the pair had become friends. It had been Lucia who had recommended the young historian to private collectors in

Hong Kong and Dubai, as well as several industry publications, after she graduated. Whenever Lucia was in the US and Kate was home in Boston, they would meet. It had been a little over four years since they'd caught up in person. Neither had had the slightest premonition back on that sunlit morning over espressos and panini that Kate's life was about to implode . . .

Turning to face her mentor once more, she said, "I'm fine." A half-truth. A lump started to form in her throat. She smoothed the curl at her temple back into her ponytail.

"When Jane called to say she was hoping to commission you to write the exclusive piece I was thrilled. You deserve this . . ." Lucia tilted her head to the side. "Make no mistake, Kate—you were granted access because your research work is the best. I know you will give these pieces the coverage they deserve."

Kate swallowed and met her mentor's eyes with a silent thanks. A shadow on the far wall caught her eye. She glanced across the room, straining to see the fine gold and enamel floral chain a dark-haired woman was stitching very precisely onto a velvet-lined board.

"We have the handful of pieces you requested laid out for you in the locked room next door. Hard to narrow it down from over four hundred items, isn't it?" Lucia gave a sympathetic smile. "The photographer is running late, I'm afraid. He came straight from Heathrow. Front desk is just trying to work out what to do with his surfboard." She tapped her left foot in frustration as she looked at her watch.

"The photographer is Marcus Holt, I gather?" Kate tried to keep her voice even, but Lucia caught her rolling her eyes.

"You know him?" Lucia cocked an eyebrow.

Everyone knew Marcus Holt's reputation as an energetic photographer who shot cover stories for every prestige publication, from *Vogue* to *National Geographic*.

"Of course! Jane introduced us a couple of years ago at a jewelry fair in Hong Kong. We've worked on a few stories . . ." Kate shrugged. "He's Australian," she added, as if that should explain everything.

Lucia's eyes met Kate's.

"He's very relaxed . . ."

"Clearly!" Lucia looked at her watch.

"He doesn't just get it done, he brings out the beauty—the magic—in his images. Marcus sees things other people miss."

"Excellent. Hopefully you'll discover something new while you are in London." Lucia's brown eyes twinkled with encouragement.

There was no need to mention the sketches tucked neatly into the back of her notebook. Not yet, anyway.

"Hope he gets here soon. I have to be at a board meeting in thirty minutes, then in the city for the rest of the afternoon trying to convince our major donors to chip in for this new site. You're coming to the party tonight at The Goldsmiths' Company, I hope?"

"Of course," Kate replied. "Sophie sent me an invitation as soon as I told her I was coming to London." She heard a card tap, a security beep, and a click as the door unlocked.

"Professor Wright. So sorry I'm late." The tall photographer strode into the room, black camera bag flung over one shoulder. He took Lucia's slender hand in his and beamed. Uncombed sandy hair just brushed his shoulders, and his dark eyes shone. "I'm Marcus Holt. Thrilled to be here. Thanks so much—"

Lucia cut him off briskly as two pink apples appeared on her cheeks. "Happy to have you." She gave a little cough to clear her throat. "And you know Dr. Kate Kirby, of course."

"Of course! Hello, Dr. Kirby."

He turned toward Kate and gave her a quick peck on the cheek, his unshaven face abrasive against her skin. He smelled of sweat and salt water.

She eyed his crumpled linen shirt and couldn't help herself. "Did you surf here?"

"Might as well have. Delays at Heathrow . . ." He dropped his smile for a moment, eyes apologetic. "Hey, I'm really sorry to keep you waiting." He casually swung the camera bag onto the table and grabbed a second bag from the security guard. "Thanks, mate."

Lucia was back to business and eager to be on her way.

"Now let me introduce you to our team." She beckoned to the pair of women who had paused in their work at Marcus's arrival. "This is Saanvi Singh, conservator of jewelry," Lucia said, introducing the dark-haired woman. "And Gayle Woods, curator of medieval arts."

Marcus and Kate shook hands with each.

"I was in Geneva last year—your paper on medieval brooch restoration was amazing," Kate told the conservator. "I've been quoting it ever since." She smiled. "Hope you don't mind if I pick your brains while I'm here. I've got a big list of questions to ask."

Saanvi blushed and nodded.

Lucia beamed at Kate. "Sounds like we got just the right person." She turned to Marcus. "Jane assured me you two make a great team."

"We do," said Marcus, smiling. "As long as I do exactly what Dr. Kirby here instructs."

Not for the first time, Kate was struck by his easy manner and casual, just-off-the-beach charm. He was comfortable around couture designers and jewelers, but equally attentive to academics and journalists.

"Now, I can't let either of you touch any of the jewels," Lucia warned. "I know you've signed the paperwork and all the non-disclosures, but I just have to make that very clear."

Kate nodded, then looked at the photographer.

He shrugged. "Sure," he agreed.

Kate's heart started to race as Lucia keyed in the code to enter the safe room. Who knew what stories she was about to uncover? When most people looked at a gemstone or a piece of jewelry they saw astonishing beauty and exquisite devotion from their creators. Love and hope. But her job as a historian was to look past the shimmer and try to work out how each piece was made—and, importantly, why. It was up to her to join the dots between the craftsman and the recipient. Sometimes she found a trail of broken hearts and betrayal. Even murder. It was a puzzle Kate never tired of trying to solve.

She took a deep breath to steady her pulse as she stepped into the vault. Her eyes jumped between three rows of tables covered with velvet displaying ribbons of enameled gold necklaces, to pools of sapphires and turquoise, from a row of gold buttons and diamond rings to the biggest emerald she'd ever seen, sitting atop a pedestal. The hairs on her forearms stood on end.

"Boom!" said Marcus as he entered the room with his camera bag. "I get how that person felt when they found the first uncut diamond rough glinting in the light. Gets me in the guts every time."

"Me too," said Kate as she steadied herself against the closest table with her hand. She didn't dare admit that sometimes her first glimpse of a famous jewel she had longed to see could be disappointing. Like meeting Tom Cruise and discovering he was much smaller in real life. Or when David Beckham started to speak with a high-pitched voice. How could reality ever compete with the retouched glossy images presented to the world?

But there was no disappointment this time.

Saanvi shot Kate a knowing look and ushered her across to the far table. "Hard to believe this collection was buried sometime in the 1600s." She waved at the enamel necklaces. "Those are pristine. They'd never have survived this long if they'd been worn. The enamel would have rubbed off, and the gold and jewels been sold or reworked and reset. If we start over here, I've laid out some of the pieces you requested. The rest are in the room we were just in for checking before they are packed back into storage. Here . . ."

Kate stepped to the edge of the velvet-draped table, angled the light, and leaned down using the eyepiece she pulled from her kit bag to study a pale cameo—a Byzantine pendant. The catalog image hadn't prepared her for the soft drape of the robes, the repentant tilt of a head.

"White sapphire?"

"Yes. It's St. Thomas. This taller figure with his hands raised is Jesus, proving to his apostle that he was nailed to the cross."

"Then rose again." Kate longed to run a finger across the relief of St. Thomas and the contours of the gold mount. Instead, she reached for her notebook and pen and started to take notes.

The Incredulity of St. Thomas—most famously painted by Caravaggio.

She paused . . .

Here, in the relief of a translucent sapphire, Kate felt witness to something intimate and tender.

Top of pendant is a single natural pearl—piety and hope.

Trust and devotion. Unconditional love and hope.

A talisman for someone to wear close to their heart?

She imagined the Byzantine jewelry workshop crammed between stalls selling squeaky white cheeses, lemon-scented honey cakes, toasted pistachios, and syrupy sweetmeats in front of the Great Palace in Constantinople. The lapidary craning over the gemstone in a sliver of light from his open window, whittling away the grooves with a tiny chisel and hammer to carve the hairline before polishing it on a stone wheel.

"Who's that?" Marcus pointed at the teardrop pendant from the far side of the table as he set up his camera and spotlights.

"Doubting Thomas," said Kate.

"Aren't we all?" he quipped as he screwed a wide lens onto his camera. He'd angled the lights over the jewelry, and a dark shadow obscured his face. There were stress lines at his eyes and across his brow.

Kate turned back to her work and scribbled *Doubting Thomas* in her notebook, and circled it.

Doubt was never far from her shoulder. Each day she asked, "What if?" in essays and articles. Her life was consumed with questions of the past. Her ex, Jonathan, had said as much the day he'd left her for New Zealand two years ago. He'd decided to take a different path to healing—apparently Kate was no match for pristine mountains and endless fly-fishing.

"Katie," he'd said with his typical surgeon's plainspeak, "you spend all this time traveling around the world chasing other people's stories. When you're home, you're hiding in that library wallowing in the past, looking at other people's treasures. When are you going to look up?"

But Jonathan could never understand what a joy it was to spend hours deep in books and archives, studying precious jewels that whispered secrets from long ago.

At the opposite table was a trio of cameos made to be worn at the neck: a Florentine portrait; Queen Elizabeth in Spanish Armada–style; and an intricate carving of Aesop's fable "The Dog and the Shadow." These spoke of seventeenth-century London. Home to immigrants and traveling artisans and craftsmen who crisscrossed the oceans and traveled silk routes, laden with wooden chests and saddlebags filled with spices, seeds, and gold.

"Kate?" Marcus had finished setting up.

He stood in front of a cluster of emerald pieces gathered together, glinting and drawing the eye like a line of showgirls.

An emerald watch, a salamander brooch, and a parrot cameo. Saanvi picked up the salamander in her gloved hand and held it up under one of the spotlights. The creature had been picked out in circles of emeralds soldered together with gold links. Kate wanted to poke her fingers into the tiny mouth dotted with black enamel because she was certain she would feel teeth. The brooch was turned over to reveal twin curved pins to secure the salamander to a hat, and more flecks of black enamel on a white belly that looked like the finest strands of hair.

"The mystical creature who rose from the fire, the salamander," said Saanvi.

Kate tilted her head. It was one of the collection's most iconic pieces, five hundred years old, and yet she didn't know what to make of it. It was trying to tell her something . . . but what?

Marcus pointed at the hexagonal emerald watch as big as a baby's fist. "I'll shoot this first. I've never seen an emerald so big. Is it Colombian?" he asked.

Saanvi nodded. "Muzo. I can't believe this stone didn't splinter when they carved out the inside for the watch. We think the watch parts could have been made and assembled in Geneva."

Kate sucked in her breath. It was the most spectacular and audacious pairing of craftsmanship and imagination she was likely to see in her lifetime. If anybody ever asked her again why she worked as a jewelry historian, she'd simply point them to this exquisite emerald-cased watch. She copied the precise dimensions from Saanvi's catalog and then jotted down some questions.

Was emerald cut in London? What cities would it have passed through?

Royalty or wealthy aristocrat?

The next display was a series of bejeweled enamel buttons, together with some enamel necklaces with flowers: roses, bluebells, and pansies.

Kate leaned over the last four buttons, gathered in a separate velvet box, and checked to see that Saanvi and Marcus were busy setting up the shot for the emerald watch. While the photographer moved to his bag to grab a different lens, she slipped the clear envelope with Essie's sketches from the back of her notebook and held it beside the buttons.

"Where'd you get that picture?" asked Marcus as he came up behind Kate's shoulder. "It's the same button, isn't it?"

Kate flinched and put her index finger to her lips as his eyes widened in recognition. She'd spent years trying to access these buttons at the museum, and the picture did appear to be similar to the jewels in front of her.

Essie—or whoever had drawn Essie's pictures—had captured the likeness. The spirit. Kate imagined a line of these beauties down the back of a prim Elizabethan gown, or used to tether a gentleman's cape as it flew behind him atop a galloping horse. Her great-grandmother could have seen a button like this anywhere. There was no proof that Essie's sketch was of a Cheapside button.

Marcus's eyes flicked across to where Saanvi was setting up a shot in the lightbox, then to Kate as he sucked in his breath. He mouthed, "Sorry," and raised an eyebrow.

Kate shrugged and slipped the image back into her notebook, hoping he would get the hint.

As Marcus left her standing beside the buttons, she realized that matching this picture to them didn't prove a thing. The buttons were similar, that was all.

She glanced at the emerald watch and thought of Essie. Her great-grandmother had had the Irish gift of the gab and would sing Kate to sleep in her crib with wild tales of leprechauns and fairy queens. She spoon-fed her folklore and history with every mouthful of boiled potatoes and onions.

But Kate's favorite was the tale of a mysterious man who bewitched Essie with his emerald eyes in Cheapside.

Chapter 3

ESTHER MURPHY

LONDON, 1912

The jewels were discovered the same day Essie Murphy fell in love. She had her brother to thank for both, of course—though in the years to come she'd often wonder which one came first.

A buried bucket of jewels.

A man with emerald eyes.

The tale would become as much a part of her Irish folklore as Midir and Étaín. Cut and polished over the years, with the roughs tossed out with the sorrow, betrayal, and loss. No one would know it had begun as equal parts tragedy and romance.

That fateful morning, Essie had pulled the front door shut behind her and prayed her mother was drunk enough to remain in bed.

Freddie had left at dawn for his long walk to work. It was up to Essie to walk her sisters to school before she too started work.

Behind her, the little twins Flora and Maggie giggled as they sat on the front step. Gertie, who was older, bent down to fasten their laces, snatching their skinny ankles and saying, "Stop moving about or I'll tie these laces together. See how far you'll get!"

The girls each lifted their pinafores to reveal boy's boots that were several sizes too big.

Gertie gave Maggie's leg a sharp tug as the little girl wriggled. "I'm warning you . . ." she said, blue eyes blazing.

Essie sighed as Flora tugged at a gaping hole in her black woolen stocking and waggled her finger like a worm. Maggie put her hands over her mouth and started to giggle, before it dissolved into a hacking cough. Essie bent down and patted Maggie's back to soothe her, worrying as she felt the child's bones jutting through the thin fabric. Their braids still reeked of sarsaparilla—remnants of the Rankin's oil Essie had massaged into everyone's heads last night to at least try to get rid of the lice that kept them scratching all night.

Gertie looked up with softer eyes and met Essie's gaze before looking away with a gulp. "Every damn day . . ." she muttered.

"Gertie. Enough!" But Essie's scolding felt hollow.

There was nothing in the house for breakfast. Ma had fed the last hard crusts to the chickens. But the chicks were so hungry they were laying only every other day, and now all residents of their Southwark garden flat were starting their day with empty stomachs. Again.

"Up you get, girls," said Gertie with a weary voice much older than her thirteen years. "Here, each of you take one of my hands."

"Sing us a song, Gertie," begged Flora.

"Please," her twin chimed in.

The trio leaped onto the footpath ahead of Essie, and Gertie started to half sing "Colcannon"—a folk song about creamy mashed potatoes stirred through with green herbs, spring onions, and kale. Essie rolled her eyes. Trust Gertie to sing about food they couldn't have. "Really, Gertie," she said, "I don't think—"

But the twins started to sing tunelessly as they stumbled along, trying to keep up with Gertie in their too-big boots, looking like a pair of sailors after too many pints.

Or their mother any day of the week.

Essie tried to swallow her anger and resentment. Ma hadn't always been like this, and she didn't want the little girls to grow up hating their mother.

Every Halloween, Ma used to mix a batch of buttery mashed potato with bacon and herbs in her favorite skillet pot and poke in a coin, a button, and a gold ring. Gertie always got the button in her bowl, and Da would tickle her tummy and declare there was no man in Ireland good enough for his girls anyway.

Essie picked her way along the footpath, trying to remember when Ma had last made up a pot of mashed potato mixed with scallions, milk, pepper, and bacon.

Not since they came to live in London.

Certainly not since Da shipped out to fight the Boers, never to return.

As the girls skipped and chanted in front, Essie stepped off the footpath to avoid a hunched man pushing a barrow of snails.

The fishmonger, Mr. Foster, tipped his hat to the girls as he finished rolling up his sleeves to add silver flounder to a mountain he'd already piled onto a wooden board—a shilling for the lot— while plates of haddock, whiting, and herring sat on his counter.

Behind him, a shelf was crowded with mustard pickles that could be added to the fish order for just a penny.

Da used to love his fish on a Friday . . .

"Don't forget to fix your account by Frid'y. There'll be none till you do." Mr. Foster waggled a warning finger at Essie as she hurried the girls past.

Essie tugged at Gertie's sleeve to cross the road to avoid the crumpet man standing on the corner in his dirty black coat with a wooden tray perched on his head. Even though the tray was covered with a length of green baize, the unmistakable smell of freshly baked dough, butter, and cinnamon filled the dusty air.

One of Gertie's classmates approached the man, and he hoisted the tray from his head and rested it at his hip as the child pulled back the cloth and took her time before clutching a crumpet with both hands. As she held it up to take a bite, Essie looked the other way.

They reached the school gate. In the playground, boys whooped as they chased metal hoops with sticks. Girls laughed and squealed as they skipped and gathered in groups, long skirts hiding skinny legs.

Essie watched the twins struggle to stand tall and straight. Flora's left eye twitched, the only hint that her bandy legs were paining her. Maggie's face was equally still. Their faces were so pale they could be carved from marble.

Essie resolved to take on more work—whatever she could find—to buy the girls fresh food and the leg braces they badly needed.

The headmaster, Mr. Morton, stood with his bucket and list. Each child had to drop thruppence into the bucket each week as they went through the school gate.

Essie stepped in front of her sisters.

"I don't have the money. But I'm off to work now and I'll have it for you tomorrow."

The headmaster snapped, "I believe you said the same thing last week. Consider this your last warning, Miss Murphy. Unless you start to pay on time I shall have no choice but to expel these three. In any case, they'll need to be punished in the usual manner. They'll continue to be punished until you pay what's due, Miss Murphy."

Essie's cheeks started to burn, and she could feel Gertie stamping her feet like a frustrated horse.

"Please—"

Gertie stepped out from behind Essie and gave her sister a nudge as she pulled Flora and Maggie with her. "You get to work, Es," she whispered behind Flora's back. "We'll be all right with Mr. Godly Gen-er-osity here . . ."

"No," said Essie, trying to wipe away the tears that had sprung into her eyes.

"Essie, you need to go," said Gertie, louder now, with as much authority as her headmaster.

"Very well."

Essie lifted the cloth on her basket and handed over three tin bottles of tea as she whispered, "I'm sorry."

Flora winked at her big sister, and flicked her braid over her shoulder as she stepped across to Mr. Morton and bent down to put her lunch at her feet. Straightening, she held both hands out, palms up and ready for a whipping.

Maggie tentatively did the same, standing shoulder to shoulder with her twin. Last to join the lineup was Gertie, who was now standing with her chin slightly lifted and cheeks flushed. Defiant.

Essie tried to turn and walk away, but her feet were lead. It was all she could do to stop herself from rushing over and scooping up each of the girls to take them home for the day.

But she needed to go to work. And besides, the girls were safer here at school than at home.

The newsstands were full of headlines trumpeting free education and housing for all, but that hadn't happened in their parts, south of the river. Miss Barnes, Gertie's kind teacher, had told Essie it might not be happening for some time yet if the rumors were to be believed. Still, Miss Barnes wanted Gertie to finish her schooling and matriculate.

Ma wouldn't hear a word of it. "It'll be the factory for Gertie, or the workhouse," she said. "Don't be putting fancy ideas in her head, Esther. No good'll come of it."

But fancy ideas filled Essie's head when it sank into her pillow in the evening. As her bones ached and her sisters coughed, spluttered, and scratched beside her, she wished more than anything for the girls to have their own beds. New shoes and a coat for winter. Most of all, she wished for them to stay in school so their days would not end up like hers.

Essie now eyed her sisters standing in a line, bravely awaiting a punishment from their headmaster they did not deserve.

Mr. Morton pulled out his short horsewhip and Maggie flinched. Flora dipped a little to one side, as if her knees were buckling under her skirts.

A whoosh and then a sharp slap as the whip hit Maggie's hand.

The child, so frail compared to Flora, started to sob and cough just as the second slap landed with a hiss. She coughed more, and the headmaster, whose face had gone red, retaliated with two more lashes, each harder than the last.

Flora trembled as it was her turn and, over their heads, Gertie looked at Essie and raised her chin a little higher, eyes glinting with anger. Her message was clear: *Leave.*

Helpless, shamed, and left with no choice, Essie forced herself to do as she was bid. She turned and hurried off to work.

Chapter 4

Essie had been sitting at her machine hemming men's evening shirtfronts for three hours when old Mrs. Ruben came and rapped her scarred knuckles on the side table.

"Enough, Miss Murphy!"

Essie stopped pedaling, but the thrumming in her ears continued. There were fifty other machinists on this sixth floor of the factory.

"I want you to do a delivery. It's urgent." Mrs. Ruben waved her hand at the table beside Essie's as she continued. "And take Miss Davis with you."

"It's Miss Avery, ma'am. Miss Davis left last week." The skinny girl with riotous ringlets bursting from her hairnet blundered on, oblivious to Mrs. Ruben turning a deeper shade of purple. "Tu-ber-cu-losis, ma'am. Remem—" The girl's sentence tripped, then stopped.

"I am well aware of the situation. I'll thank you not to bring it up again." Mrs. Ruben squared her hefty frame and eyed Essie. "I need you both to take these to The Goldsmiths' Company in Foster Lane off Cheapside."

She wheeled over a rack with a black tailcoat, white bow ties with matching waistcoats, and half a dozen stiffly starched white shirtfronts and collars.

"Mr. Ruben's automobile and driver are waiting for you downstairs. You'll make your own way home. Now be gone with you. Don't be getting any ideas, mind. This is a friend of Mr. Ruben's who is over from Antwerp and needs a dinner suit for tonight. And Miss Murphy . . ."

"Yes, ma'am?"

"They'll pay you a tuppenny at the other end for your trouble. Don't embarrass the firm. No creases." She was yelling now across the noise of the unending machines. "Do not disappoint me."

The girls carried the rack slowly down the six flights of stairs, stopping for a rest on each landing. Judging by Miss Avery's bagging sleeves and pinned skirts, there was as little for breakfast at her house as at the Murphys'.

"I'm Essie," Essie volunteered.

"Bridget," the other girl replied breathlessly as they wheeled the rack out of the factory to the waiting car.

They loaded the pieces carefully into the middle of the back seat, then, as the driver held the door open for them, the two girls slid onto the buttery leather seats. Essie had never been in a motorcar and, if Bridget's saucer-wide eyes were anything to go by, she never had either.

Both girls were too nervous to speak, so they sat stiffly in their patched pinafores and scuffed boots as the car motored away from the warehouse on the Thames, passing other automobiles, horses and carts loaded with wooden barrels, and tired, filthy navvies.

Essie thought of her brother, Freddie, gone with his pickaxe before dawn. Nothing but a bottle of tea for his break.

If she was going past Cheapside, perhaps she could stop by with some food on her walk back.

"Essie." Bridget touched her arm and shook her out of her daydream. "Look!"

A crowd of women closed in around their vehicle, causing the driver to slam on the brakes. Most wore white dresses, wide-brimmed hats clad with green and purple ribbons, or a ribbon fixed at the waist. The dresses tapered at the ankles, and Essie noted with a twinge of jealousy that most had fine stockings and pretty shoes with the latest French heel.

What would it feel like to have a spare change of fresh clothes and silk stockings? she wondered, as she tried to hide her calloused hands in her rough skirts.

The driver cursed under his breath and muttered, "Bloody suffragettes. Clogging up the streets like this. Should be slammed in the clink, the lot o' them."

Several women were wearing placards dangling from thick straps at their shoulders emblazoned with the words: vote s for wo me n.

"What do they say?" Bridget whispered, cheeks pink with embarrassment.

Essie read the nearest placard. "They're inviting us to a procession. This Friday evening at five thirty in Knightsbridge."

"*Us?* In *Knightsbridge?*" Bridget adjusted her hairnet and giggled. "Don't think they'll be wanting the likes of us, do you?"

Essie shrugged. Even if she'd wanted to attend, she had coal to fetch and supper to cook, then bathing and delousing the little ones before washing out their clothes for the week and hanging them over the fire.

Friday nights were always the same for Essie. The only highlight was a scrap of mackerel instead of turnip soup—if she could convince old Mr. Foster to extend their credit for another week.

The driver leaned on his horn as the women walked in front of the vehicle, filling the pavement with linked arms, chanting: "Votes for women."

Who were these immaculate women with time to protest in the streets? No jobs here—or in the home, she reckoned with a quick glimpse of their neatly gloved hands. A row of police riding on black Clydesdales started to appear from a distance, and the women in white started to move in circles, as if in a butter churn.

Soaring above them all was the Monument, Wren's beautiful sculpture commemorating the Great Fire, golden urn glittering in the sunshine. Essie walked past it every day on her way to and from work, and often stopped to admire the frieze on the base, in which London was portrayed as a woman languishing, disrobed, on a pile of rubble. Bishops, king, architects, and soldiers all crowded around to lift her to her feet. The woman—London—looked tired. Defeated. Probed and pulled by too many people.

Essie knew what it meant to have so many regarding you with expectant faces. Depending on you to keep going.

She'd heard it said that this sculpture represented the might of London. She would recover, pick herself up, and fight again. But the sad line of London's cheek—so many hands pushing and pulling at her shoulders—made it hard for Essie to breathe.

"Eel, thanks, sir." Essie handed over her precious tuppence and tried to ignore her own hunger pangs as the pie man wrapped the pie in newspaper. She slipped the warm parcel into her apron pocket and felt the comforting weight against her leg.

"I hope your brother knows how lucky he is," Bridget remarked. "I'd best be getting on. It's mid-afternoon . . . If I walk back to work then 'ome again it'll be long past dark. My babies are with Mother and she'll be in a right state. Who'd've known the gentleman would take so long to choose his shirtfront? Tell you what, there was more gold in those columns at that Goldsmiths' 'ouse than in the Crown Jewels. Surely the butler could have done his bidding today?"

"You go." Essie shooed her along, wishing she had a second tuppenny to buy her new too-skinny friend a pie as well. "I'll tell Mrs. Ruben it was my fault."

"But she'll dock your pay . . ."

"Shush. Go."

Bridget mouthed a thank-you, fist clinging tight to her tuppence. She refused to slip the coin into her pocket in case it got lost. Closer to home, Bridget would probably buy some potatoes, a turnip, and perhaps some salmon. For her babies. For her ailing mother. It wouldn't go far enough . . .

Essie walked along Cheapside, scanning the demolition sites and listening for the telltale *tink* of pickaxes striking rock and rubble. Eventually she came to Freddie's site, and was surprised to see that in the past week they had razed almost all the walls and floors of the old line of shops, except the cellar.

Her brother had removed his shirt, revealing ribs and sinewy arms. His best friend Danny looked the same, only with sandy hair rather than her brother's dark Murphy curls. Beside them stood a row of navvies in an assortment of patched overalls, torn shirts, and waistcoats and filthy boots. Everyone was bent over, digging through clumps of soil and stone with their picks.

"Tea break," boomed the foreman from the lip of the cellar, just a few feet from where Essie stood.

There was a collective sigh of relief as tools were dropped, and men tried to straighten backs bent stiff from hours of toil.

Essie looked across to the foreman, noticed his thick dark hair, green eyes. He had removed a fob watch from the pocket of his smart waistcoat and was making a show of looking at the time, holding it up to the light.

Freddie waved and walked over to her.

Danny found an old metal bucket, brushed it clean, and turned it over to make a seat. "Sit, here, Miss Essie."

"Thank you, Danny," she said as his ears reddened. Essie reached into her pocket and handed her special parcel to Freddie. "Lunch—special delivery," she joked.

Freddie beamed as he placed the parcel on his lap, carefully unwrapped the newspaper, and split the pie into three with his pocketknife. He handed a piece to Essie.

She shook her head.

"Es, you've been working just as hard as me."

"You lads split my share. I'll get another on the way home."

All three knew she wouldn't, and Freddie pulled a pained face at the rest of the pie, torn between gobbling it up and forcing his little sister to eat.

"No fraternizing on-site, Murphy. Don't care if it is tea. Y'know the rules," a voice boomed over Essie's shoulder.

Startled, she jumped up and knocked over the bucket.

Standing behind her with his hands on his hips was the foreman. Up close, he was younger than she expected. Perhaps a year or so older than her brother, with neatly combed dark hair and a ribbon of dark freckles over his nose.

"Sorry, sir. I'm Freddie's sister. It's my fault. He didn't know I was coming. I surprised him with a pie."

"A pie!" He looked bemused. "Wouldn't have picked you to have your sister running your errands, Murphy." He glanced over her shoulder at Freddie.

"Sorry, sir."

"Back to work, the lot o' you."

Danny started to protest. "But, sir, it's only been—"

"I take it you want a job tomorrow, O'Brien?"

"Yes, sir."

"Then get moving. You too, Murphy."

The young men walked in single file back into the cellar. Essie could hear them cursing and muttering under their breath.

No doubt the foreman could too. But when he turned back to face her, he was wearing a wide smile. He didn't run his eyes over her threadbare pinafore or comment on her too-big boots. Instead he extended a hand and said politely, "I'm Edward Hepplestone." He tilted his head at where Freddie and the navvies were digging. "Sorry if I sounded a bit gruff. It's just that I'm under a bit of pressure to finish this job and move to the next. We're a few weeks behind, you see?"

"Esther Murphy," she replied, feeling his warmth as she put her small hand into his larger one and he shook it. With his touch, she tilted her chin a fraction, as she imagined a proper lady might.

He smiled—relaxed and easy—and she noticed how the smile reached all the way to his eyes. They stood studying each other in silence for a few beats before the spell was shattered.

"Sir! Sir!" called Danny.

"What is it?" said Edward, clearly annoyed at being interrupted.

Essie stepped sideways so she could see over Edward's broad shoulder to Danny, who was shouting and waving his arms.

Freddie dropped his pick and reached down to pull out a clump of dirt bigger than his head.

Essie swallowed and blinked, not trusting what she saw.

When she looked again, Freddie was holding his find above his head. Dripping like water from the soil were loops of gold chains, giant green stones, cameos, some buttons and rings, a gush of sparkling colored gemstones, and what looked from a distance to be some small jeweled silver hooks.

The navvies tossed their picks and shovels aside and clambered across to Freddie from their section in the cellar, rubbing their hands together and craning their necks over the man in front of them to get a closer look, theorizing about what had been found.

"A green stone as big as m'fist!"

"Chains of flowers as long as your arm."

"Looks like a perfume bottle."

"I swear on my life—they're diamonds. Handfuls of 'em."

Among the chaos and high-pitched chatter, the navvies pulled clumps of soil from the debris. Mr. Hepplestone had rolled up his sleeves, and was squatting and pointing into the hole—shouting at everyone to leave the soil where it lay. At one point, he looked up and squinted across to where Essie stood just to one side of the jostling navvies. He raised a hand and gave her a small smile.

But was it meant as a friendly gesture or as an instruction for her to leave?

Essie lifted a hand and waved back, but then noticed Freddie and Danny staring at her, Freddie frowning and Danny looking a little forlorn.

"Best be getting along, Es," said Freddie as he blocked her view of Mr. Hepplestone. "You'll be needing to get the girls from school. The lads are getting a bit—"

Before he could finish she was knocked in the side of her head by two men shoving each other.

"Hey! Watch the lady," said Danny, giving one of the navvies a push.

But they ignored him.

"Give it back. I saw it first."

"Pity your fat hand didn't grab it!"

The filthy pair sounded like the twins fighting over Papa's medals as they played cross-legged on the floor.

Danny offered to fetch a cool cloth for Essie and find somewhere for her to sit, but she assured him she was fine as she turned to walk away down Cheapside. Rubbing the side of her head, where a bit of an egg had developed, she glanced back over her shoulder at Danny, who was still watching her. She gave him a smile, and then looked across to where Mr. Hepplestone stood knee-deep in the pit, his dark hair curling over his collar and the muscles in his arms visible beneath his rolled-up sleeves. He didn't notice her leave.

Chapter 5

KATE

LONDON, PRESENT DAY

Kate's stomach growled and she looked at her watch: 3:30 p.m. She had been taking notes all day without a break, interviewing Saanvi and Gayle while Marcus set up each shot.

It was almost time to go—their security pass required them to leave by 4 p.m.—but she wanted to squeeze in a couple more pieces.

To their left was a gold pomander, or scent bottle, studded with diamonds, rubies, emeralds, sapphires, and spinels. Kate imagined an aristocratic woman holding this bottle under her nose and sniffing ambergris, clove oil, and cinnamon to mask the stench of rotting corpses blackened by the plague as she traveled through London in her carriage.

And there, sitting quietly on the last pedestal, was a tiny diamond ring: a solitaire.

The diamond was set into the gold bezel, and the gold band had been coated with white enamel. The ring was so simple. So small. Was it a mourning ring, or did it symbolize love?

It struck Kate that if she were to choose an engagement ring it would look something like this. She swallowed, feeling dehydrated and dizzy as memories of Jonathan continued to press down with the hot air in this tiny room. She could smell the linseed and oak in Jonathan's hair as he finished sanding and installing the last of the kitchen cabinets in her brownstone, then lifted Kate onto a benchtop and proposed. Those warm eyes and impish smile . . .

Kate had accepted the proposal but was secretly disappointed it had not been accompanied by a ring. It turned out that the dreamy little girl sitting at Essie's dressing table rummaging through beaded necklaces and colorful earrings had not disappeared completely underneath the tailored suits and silk shirts.

Jonathan must have read her feelings in her face, and who could blame her fiancé for looking bewildered? "But I thought you'd know exactly what you wanted. That's why I didn't—"

She'd stopped him midsentence with a long, slow kiss. Drew him closer with her legs and wrapped them around him as she ripped his work shirt off, showering them both with sawdust.

She took a deep breath.

Kate stepped back from the pedestal and tried to blink away her tears. Her grief felt exposed under the harsh fluorescent lights. She had managed to sign the divorce papers before she left, but she hadn't yet mailed them back to Jonathan's lawyer.

"Are you okay?" Marcus glanced up from the emerald watch he was studying from every angle, as he tried to position his lights and lightbox for a few more shots.

Saanvi stepped toward Kate and put a steadying hand on her arm.

Embarrassed, Kate shrugged and lied, "Jetlag. Sorry!"

Marcus held her gaze for a beat, brows creased with concern. "We can finish this tomorrow, if you like."

"I'm fine, honestly. I don't want to miss a thing here . . ." She stretched and examined the table, taking in the cameos, the salamander, the emerald watch . . . the pomander.

Where to start?

Every story needed a big opener. The emerald watch seemed the obvious choice, but her eye kept being drawn back to the little black-and-white ring. The simplicity of it touched her.

At Kate's nod, Saanvi picked it up in her gloved hand and held it under the light. As the ring turned and the diamond flickered like a flame Kate wondered why this simple ring had been buried in a damp cellar with the much more valuable pendants and the watch.

The diamond was table-cut and clear. Kate used her eyepiece to scan the stone for variations. Flaws. Nowadays a diamond could be filled and baked, then sent off for certification that it was perfect; the rough would be brilliant-cut to throw sparkle around the room.

Kate made careful notes.

3–4 ct, late 16th century or early 17th century?

Small gold band. Possibly for child or small woman. Champlevé enamel. Mannerist style. Black flowers painted onto white. Pansies? Forget-me-nots?

Engagement, or memento mori ring?

What promises were made with this ring? How had it ended up in the Museum of London?

"Saanvi, do you know where this stone is from?"

The conservator smiled. "That I *can* tell you," she said. "We've had this stone tested alongside some others, and we know the rough was from Golconda. So this ring"—she held it up to the light so it glowed with the warmth of a candle—"started its life in India."

THE DIAMOND ROUGH

GOLCONDA, INDIA, 1630

The boy woke to the screams of his brother. It had been this way since the last moon.

Sachin rose from the straw mat he shared with his father, fastened his leather belt around his waist in a knot, and padded quietly across the dirt to where his older brother Arjun lay in the corner, his hands and feet bound with twine.

Kneeling, Sachin placed a hand gently on the young man's thigh to calm his thrashing. Next, the boy loosened the ropes from around Arjun's ankles before cradling his brother's head in his arms. He kissed the top of Arjun's head and whispered a prayer to Mahadeva.

Arjun knocked the boy off balance with his closed fists, but the whites of his eyes were like those of a frightened animal. He whimpered and tried to curl himself into a tighter ball.

Sachin could smell dried piss on his brother's skin. He stood, then helped Arjun to his feet. He'd take him to the river's edge to finish his ablutions and pray.

In the opposite corner of their mud hut, his mother and sister were kneeling next to the hearth. The younger woman was rolling out balls of wheat dough and black sugar with the heel of her palm. Their mother was dropping spices into the large clay pot of tea simmering over the coals: a stick of precious cinnamon, a thumb of ginger, a fistful of cloves and cardamom buds. Already the spices were mixing with the smoke and a sweet woody scent filled the hut. Geetha, his eldest sister, would go out to their shared village cow and return with a tiny pitcher of warm, creamy milk to finish their chai.

As they walked outside into the air, Arjun turned his head and sniffed—like a camel might sniff the wind—then visibly relaxed. He giggled as his breath floated up to the clouds, lifting his bound hands to catch the white puffs as though they were butterflies.

Sachin's chest tightened as he glimpsed the weeping red welts on his brother's wrists. He wondered if his mother could spare him a little turmeric and ghee to massage into these wounds.

How he wished he could unbind Arjun's wrists. But ever since his brother had shoved the village Brahmin up against a stone wall when the priest came to offer prayers, their father had promised to keep his eldest son bound up like he was a beast.

The priest said Arjun had the devil's fever, but he was wrong. Arjun wasn't evil. He was just scared and broken since the accident in the mine the year before. It was a wonder he hadn't died, Sachin thought. Arjun had been buried beneath a pile of rubble when the edge of the pit he was working in had collapsed. He hadn't been the same since.

Nobody met their eyes as they walked past hundreds of huts just like theirs to the river's edge.

The mountain escarpment loomed up from the foothills, smothered by jungle. The air was thick and humid, and beads of sweat were already forming at his brow. Morning birdsong and the screeches of wild monkeys rang out from deep in the rainforest. Not for the first time, Sachin wondered what it would be like to walk beyond the fringe of these lush trees and vines. To lose himself among the foliage.

What lands—what kingdoms—lay beyond these mountains?

They walked past a wooden caravan pulled by a dozen dusty oxen. The road between the mines, Golconda forts, Hyderabad, and the port of Goa was a steady parade of caravans loaded with cotton, silk, rice, corn, and salt. Others would carry spices with the scent of foreign lands, plus sugar and mace. Mostly the merchants were nomads or Persians. But lately there had been an assortment of foreigners dressed in strange dainty shoes, sweating in long stockings, woolen pantaloons, and waistcoats, curled hair plastered to their foreheads.

These fleshy pink men who stank like pork would walk through this village of mud huts and thatched roofs, cursing and swatting away the goats and chicks in their dusty path. They tried to bribe their way into the mines studded between the riverbank and the foothills, but the merchants and guards would have none of it. These mines belonged to the king of Golconda, and if the foreigners wanted to view the diamond roughs they had to go to the village bazaar with all the other merchants.

An ox flicked its tail, listless, as one of the foreigners ordered bags of millet to be unloaded from his wagon. Sachin had heard that this man with pale skin and sunburned nose and cheeks had paid twenty thousand gold pagodas for a ruby and a handful of rough gemstones at the bazaar. He tried to imagine the weight of that gold, and what it would buy for his parents and siblings. They could have Arjun treated by one of the city healers. Buy a herd of cattle for milking and soft curd cheese. Perhaps a field to sow rice or millet. For certainly his parents were aged and hunched before their time, and had just three pagodas a year to thank for their efforts in the mines.

Sachin walked slowly downhill to where the Krishna River roared over its bed of pebbles. Arjun kept tugging him, eager to reach the water. This shared morning ritual of bathing in the river would be the only happy interlude in Sachin's day before he kneeled for prayers, then went to work in the pits.

After bathing, Sachin kneeled beside his brother on the muddy riverbank to give thanks before he spent the day digging up the gravel in their new pit. He could hear women nearby winnowing gravel in straw baskets, then tossing it onto the flat bed of prepared dirt for it to dry. As it dried, children would rake the gravel, turning it over and over in the hot air before their mothers would push them aside to beat the gravel with wooden batons. When this was done, the gravel would be scooped into baskets, and the winnowing would begin again.

Sounds of endless scratching filled the heavy, humid air as he started to pray, bowing three times before the statue of the goddess Lakshmi. After prayers, the Brahmin daubed their brows with sticky orange paste of saffron and ghee and pressed seven grains of rice onto each forehead to bring strength and prosperity.

Sachin had lost count of the grains of rice he'd had pressed into his brow. All the gemstone roughs they had picked from their dried and raked beds of gravel had been dark and muddy, yielding only a new turban and a few lengths of cotton.

Sachin and his family washed their hands and feet with water, before the Brahmin handed them their only meal for the day: a scoop of rice on woven sál leaves. This morning they were gifted a copper cup of warm ghee mixed with sugar and cinnamon to pour over the rice.

Sachin looked across to where Arjun was tethered to the nearest banyan tree, curled up asleep in the shade. This was their life now: working the mines for clear stones and yanking their prized son and his brother to the pits like a belligerent goat.

The sun rose higher and the gravel started to grow warmer. Sachin moved quickly to stop the tips of his fingers burning. His throat turned dry. He struggled to swallow, and longed to plunge into the shallows of the Krishna River below.

Arjun lay moaning, hair plastered to his face.

Sachin scooped up a handful of gravel. He let it flow through his fingers, shaking his hands and watching for a hint of light. He did this over and over—until his skin was raw and chafed—before he caught a rough between his fingers. He rubbed the stone on his loincloth and held it up to the light. The guards had spotted him, and they moved closer to ensure he didn't swallow it.

Sachin nodded, heart starting to race as the head guard produced a banyan leaf and held the stone against the leaf to check it ran clear, not blue. The boy craned for a look, but was given a swift kick and ordered back to work. The guard grinned, and the rough was slipped into a leather pouch on his belt.

The rest of the guards made a wall behind Sachin, peering over him as he resumed sorting through the gravel, hoping for more . . .

Sweat dripped from his brow. If only he could sip some water. Or at least give some to his mother and sister.

Under the tree, Arjun started to stir. He stood and tugged at the twine that bound him to the tree.

The guards turned to watch, laughing. Arjun was nothing more than an amusement for them, like a dancing monkey at the bazaar.

Sachin swallowed, turning from the cruel scene, then spotted a glimmer in the gravel. He shifted sideways to throw a shadow and hide the stone.

Arjun started to moan and kick. He leaned back, breaking his twine, and then ran toward the guards. They left their positions behind Sachin and moved forward to restrain him.

"Shabdkosh! Shabdkosh!"

Devil.

A guard tackled Arjun to the ground and another grabbed his feet. A third pulled his pistol.

Sachin's father appeared out of the pit and ran across to the guards, placing himself between the pistol and his eldest boy, hands in the air. He raised his voice, arguing with the head guard as the other two tied Arjun to the tree once more.

As his mother put down her basket and hurried over to soothe her son, Sachin crouched down, plucked the clear rough from the gravel, and gasped. This stone was of the clearest water, glowing as if it housed a flame.

He stared, entranced. He'd never seen such a pure light.

Without even a touch of the polishing wheels spinning to the side of the pits, Sachin knew at once that the stone he held was special.

For the first time, he believed the Brahmin's insistence that the Golconda stones were the most powerful of all. He clasped it in his fist, calling on the power of the stone, of the crown chakra, to protect his brother.

Behind him Arjun moaned and thrashed as Sachin's mother cried out to the Divine Mother.

The head guard shouted a warning. Father turned to the thrashing Arjun, pleading with his son to be silent.

Sachin lifted his eyelid and slipped the rough into the corner of his eye, then he turned and ran toward his brother. The stone scratched his eyeball and tears started to form but he wiped them away with the back of his arm. This stone would save them.

"Arjun!" Sachin pleaded as he moved closer to his brother.

Arjun's hands were tied, and he kneeled with his feet bound behind him. His mouth was frothing with spit and his neck strained tight as he thrashed at the soldiers who were kicking and taunting him as if they were at a cockfight.

"Stop!" Sachin tried to throw himself between the soldiers and his kneeling brother, as his father had done before.

The guards kicked Sachin down into the dirt.

"Shabdkosh!" yelled the guard, and Arjun lunged for the man's ankle and bit hard.

The guard threw his red face back and roared like a wolf.

Sachin felt the stone digging deep into his eyeball as he fell onto Arjun to protect him from another beating and their sweaty bodies wrestled together in the dirt.

The last thing Sachin heard was the shot of a pistol.

Once, then twice.

Chapter 6

KATE

LONDON, PRESENT DAY

"Welcome to The Goldsmiths' Company."

A footman in Elizabethan pantaloons, white stockings, and a red coat greeted Kate, checked her ID, and handed her an elegant nosegay of rosemary, lavender, rue, and a white rose wound in a circle and tied with a navy ribbon. She slipped the ribbon over her wrist and held it to her nose, inhaling the scent of the herbs as she crossed the marble foyer and strode up the grand staircase to the Livery Room.

It was like she'd entered a giant jewel box, with pink marble Corinthian columns, red velvet curtains set within golden arches, and soaring molded ceilings detailed with gold leaf. Four enormous crystal chandeliers set the room ablaze.

But the old-world formality was shattered by the beats being pumped out by a six-foot RuPaul-look-alike DJ in the far corner.

The room seemed to spin, thanks to a slide show of antique rings, necklaces, and brooches blown up and projected onto the walls at all angles.

Every June for the last decade, Shaw & Sons Jewellers had hosted the Bijoux Gala at The Goldsmiths' Company—the fanciest guild in London, just a block from St. Paul's Cathedral—and it was a highlight of London's summer season. Kate's best friend and host, Sophie Shaw, had managed to transform her conservative family business into *the* jewelry house in London in less than a decade, with zero brothers or sons to help her.

Kate elbowed her way through the crowd of jewelers, aristocrats, and some elegant Chinese billionaires—some she recognized as her own clients—sipping Krug underneath green archways of star jasmine and bougainvillea. Spying her friend, she grinned like a maniac and waved.

Sophie Shaw was wrapped in a hot pink sari, sported a new turquoise bob cut at an angle along her jawline, and wore a tiny emerald nose stud. On catching sight of Kate, she returned the wave, grimaced, and pointed at the next room, mouthing, "See you in there," before miming downing a glass of champagne. Some things never changed.

Among the crowd walked actors dressed in golden silk skirts and suits. The men wore white ruffs at their wrists and necks, and genuine longswords at their hips. The women's bodices were so tight Kate worried a perky breast might pop out from the corsetry at any minute. Fashioned onto these Elizabethan costumes were pieces from Sophie's latest collection. Chunky emerald rings were stitched into the neck ruffs, angular gold brooches sat at the breast, and long swathes of gold chains and pearls were strung over shoulders and swung down to waists. It was contemporary jewelry worn as in the seventeenth century, when Queen Elizabeth I's ships ruled the seas. The women's earlobes sparkled with an assortment of modern gold hoops and diamonds, and the black-clad bodyguards standing in every corner looked nervous.

"Kate. Hello again." Lucia Wright kissed her on both cheeks. "Isn't Sophie amazing?"

They both watched Sophie dance like a robot for a few steps while celebrities and pop stars looked on, laughing and clapping.

"I love her. I mean, look . . ." Lucia turned to survey the crowd. "She asked to borrow some slides from the museum—she wanted to project London's jewelry through the ages onto the walls. Watch out for them." As she spoke an image of diamond and pearl brooches taken from the Crown Jewels flashed onto the wall in front of them. "Oh, and here's someone I'd like you to meet . . ."

A short, rotund man was approaching them, smiling shyly.

"Kate, this is the librarian here at Goldsmiths', Thomas Green. He might be able to help you with your feature. Thomas, this is Kate Kirby, a brilliant former student. She's writing about the Cheapside jewels for an American magazine. I'll leave you to it." This last line was shouted over the top of an Eminem grind as Lucia turned and headed toward a group of snappily dressed young men.

"How can I help?" Thomas asked kindly, and Kate liked him immediately. Librarians were some of her favorite people.

Kate leaned close so he could hear her and asked, "I wonder if you could help me identify who owned the site where the Cheapside jewels were found?"

"Well, that's a complicated question. We think the cache was dug up at 30–32 Cheapside . . ."

"Saanvi gave me the address and I walked past it on my way here," Kate told him. It was a stone's throw from The Goldsmiths' Company—opposite St. Paul's Cathedral.

"Did you take the escalator to the basement? It's right near the Marks and Sparks Food Hall."

"I did, but it's hard to get the seventeenth-century vibe standing between the restrooms and a discount shoe store. The only sense of the past was St. Paul's dome framed between the glass walls of the escalator." She wondered how many Londoners knew they were literally pissing on their own history.

"The problem is, there was more than one tenant on the premises. Rent books show a complex web of letting and subletting. There were local goldsmiths and *stranger*—that is, foreign—jewelers sharing quarters. Perhaps a group of jewelers combined their working stock in trade and it was those jewels that comprised the jewels dug up by the builder's laborers hundreds of years later . . ."

The museum staff had painstakingly identified and cataloged the more than five hundred pieces. It seemed decadent—until you walked into any jewelry store on Bond Street or Park Avenue and counted just how many pieces were on display. And that didn't include any special stock tucked away in safes.

"Next week I'll have another look at the rent books for the 1600s, see what else I can find."

"Thank you," said Kate.

Mr. Green continued carefully, "But there's no record of the navvies who allegedly found the stash. And we don't *know* the discovery site for certain. Someone could have been covering their tracks. Made up the location so as not to reveal the true source of the treasure . . ."

"If there are no records, then how do you know the jewels I saw at the museum were all part of the same cache?"

"Good question. We don't. The workmen were all digging in the same cellar on Cheapside around 1912. They pocketed clumps of dirt and tied up the jewelry in socks, shirts, and handkerchiefs. Most of the jewels were acquired for the new London Museum over a number of months by an, ah, antiquarian called George Fabian Lawrence—otherwise known as Stony Jack."

Kate pulled her notebook out and wrote the dealer's name on a new page. As she wrote, she asked, "Did all the jewels from that Cheapside site go to him? Could the navvies have sold gemstones or jewels to someone else? Or kept them?" She tried to keep her voice even, but she held her breath, thinking of Essie's sketches of jewels and remembering the articles and notices she'd read back in Boston: *Such articles belong to the City of London . . . liable to prosecution.*

"How would we ever know?" He shrugged. "It's possible that we'll *never* know every piece. One of the workmen could have given a ring to their sweetheart or sold some gemstones to a dodgy diamond dealer on Cheapside. It was known as Goldsmiths' Row, so there was no shortage of potential buyers."

"So some pieces of jewelry connected with the collection could be anywhere in the world?"

"Exactly." The librarian smiled and excused himself as one of the actors brushed uncomfortably close. Kate suspected the librarian was eager to escape the surging crowds.

"Was Thomas helpful?" Lucia was back.

"Yes. I've got plenty to follow up on when I'm back in London in a couple of weeks."

"Back? Where're you off to?" asked Lucia.

"Jane has instructed us to go to the source."

"But the jewels come from everywhere—Colombian mountains, Indian valleys, and Sri Lankan beaches. Pearls from the Persian Gulf and Scottish Isles . . ."

"I've decided to focus on a single piece to start with: one of the little champlevé rings."

"The black-and-white solitaire?"

"Yes. The diamond is from Golconda."

"India. Yes, it's one of our finest diamonds. But no one knows the exact locations of the mines . . . and they don't mine in the area anymore."

"I know. I'm taking a slightly different approach. I want to see the bazaar of Hyderabad where the diamonds of Golconda were traded. I've read so much about the famous European gemstone merchants traveling through Asia and Persia along the trade routes. Jane wants me—and Marcus—to investigate the source . . . so I want to get a feel for the place. Try to capture the hands that traded the stone—then created this ring—between India and London.

"I'm also going to head to Sri Lanka. Up near Ratnapura, where Marcus says he has some contacts he can introduce me to. I'd like to see how the gemstones are mined today. Saanvi said some of the gemstones from Cheapside were possibly from that region."

"Sounds fascinating. Very different angle . . . can't wait to see what you uncover!" Lucia glanced at Kate's earrings. "Gorgeous sapphires by the way."

"Thanks. They belonged to my great-grandmother."

"I bet there's a lovely story behind them. From the cornflower color . . . I'd say Sri Lanka?"

"Perhaps." Kate felt her face grow hot. She knew how ridiculous it sounded. She spent her life flying around the world researching rare jewels, hunting stories, yet she didn't know the first thing about these earrings. The sapphires were a daily reminder of how little she really knew of her great-grandmother Essie's story. "I don't really know," she muttered, embarrassed.

"Nothing at all?"

"My great-grandfather Niall Kirby was a merchant seaman who went into shipping out of Boston. These were his gift to Essie on their fiftieth wedding anniversary." Had the seaman known of the Ancient Greek belief that the *sappheiros* was the symbol of sincerity and faithfulness?

"He died in his sleep soon afterward, so nobody knows where the sapphires actually came from. I suspect you're correct, though, and they were picked up for a song in Sri Lanka."

"It does sound likely," said Lucia. She took a sip of champagne.

"Apparently Niall called Essie, *Mo stóirín.*"

"Irish. 'My treasure' or 'my love,'" Lucia translated. "Now *that's* a beautiful story for those earrings."

Lucia turned her head and surveyed the room. "We have a roomful of stories here tonight, don't we? Look at all these people tripping over themselves to touch Sophie's pieces. I bet they wish they could touch the images on the wall too." She gestured to where a group was staring openmouthed at an image of some enamel and bejeweled gold necklace blinking on the wall. "I mean, the lure of priceless jewels is one thing, but each of these antique pieces was designed for one person and crafted by another. Each piece has a special story."

Kate nodded. This was probably why she was so intrigued by the little diamond ring.

"That individual piece becomes an heirloom," she continued. "Like your sapphires."

Kate swallowed as she recalled the broad laugh and untamed curls of her great-grandmother Essie. The same curls had covered Noah's tiny head.

"When people pass"—Lucia was speaking softly now, and Kate had to strain to hear her over the music—"sometimes it is enough just to bury yourself in something so exquisite, so beautiful, that it reminds us that there is hope. That people *can* be beautiful, thoughtful, and kind." The older woman put her hand on Kate's arm. "Keats was right, you know: *Beauty is truth, truth beauty* and all that."

Beauty is truth, truth beauty . . . The words drew Kate back to another party, another time.

It was too late by then, of course. You could unpick the past, but never undo it.

Chapter 7

KATE

LOUISBURG SQUARE, BOSTON, 2002

Kate hadn't known that her eighteenth birthday would be the last time she'd see Essie.

"Here you are!" Kate grinned as she poked her head around the study door and saw her great-grandmother standing in front of the bill of sale for the SS *Esther Rose*. "The party has started without you. They're all in the conservatory admiring the croquembouche. I brought you a glass of champagne." Kate held out a cut-glass flute.

"Thank you, my dear. Happy birthday!"

They clinked glasses.

"What's that?" Kate pointed inside the desk drawer her great-grandmother had just opened.

"Oh, just random clippings and pictures from England that take my fancy. I never returned to London. It's my biggest regret—and that door has closed to me now." She smiled wistfully. "Still, I like to know what's happening in my homeland . . ."

Essie pushed the drawer closed with her hip, but not before removing something.

"These are for you." She passed Kate a tiny wooden jewelry box. "Consider it an eighteenth-birthday present . . . coming of age, whatever you want." She waved her hand and collapsed onto the couch with a sigh.

"Essie, you're already giving me this party," Kate said in protest. "I don't need another gift."

"Pfft. I just couldn't fathom the thought of standing around in that concrete and glass mausoleum your mother insists on calling a home."

"It won *Wallpaper* House of the Year!"

"I have no idea what that means, my darling. Your mother doesn't design homes. A *home* has spirit and warmth. A history. I'm always afraid if I stay at your house too long she'll whisk me into one of those hidden storage cupboards. Now, open the box!"

Kate chuckled and opened the box to find a pair of sapphire earrings. And not just any earrings—they were Essie's favorites. She snapped it closed. "I can't accept these. Niall gave them to you."

"Nonsense. I insist. I never had any heirloom passed to me except trouble, if you count that . . ." She looked sad, and suddenly a decade older. "Besides, I can't wear them anymore; my earlobes touch my shoulders. Look!" Essie tugged an earlobe under her mop of wild white curls.

Kate laughed. "They do not." She unfastened the earrings from the box and held the sapphires up to the light. It felt like gazing into the ocean. She'd played with these very earrings hundreds of times as a little girl, rolling them around on her great-grandmother's dressing table.

Essie's expression was a strange mix of love and melancholy as she drew out a long necklace tucked under her collar and let the gold run through her fingers. As if somehow she didn't quite deserve it.

"Take the sapphires, Katherine. I insist. Every young woman needs a little something in the hem of her skirt when she sets sail. And you, my dear, are setting sail."

Kate sat on the arm of the couch, touched by the gift, but slightly confused. Essie's quip about jewels in the hem of her skirt seemed an odd thing to say. Then again, she was always repeating little Irish sayings . . . Essie wrapped her arm around her great-granddaughter's waist.

"They're beautiful—thank you," said Kate as the tears welled in her eyes. She'd miss her weekly visits with Essie. "Will you phone me every week?"

"I certainly will *not*! I detest those handheld phones, or whatever it is you young people use. I only have a phone because your father insisted on being able to contact me at all times. But who wants that? It's none of your father's business what I get up to."

"What if they can't reach you in an emergency?"

"A woman has to keep a little mystery about her."

"Speaking of mysteries, remember how I asked for your permission to write about you in my college admissions paper?"

"You had my blessing, child. Lord only knows why you wanted to. There are far more interesting women getting about than me."

"You've never much talked about your life in London. Why you left all by yourself . . ."

Kate hesitated, regretting her lack of subtlety. She knew the bare bones of Essie's childhood: kippers on Fridays, the clanging sound of Big Ben striking on the hour, suffragettes in white striding around the Monument. Skinny kids kicking a football made from sheep guts in narrow cobbled lanes. A poor Irish immigrant family crowded into a garden flat. Some of the siblings never made it to adulthood. No wonder Essie preferred to make her early years in London sound like a fairy tale—the reality must have been awful.

"Sorry, I didn't mean to pry. It's just that I've always been curious about how you made a new life on the other side of the world. Colleges want to know how we overcome challenges, but . . ."

She blushed as her great-grandmother sipped champagne.

Kate pulled a copy of her college entrance essay from her purse. "I brought you a copy. I thought you might like to read it sometime."

"You read it to me now."

"No!" said Kate.

"Please? My eyesight is so poor . . ."

There was no use arguing. Kate cleared her throat and began to read:

"Perhaps it is the Irish blood in my veins that makes me yearn to tell stories. My Irish great-grandmother, Essie, crossed the Atlantic to find a better life in the New World for herself and the family that was to come.

"This story of a girl, a boat, and a heart full of hope is as much a part of me as my left arm. And yet stories from her old world were spun into fairy tales, and I've never been sure where the fantasy ended and the truth began."

Kate looked over the top of her page and saw that Essie had closed her eyes and was nodding. There was a trace of a smile—or was she asleep?

Essie's eyes snapped open as she barked, "Well, don't stop."

"I just thought—"

"Carry on, Katherine," she demanded imperiously, and Kate obeyed.

"*My great-grandmother's stories of childhood are rich with colcannon, sticky apple pie, and handfuls of buried treasure plucked from the soil. Yet the scars on her hands and scant details about the people she left behind suggest a different, darker tale.*"

Essie snorted. "A touch dramatic, don't you think, dear? You get that from your mother." She waved her hand for Kate to keep reading.

"*I've learned that people polish some stories and bury others. As if by burying the past, they can stop trauma from being passed down the line. But I wonder if this recasting of history really helps us find that perfect future.*"

Kate paused, wondering how much more to read . . .

Essie had straightened and clasped her hands together. When she looked up there were tears in her eyes.

"Continue, child."

"Um, okay . . ."

"*When I go to visit my great-grandmother, I stop and sit on her front stoop and look over to the two statues standing in the park outside her house. I used to play soccer in Louisburg Square with my sister when we were children. We'd climb these statues.*

"*Christopher Columbus stands proud, wet, and mossy at the northern end, and Aristides the Just at the other. Men who were unquestionably brave. Men who sought new worlds. But both men also left a trail of mystery, darkness, and deception in their wake."*

Essie raised a snowy eyebrow and said wryly, "I have no idea where this is going."

Kate's hands were shaking and she found it hard to keep the paper still and read. Her voice strained like a middle-school kid onstage at assembly.

"There are lots of records of great men. But what about the ordinary women who made new lives in faraway countries? Where are their histories?"

"Ordinary!" repeated Essie with a humph, and this time Kate ignored her great-grandmother, as she was getting to her main point.

"I want to immerse myself in the study of history to explore the ways people constructed their lives, their worlds . . . their stories. To compare conflicting tales against the evidence available. I want to study people who have weathered adversity, overcome moral dilemmas, and had the courage to take risks—to follow a different path from the one mapped out.

"My story is folded into my great-grandmother's story. One day, I hope to solve the riddles of the past for my future."

"Well, that's quite the essay." Essie gave an uneasy chortle. "It seems you've inherited the Irish gift of the gab. Perhaps you'll be a writer one day? Have you thought of that? If not, you should. I never realized you were so . . ."

"Interested?"

"Nosy, more like it." Essie laughed. "My bonnie lass, you didn't *believe* the fairy tales I told you and Molly, did you?"

"Well . . ." Kate shrugged, embarrassed.

"Let me tell you something, Katherine." Essie was leaning forward. "I've had a good life in Boston. Beautiful family—roguish great-grandchildren." She tapped Kate's leg. "Your great-grandfather and I managed to make something from nothing—with a bit of . . . luck. Now I'm supposed to say, *May the road rise up to meet you* and so forth on your eighteenth. I've got a whole speech prepared for after dinner, you know?"

"I don't doubt it!" said Kate with a touch of nerves. Essie's speeches were legendary. She always claimed she was making up for lost time.

Essie stood up, reached for her walking stick with one hand, and put her other over the box in Kate's hand. "I've watched you grow into a thoughtful young woman. That essay . . ." She hesitated, then reached up to touch Kate's cheek. "I think you are perhaps starting to see that not everything in life is black and white. Now that you're eighteen, I think I can share with you a little more of my early years . . . Perhaps then you'll understand why I never returned to London—though it broke my heart to leave. I made a *terrible* mistake, and I live with that guilt each and every day."

Essie's eyes looked haunted, and her voice quivered as she continued: "In eighty years nobody has ever really asked. Not your grandfather or father—they've always had their heads full of shipping lanes and ports.

"My bones ache with regret, Katherine. But I also know that to turn my back on London forever was the right decision. Both things can be true, my love. It's possible to live with a heart heavy with grief and loss, but also brimming with love and hope."

"I don't understand," said Kate, frowning. "Why didn't you just go? It's not like you couldn't get a berth!"

"I'll tell you what: how about next time you're home I'll fix us some colcannon and I'll tell you my story. From the very beginning."

"Including the man with the green eyes from Cheapside?"

Essie's eyes narrowed. "Where'd you get that from? I think you've got your folklore in a muddle, my beautiful girl."

"But you used to tell those fairy tales when Molly and I were little."

Essie's smile relaxed. "My darling, we all need to believe in something beautiful. A little magic. It's what keeps us going during the dark times . . ."

Chapter 8

KATE

LONDON, PRESENT DAY

The DJ picked up the beat in the Livery Room and the crowd started to roar and dance. Kate walked into the oak-paneled drawing room looking for Sophie. As the music reverberated off the marble columns, Kate touched her sapphires. She recognized something of herself in Essie; perhaps a desire to keep her innermost thoughts—her trauma—to herself. Essie had filled her days with work projects and charities. Were all these accomplishments a coping strategy for Essie, too, as she poured herself into a new life on the other side of the Atlantic?

Kate was sorry that she never did end up hearing Essie's promised story about why her great-grandmother had left London and never returned. Essie's secrets were buried with her.

Standing in the corner, under jasmine vines suspended from the ceiling, Kate opened her notebook and flipped through the pages, before having a peek at the sketch of the button. Could Essie have seen some of the cache of jewels found in Cheapside? She snapped her notebook closed and tucked it into her purse, then went to join Sophie and her husband, George.

Kate had met Sophie during summer school at Oxford, when they were both preparing for their doctorates in Elizabethan history. They'd bonded over lukewarm beer and a mutual loathing of rugby. Sophie was thin and shared the luminous skin of her Indian mother, with cheekbones that belonged on-screen and a throaty Greta Garbo laugh. After two years roaming Southeast Asia with a backpack, Sophie had ditched the Dutch husband she'd impulsively acquired after a full moon party in Thailand, along with her dreadlocks and a filthy clove cigarette habit. She'd returned home to take over the family's appointment-only antique jewelry business in an elegant set of rooms just off New Bond Street. Last year, she'd married George Bailey—a diamond dealer based in Hatton Garden and confirmed rugby fanatic.

"I'm so excited to see you," said Sophie as she threw her arms around Kate. "You look fantastic."

"Love a woman in a tux. Very chic," said George as he kissed Kate on both cheeks. "Good to see you."

"It means so much that you could come, Kate." Sophie squeezed Kate's arm.

"My pleasure. It's a pity I can't stay longer. I leave for India in a few days." She ushered them to the middle of the room, where images of three pieces from the Cheapside collection were flickering on the walls.

George pointed to the vision of a pomander gliding across the ceiling. "This scent bottle takes the cake."

Kate eyed the tiny blooms painted in the enamel then studded with opals, rubies, diamonds, and pink sapphires to give it a vibrant botanical feel. It felt like spring. "Trust you to choose the most precious of all." Kate winked at Sophie behind George's back. "I'd wear this on a long chain today."

"So would I," said Sophie.

Kate's chest tightened at the thought of a woman clinging to something so exquisite—clinging to hope—when London's cobbled streets were blocked with sewage and garbage, beggars, rats, and festering bodies during the Black Death.

"I wonder if she survived," said Sophie wistfully.

"I doubt it! No jewel immunizes against bacteria. But rubies were seen as amulets against the plague. Diamonds protect—I mean they are invincible, right? And opals ease a sore head, apparently."

"Good for a hangover," said George as he collected three fresh glasses of champagne from a passing silver tray and handed one to Kate as the image of the black-and-white diamond solitaire from the Museum of London flashed in multiples around the room.

Who was it made for?

"Did you know that's a Golconda diamond?" Kate asked, pointing to the image.

"Ah," said George, eyeing the ring. "So that's why you're going to India. I have clients who would pay any price for a Golconda diamond—they're so rare. The only one I've heard of on the market in the past couple of years was just over ten carats. It sold at Christie's in New York for about twelve million dollars. But now there's talk that, today, the price could be worth that amount per carat." He shrugged. "Nobody wants to sell. They stopped mining them in the early eighteenth century."

"Wasn't it Alexander the Great who recorded that the Golconda locals threw chunks of meat down to a valley floor swarming with snakes, then sent eagles to lift the meat back up the mountain, studded with the clearest stones ever seen?"

"Cheers to tall tales." George laughed as they clinked glasses.

"But they're not always white, are they?" asked Kate, thinking of the legendary Hope Diamond, which was blue and rumored to have been found in Golconda.

"Correct. But all Golconda gems share a magical quality. It's like looking into the purest river moving through the stone. Clear water, they called it back in the day. If I did have one to sell, I wouldn't just sell it to the highest bidder. They'd have to appreciate the beauty . . ."

Sophie beamed at George. "You old romantic."

Kate studied her friends. George looked at Sophie as if he could gaze at her forever. He was proud of his clever wife, and Kate couldn't help but feel a tinge of jealousy whenever she was around this flamboyant couple. She loved them both dearly, of course. It was just that when she was near them, Kate wondered if she would feel that kind of deep connection ever again.

They all paused to look at the diamond ring flashing on the wall.

"Who created this?" Sophie wondered aloud. "The peasecods are exquisite. It took time to make this ring. Whoever it was intended for must have been deeply loved." She squeezed George's hand and he leaned in and gave her a tender peck on the lips.

Kate took a sip of champagne and turned her head. Out of the corner of her eye she spotted Marcus talking with Lucia and a circle of men. As if sensing her gaze, he looked over and gave her a wave before returning to the conversation. Kate couldn't work out what surprised her more: that Marcus had brought a tux to London or that he looked so at ease in it.

She turned back to her own conversation in time to see Sophie raise her champagne glass and say, "To Golconda. May it surprise you."

Chapter 9

ESSIE

LONDON, 1912

It was Friday afternoon and Essie was kneeling beside a desk in Miss Barnes's classroom, helping a student with his spelling list—an arrangement Miss Barnes had kindly negotiated with the headmaster the day before so the twins and Gertie could stay in school until the end of term. But, the headmaster had warned, if Essie failed to pay the thruppence a week owed for each girl, they would all have to leave at once.

When term finished, Gertie would finish school and start at the factory alongside Essie. Ma had agreed to Gertie's weekly pay and start date in writing with Mrs. Ruben, despite Essie's protestations that Gertie should stay at school until at least the end of the year.

"And how would we be paying for that, Essie?" Ma had snapped.

Essie shifted her weight on her knees as she leaned across the desk to help a little boy remember his alphabet.

When Essie had approached her manager to request an afternoon off so she could assist at the school, Mrs. Ruben had been initially reluctant. "I'll be having to dock your pay." But when Essie suggested that Mrs. Ruben instead pay Essie a little extra to cover her sisters' schooling, Mrs. Ruben bristled. "This factory is not a charity, young lady. I'll thank you for not taking advantage of my good nature." She did, however, agree to the afternoon off.

Still, Essie couldn't help thinking that this small concession would not be shared with Mr. Ruben. Mrs. Ruben was a battle-axe to be sure, but she looked after her workers in her own way. Last week, Bridget had found a large remnant of wool felt folded and tucked into her basket. When Bridget asked Mrs. Ruben about it, she was batted away with a stiff, "It was going to be tossed out, so it might as well be fashioned into a baby's blanket."

And so it came to be that Essie had agreed to help Miss Barnes with reading and writing on Friday afternoons in the classroom as part-payment for the girls' tuition.

"*H*," said Essie softly as the boy nodded and started to scratch the letter with a flourish, trying not to smudge his chalk across the slate.

"Can you think of three words that begin with an *H*, Jack?"

He scratched his head, and his legs jittered so hard they hit the desk.

"'Istory, miss. And 'orrible—like my dad." He looked around the room sheepishly in case the teacher had heard. But there was no need as Miss Barnes had moved to a different room.

"One more," coaxed Essie.

"'Appy." He gave her a gap-toothed grin. "Like you, miss. You always wear your best smile in 'ere. Not like Mr. Morton," he whispered in a conspiratorial voice before starting to scratch out a row of wobbly *I*'s.

"Ah, well." Essie patted his back as she stood up. "Thank you, Master Wainwright. You are most kind," she said in a mock-official voice.

The boy giggled, and Essie gave him a wistful smile. She wished she could keep him at this desk farting, smudging his chalk, and scrawling illegible letters forever. Instead, he'd be turning eleven soon enough and laboring down at the docks with his four older brothers.

How could Essie prevent her sisters from sharing his fate?

As she walked to the front of the room Essie counted the children with knock-knees, lame legs, missing teeth, and hunched backs. It was at least half the class.

Still more had bare feet.

Essie counted her family's blessings. Maggie would be fine once she got over her cold. The girls would be much stronger once their leg braces were fitted—when she could find the extra money. At least they all had shoes. That was something . . .

She pointed to the board where a spelling list ran down the side in Miss Barnes's immaculate script.

"When you are finished with your alphabet and your letters, I'd like you to copy this spelling list onto your slates."

Over in the back corner a trio of fair-haired boys who spent alternate mornings and afternoons working in the mills were fast asleep. The sun streamed in the window, and a smattering of freckles rained across the face of the youngest. He looked serene, younger than his eleven years. He spluttered a little and lifted his hand to scratch his nose. Essie grimaced. His hands were red and cracked, wrinkled like an old man's.

Like hers. She pulled the jar of beeswax and almond oil salve from her apron pocket, given to her by her neighbor Mrs. Yarwood, and tapped the boy on the shoulder. "Here, Jimmy, rub this on your hands. It'll make them feel better."

"Thanks, miss," said the boy gratefully as he scooped a glob onto his palm and rubbed it into his work-roughened hands.

Essie smoothed her skirts and walked over to where Gertie was working her way through a list. Where all the other children worked on slates, Gertie worked in a book gifted to her by the Yarwoods. The page of her ledger book was divided into three columns. In one column was a list of English words; in the other two columns Gertie would write the translation of each word into both Latin and French. Essie felt a wave of pride, before noticing a glint of gold under Gertie's sleeve.

It was the button from last night.

Freddie had arrived home filthy from a day's digging and gone straight to where the three girls were huddled around the kitchen table. Usually he was weary and wanted a wash and supper before collapsing straight into bed, but today he seemed excited. His arms twitched as his hands remained in his pockets. Essie narrowed her eyes and thought about the handfuls of jewels the men had plucked from the soil over on Cheapside . . .

Gertie had finished the extra mathematics Miss Barnes had set her and had begun to sketch the twins with their heads together in mischief, braids tumbling down their shoulders.

Essie stood at the table bruising a handful of ivy leaves with a wooden roller before dropping them into a pot of boiling port and cinnamon. The kitchen air smelled thick, sweet, and woody—like Christmas. Mrs. Yarwood, from next door, had shown Essie how to make the blend. "A draught of the liquor infused with a generous helping of ivy is the speediest cure for too much wine, love."

Either way, Ma was in a bitter mood, and a cup of this brew would see her off to sleep until morning. The house was calmer—quieter—when she slept.

Essie tried to quell her frustration that their mother had spent a day's spinning wages on half a flagon. More's the pity there was not a tea that could drain away her sadness.

The twins were reverently watching Gertie. There was only the mildest pushing and squabbling and bony elbow in the guts as they took turns to pass the ink to their older sister.

Freddie boomed, "Who wants to play the button game?" Their pa had taught it to Gertie, Maggie, and Flora when a brass button from his dress uniform had fallen off right before he shipped out—before Ma ushered the girls away and carefully stitched the button back on with a tender smile.

"Me!" they all squealed. Maggie jumped up and wrapped her arms around her brother's legs, dark braids dangling over her shoulders.

"Now remember, just like Pa did it. Nice and fast. Hold your hands out, young ladies. Both hands. Now close your eyes. And I mean close them properly—I can see you squinting, Miss Flora

Murphy." He tickled her tummy, and she howled with laughter as she tried to wiggle away.

"Honestly, Freddie," Essie sighed as she prepared the tea for her mother. "I was trying to keep them quiet before bed, not stir them up so they won't sleep." But even as she tried to scold her brother, her shoulders softened at the sight of his wan cheeks and tired eyes. Freddie had tried to step into Pa's shoes and find a job that paid enough to support them all, but he was still just a lad himself, with no skills or education, and with his dreamy demeanor and hapless optimism he had more in common with Gertie than their soldier father. Still, he was trying.

"Freddie," Essie said softly. "You need to eat . . ."

"Shh," said Freddie as he held a finger up to his mouth.

Essie held her breath as she noticed how like their father her older brother looked. The bridge of the nose, square jaw, and strong hands. In different clothes he could be an aristocrat.

"Hands," he barked, like their pa used to, and the girls straightened like soldiers and obediently held their hands out and closed their eyes. Maggie popped one open before squeezing it shut.

"Button, button . . . who has the button?"

He dropped the button into Gertie's hand and she clasped her fingers around it, squeezing it for a few beats before opening her eyes.

If Gertie were the God-fearing type, Essie would have sworn her sister was praying for something. More food, most likely.

"Right, now you play with your sisters, Gertie-girl, while I have my wash," instructed Freddie as he tried to peel the twins from his legs. But the twins were having none of it. They ignored

Gertie and dropped to their brother's feet, kneeling on the cold dirt floor like a couple of puppies and bickering over who would be the one to untie the laces of his filthy boots.

As Essie pulled the bathtub from its hook on the wall and turned to boil up hot water for Freddie to bathe, she noticed Gertie's usually composed face light up with a smile as she slipped a shining gold button into her apron pocket. For a moment Essie glimpsed the cheeky, carefree girl Gertie kept hidden away under her pinafore.

Gertie must have forgotten to return the button to Freddie, though, because here it was now, tucked under the corner of her book.

Carefully, so as not to distract her sister, Essie moved forward for a closer look.

The button was a double-layered flower: a rose fashioned from gold, with just the faintest traces of blue and white paint. At the center of the flower and dotted along the petals were blue, red, and white stones. Were they precious stones, or colored paste? Each of the inner circles also had gold indents, as if there were more to come.

Who did this button belong to? Also, if this was just a button, what on earth had the dress it was intended for looked like?

Freddie must have accidentally pocketed this on his worksite yesterday and then, in his excitement upon finding it, hadn't been able to resist showing it off to the girls. It was so typical of Freddie to forget to take it back from Gertie when they'd finished their game. Instead, he'd wearily trudged straight upstairs to bed after his supper of bread and dripping. Essie would force Gertie to give the button back to Freddie the minute he arrived home this evening.

She took a minute to look at a sketch of the button Gertie had made below her spelling list. Their accountant neighbor, Mr. Yarwood, had insisted on giving Gertie the ledger book to use for her drawings when she and her sisters had been over for a supper of pea and ham soup, followed by a sponge cake loaded with bilberries and cream last week. "Silly me, I bought the wrong one. Only good for your sketches, Miss Gertie."

Even in black ink, Gertie had managed to capture the curve of the petal, the grand skeleton of the gold framework. The divots for the missing parts had been marked with shadows to indicate their depth.

Essie remembered Freddie holding the clump of soil over his head yesterday. The river of gemstones and jewelry falling from the soil.

The man with green eyes.

Freddie had taken this button from that soil. Stolen it.

Had he taken anything else?

Essie felt her chest tighten with a dangerous mix of fear and hope as she looked across the classroom to where the twins were squabbling. They knew their days in this classroom were nearing an end.

She looked at the button and resolved to speak with Freddie tonight. Were the pretty jewels colored glass paste, or precious stones? Freddie wasn't reckless and wouldn't intentionally forget something so valuable; it was just that, like their ma used to say when Essie and her brother were small, he was away with the fairies half the time.

Essie was just reaching for Gertie's shoulder to say something about the button when Miss Barnes entered the room wearing a big smile and holding two enormous red apples up in the air.

"Who would like a slice of apple?" she asked as she pulled a penknife from the drawer of her desk and proceeded to slice the fruit.

Chaos ensued, as chairs were scraped back and a sea of grubby hands shot into the air.

"Me, please!"

"Miss, me!"

When Essie looked back at her sister, Gertie was gazing out the window, lost in a daydream. But the book was closed, and the button was nowhere to be seen.

The bell rang loudly and a tangle of children rushed to the door, eager to be outside before the afternoon started to fade.

Miss Barnes, who was packing up her desk, beckoned to Essie to join her.

"We have our annual summer excursion coming up. Mr. Morton has insisted that we take the children to Greenwich on Saturday fortnight. I was wondering whether you might be able to join us?"

"Certainly," Essie replied as she looked over her shoulder and saw that Gertie had paid no heed at all to the bell. She was still at her book finishing the extra algebra questions Miss Barnes had written on the board just for her. The twins were outside watching the boys roll a hoop across the gravel.

A shaft of light came in the window, and Essie thought how peaceful Gertie seemed. Her frustrated jostling with the twins as they tied their boots and dressed, and her constant ribbing as they walked to school, calmed as soon as they entered the school gates.

"I've been meaning to ask whether your mother has read the letter I gave you," Miss Barnes remarked.

Essie squirmed a little and glanced again at Gertie. The girl's gaze was fixed on her book, but she had gone very still. She was listening to every word the teacher was saying, Essie knew. Not much escaped Gertie, despite her dreamy demeanor.

"Sorry, Miss Barnes. I did pass it on, but Ma's been rather . . . busy."

Essie hoped the young teacher did not pick up on her hesitation. She looked at this neat young woman, with smart heels and an open face full of possibility.

"I see," said Miss Barnes, even though she clearly didn't. "I thought something like that might be the case." She spoke softly, with a slight quiver—as if she were nervous. "I'm leaving at the end of term. Just before Christmas. I've been offered a position at another school."

"Congratulations," stammered Essie, sad for the girls to lose such a valued teacher.

"It's a school just for girls. Clever girls, in fact."

The shock must have been written on Essie's face as Miss Barnes continued: "It's been running for quite some time. Miss Beale—the previous principal—even set up a college at Oxford: St. Hilda's."

"I've never heard of a school where girls go right to the end," said Essie shyly. "Though I suppose they exist, otherwise how would we have wonderful teachers like you?"

Miss Barnes blushed.

"The children will miss you," said Essie with a sad smile. "We all will."

Gertie had stopped pretending not to listen, and was staring at them both, openmouthed and red-faced.

"You can't leave!" spluttered Gertie.

"Gertie!" warned Essie.

"What, Essie?" said Gertie as she lifted her book and slapped it back onto the desk. "There's no point to this if Miss Barnes is leaving. And Mr. Morton is about to throw us out." She burst into tears.

"I'm sorry, Gertrude. I understand you're upset. I'm sorry to be leaving too. I'll miss everyone, especially you." Miss Barnes wrung her hands together before she walked across to Gertie and placed a gentle hand on her shoulder. The teacher's fervor reminded Essie of the determined women in the parade near the Monument, arms linked and chanting. Women who had new shoes, read books, continued their studies. Or, at the very least, finished school.

Miss Barnes took a deep breath and looked at Essie. "I've known for some weeks now, though I couldn't say. That was why I passed you the note with my new school's information and entrance exam slips for Mrs. Murphy—it's a shame she hasn't had a chance to read it. I'd like Gertrude to sit the entrance exams."

Gertie's head shot up and she looked from Essie to Miss Barnes, astonished and elated in equal measure. "Oh, can I, Essie? Please?" Gertie clapped her hands together and her stormy expression switched to delight as she bobbed up and down in her seat.

"It's not up to me, Gertie. We'll have to speak with Ma . . ."

As soon as Essie said it, the smile slipped from Gertie's face and the child closed her book, eager to be gone.

Miss Barnes walked back to her desk and reached down into her bag. As she rummaged around Essie saw green and purple ribbons and felt a flash of envy. Miss Barnes tucked them back into her bag and retrieved a crisp new envelope with neatly stenciled letters on the front: *For the parents/guardians of Gertrude Murphy.* She handed the envelope to Essie.

"I had Gertrude sit some short tests, in class last week when the others were taking their arithmetic test, and the results were very promising. I can't say for certain, of course, but I know there are scholarships for a few students every year. You'd have to come to the school in Cheltenham for a weekend . . ."

Essie quietly shook her head, and Miss Barnes turned pink, realizing her mistake as soon as she said it. She shuffled some papers on her desk and avoided eye contact as she said under her breath, "I understand. Of course. How thoughtless of me." She finished shuffling her papers and placed them in a pile on her desk. Then she ran her hands over her hair, fixing an imaginary stray strand into her bun.

Miss Barnes lowered her voice so far that Essie had to lean in to hear.

"What if I were to arrange for the entrance exams to be done here, during school hours? I could do it on a Thursday when Mr. Morton has his weekly meeting with Father McGuire."

Gertie had finished packing her bag and stood outside the classroom window, wisps of disheveled hair moving with the breeze. Essie studied the line of Gertie: her shoulders were starting to stoop, her hair was growing dull. As the clever child was becoming a young woman, all hope was being leached away.

Essie wanted her sister to stand tall. Perhaps she could even become a teacher, like Miss Barnes.

Essie studied her own scarred palms and knew that Gertie deserved better than a life lived on the factory floor. And Essie was determined she would have it.

Essie took the letter from Miss Barnes's hand. "Thank you. You are so kind. Our mother, she can be diffi—"

"I understand . . . Honestly, Essie. If I could take everyone in this class with me I would. But trust me when I say Gertrude is special. She has a magnificent mind. Deft and curious. Do you know, every day I leave here and I go to a meeting—"

"The suffragettes?" whispered Essie, as if she might be arrested for the mere mention of the word.

"Yes. And do you know *why* I go to those meetings?"

"For women to have the vote?"

"Partly. But I go to different meetings in the East End, with Sylvia Pankhurst. Miss Pankhurst is arranging for children to be cared for while women work or study. Soup kitchens. Clean clothes.

Forget about what you see in the newspaper, Essie: this isn't just girls in pretty petticoats and ribbons. We want change. Education. Choices. And the best thing I can do to further our cause is to educate girls. Those girls will educate more girls. Then they will demand a voice in parliament. Law courts. Hospitals. Anywhere you name, they will have to let women work there one day."

Essie studied her too-big boots, hoping Miss Barnes could not see the doubt on her face. University for women? Higher office? Both seemed less likely than the vote for anyone from Essie's part of London.

Miss Barnes placed her hands over Essie's. They were warm.

"Please, I beg you. Find a way for your mother to sign that letter."

"I will do my best."

And she meant it. Gertie could finish her page of translations, spelling lists, and algebra before most children finished the first set task. When Gertie drew a portrait it was as if she captured a person's very soul. Gertie was more than clever—there were plenty of children in the class who were sharp-tongued, could do arithmetic in their heads, or had the gift of the gab. But like Miss Barnes said, Gertie was special. Gertie's sense of justice raged within her skinny chest like a candlewick just waiting to be lit. She belonged with Miss Barnes and those fierce women in white. Gertie could have a life beyond the factories and the stinking lanes of Southwark. Essie was going to find a way for Gertie not just to stay in school until she was fourteen, but to get the education she deserved.

Chapter 10

KATE

LONDON, PRESENT DAY

Kate had arranged to meet Bella Scott—her third cousin—for dinner at Covent Garden after work. They'd met as teenagers one summer at Rhode Island, when Bella's mother had decided to research her family tree then proceeded to drag her reluctant children all about the UK—and occasionally the US—to meet bewildered relatives and present them with a thoughtfully bound color-coded copy.

Fortunately, Bella was close in age to Kate and Molly, and shared a love of surfing and romance novels. They'd swipe the books Bella's mother, Mary, had bought at the secondhand bookstore and escape to the pier to suck on milkshakes and swing their sandy legs in the wind as they devoured novel after novel, comparing plot points.

Molly would criticize the plots stridently: the heroine should rescue herself, she insisted, not wait to be rescued. Bella agreed. Kate was less concerned about plotlines; she'd developed an obsession with a series of racy novels set in Tudor times. Perhaps there was something in the water that summer, as she'd made a life's work of other people's histories.

Bella had never summered with the Kirbys in Rhode Island again; Mary had moved up the ladder to second and first cousins in Africa and the Bahamas. But Bella, Molly, and Kate had remained firm friends, catching up whenever they found themselves in the same part of the world. Like Molly, Bella had become a lawyer, and Kate spent a few weeks in Bella's first flat in Brixton when she'd interned at Christie's one summer.

On this particular evening, Bella had texted to say she was running half an hour late for dinner, so Kate stood at the crowded bar of La Goccia and ordered a pink gin and tonic. The bar itself was a masterpiece—boasting oversize leaves and petals cast in bronze, with a matching bronze countertop, it was a botanical homage to the bar's Covent Garden roots. Kate reached underneath the lip of the counter to trace her finger along the spine of an oak leaf.

She made a note to tell Marcus about this bar—it would be great to photograph the detail—but she pushed all thoughts of the photographer out of her mind as her drink arrived in a cut-glass tumbler with a sprig of rosemary for stirring.

Kate carried her drink through the after-work crowd milling about under the chandeliers and out to a courtyard, where she sat at a table tucked between two oversize terracotta pots sprouting ferns and magnolias. Twilight bathed the cream walls, and the summer air was thick with the smell of jasmine and japonica. It was hard to believe, in this haven of tranquility, that only feet away people were hurrying across ancient cobblestones on their way home from work or school or perhaps a shopping trip, pouring downstairs into the tube that would funnel them across London and beyond.

A waiter passed with a tray of onion and rosemary focaccia still fragrant from the pizza oven, and Kate ordered a serving for herself, along with some olives, before pulling her notebook from the tote at her feet. She hesitated for a moment, touching the second, more personal journal that lay underneath, still unopened.

Not yet.

She flipped open her workbook, leafing through the pages until she found the notes she was looking for. Underneath Essie's sketches was a series of newspaper clippings she'd found in a manila folder titled *London* in her great-grandmother's filing cabinet. She sipped on her gin as she flipped open the folder and scanned the faded newspaper clippings.

GERTRUDE FORD OPENS WOMEN'S CRISIS CENTER IN SOUTHWARK.

JUSTICE GERTRUDE FORD APPOINTED TO BENCH IN EAST LONDON FAMILY COURT. CREDITS SUFFRAGETTES, HER TEACHER AND FAMILY.

GERTRUDE FORD BEQUESTS MEANS-TESTED SCHOLARSHIP TO ST HILDA'S COLLEGE, OXFORD.

Esther Kirby had been the mouthpiece for Boston suffragettes, so it didn't seem unusual she would collect articles from her homeland about the education of women and the suffragette movement. Or her sister.

Kate felt her throat constrict, like someone was pressing against her thorax. She struggled to swallow and allowed the conversations swilling around the courtyard to wash over her. A waitress placed a bowl of black olives and warm focaccia on the table and Kate forced herself to speak. "Thank you."

What would her life look like without Molly?

She remembered Molly snatching the Harvard-stamped envelope from Kate's hand, ripping it open, and her face falling as she realized that what it contained was not an acceptance letter identical to the one she herself had received the year before, but a rejection. "Oh, Kate. I'm sorry. That sucks . . ."

And again, just four years ago, as Molly had clutched the newborn Emma to her chest, trying to work out how to nurse her. Exhausted and clammy, with strands of hair stuck to her forehead, Molly had reached up to Kate and touched her cheek. Kate had lain down beside her sister on the narrow hospital bed with an arm cradled across Emma as she helped the baby attach to Molly's raw nipple. Kate had remained on the bed, cradling her older sister and her sticky newborn niece, heart flooded with love, promising to keep them safe.

A life without Molly, her partner, Jessica, and little Emma didn't bear thinking about.

She looked closely at the clipping photograph of the young Gertrude wearing a mortarboard and academic gown. The law graduate had gleaming eyes and creases at her temples that hinted at the anticipation and sadness she recognized in the lines on Essie's wrinkled face.

Gertrude Murphy had been the only female graduate in her class. Kate wondered what it would have been like to be the lone woman among all those young men in stiff shirts and ties. She thought of her own art history classes—the ones she made it to—where it was commonplace for the class to be filled mostly with women, slouched low at their desks in the unisex Californian uniform of denim cutoffs, sandals, and a loose T-shirt.

It had been refreshing to go to college on the West Coast. Kate took student loans and paid her own way like any other student. It was liberating to be unhooked from the Kirby family back in Boston and the expectations that came with it; to be free to surf and to study whatever subject piqued her interest, from French to Elizabethan Jewelry to Life Drawing.

But lately the tide had turned. Perhaps it was living in the old Louisburg Square house, or a mellowing that came with age, but Kate wanted to lean in toward Essie and her family. Unscrambling the London secrets would be a start.

As she reached for an olive, Kate saw out of the corner of her eye a tall, striking woman in elegant wide-legged pants, heels, and a green blazer striding toward her, briefcase in hand.

"Sorry!" said Bella as she bent to kiss Kate on both cheeks before sitting down. "It's been quite the afternoon."

"Tough case?"

"Is there any other kind in family law?" Bella grimaced and waved at the waiter, then pointed to Kate's drink to indicate she'd like one of the same.

"I guess not."

Bella leaned back in her chair and breathed in the warm air. "Had to extricate myself from the bailiff, then console a distraught father."

"God, how awful . . . I'm sorry," said Kate, thinking of her own father and grandfather. Her grandfather had spent hours every summer teaching Kate and her sister to sail, while the girls' father had taught them to surf.

Bella noticed the notebooks. "Looks serious! You mentioned in your email that you're interested in my great-grandmother Gertrude. I've been waiting for years for someone to ask me about her! Before she and Dad retired to Majorca, Mum left me with a box full of papers from her family history years; she's more into scrapbooking and Pilates these days."

Bella reached down into her bag and pulled out a manila folder on which was written in neat capitals: mur ph y f a mil y tr ee. She handed it to Kate, who opened it out on her knees and unfolded the family tree that had been laminated into three sections.

Bella smiled. "So, we share great-great-grandparents, Clementine and Conrad Murphy. Clementine was widowed when Conrad died in the Boer War. She had seven children, and the only ones that seem to have survived into adulthood were our great-grandmothers, Gertrude and Esther. See here." She tapped the first branch of the tree. "Freddie, the eldest, was killed on a worksite near St. Paul's Cathedral when he was nineteen. Crushed when an unsecured wall of bricks toppled down on him, poor bugger."

"Then there's Esther Rose, my great-grandmother," Kate observed, "followed by Gertrude, who was yours."

"They were the lucky pair. Their younger sisters Flora and Maggie—twins—didn't even make it into their teens, and two little girls either side of Gertrude died of measles and whooping cough as babies."

The spider's web of lines below Clementine and Conrad Murphy gnawed at Kate. She imagined tiny coffins in the back of a horse and cart bobbing and swaying over cobblestones, headed to a pauper's graveyard somewhere on the outskirts of London.

Bella caught her eye and winced. "But they did have some happier times. Gertrude and Essie met in Hawaii for a holiday together once a year after they both turned fifty. I guess they were too busy with work and family before that. Gertrude's notebook and her letters to Essie are now part of a permanent collection at the Serpentine, along with her paintings. We can go together when you're back in London, if you like?"

"There are paintings too?"

"In her later life she became an artist. Her work is very Modigliani meets Yves Klein. Mum can't stand them, but I quite like her paintings. I have a couple in my study at home. They feel happy . . . kind of buoyant, if that makes any sense?"

"Looks like the talent ran in the family. I think these were drawn by Essie." Kate pulled some protective envelopes from her notebook and showed her cousin the sketch of the two laughing girls.

Bella frowned. "That's Flora and Maggie, I'm sure of it. The notebook gifted to the Serpentine was lined, just like this page, and there are pictures of the girls that look very similar. They could even be the same hand. The notebook definitely belonged to Gertrude, though; her name is written on the front."

"You think Gertrude drew these, not Essie?" asked Kate, feeling the familiar rush of adrenaline that coursed through her when she made a historical connection between artwork or jewelry, no matter how tenuous. "Would it be possible to compare them with the drawings in the notebook?"

"Of course! I'll call my contact at the gallery and request access."

Kate reached for her drink and took a sip, enjoying her gin. The sun was low, softening to twilight, and as she sat across from Bella, something metallic caught her eye.

Kate leaned forward, shading her eyes with her hand. "Your necklace—may I have a look, please?"

"This?" Bella pulled a gold chain from underneath her silk shirt. "It's a pendant my mother gave me as a graduation present when I finished law school. Her mother gave it to her. It belonged to Gertrude, apparently." Bella looked down as she continued, "Bit big for me—too flashy for court. But I like it close to my skin for some reason, so I just tuck it under my shirt. Here . . ." She lifted the gold chain over her head and passed it to Kate.

Kate ran her thumb over the gold chain and held the pendant in her palm, her heart fluttering. The pendant was gold, with layers of petals resembling a rose. There were a couple of flecks of white and blue enamel, but otherwise the pendant was bare.

"See these tiny squares?" Kate pointed to a grid pattern in the petals with square shapes. "These indentations in the gold suggest that it was studded with table-cut stones, but they must have been removed at some stage. And this isn't actually a pendant—it was originally a button." Kate flipped the pendant over and pointed to the telltale soldering marks at the base of gold hoops that enabled it to be stitched onto cloth. "See?"

Bella's eyes were wide. "I had no idea. I'm not sure what happened to the original stones; I didn't know there were any—I just assumed those marks were a pattern. Gertrude was one of the first women at Oxford to read law, so perhaps she flogged them to play for her education? Although it seems unlikely." She tapped the family tree. "There's nothing here to suggest the Murphys had two pennies to rub together, let alone a fancy button filled with gemstones. Gertrude's mother, Clementine, died of liver failure in the workhouse, so they weren't exactly well off. I'd always assumed this was a present from Granny Gertie's husband—my great-grandfather Hubert."

"Perhaps there were no stones in *this* button," said Kate, "but she might have seen one with the gemstones in place." She slipped another envelope from her notebook and handed it to Bella. "This sketch was also among Essie's papers."

Bella studied the image. "It's identical. Except for these stones." She tapped the drawing. "What does it mean? Where did this pendant *come* from?"

"I don't know. But apart from the missing gemstones, it's identical to a collection of buttons I saw at the Museum of London."

"The same? That could mean . . ."

They sat in silence, both looking from the drawing to the button in Kate's hand. Kate tried to push away the whispered thought: *liable to prosecution.* Essie's family had been poor. Was it such a stretch to imagine she might have kept something precious that she stumbled across at work or found in the street—or that had been dug up, by someone she knew, from a cellar near Cheapside? Or stolen it? And, if so, who was the rightful owner now?

For the insurance report for her Swiss client, Kate had been tracing the origin of a medieval skull ring over the last few months, a memento mori, distinguished by the engraved words nosc e te ipsum. *Know thyself.* The ring was featured in a 1574 oil painting of a Flemish gentleman before being sold on to a Jewish collector in Holland. The paper trail had stopped abruptly in 1940. Her client looked embarrassed at the suggestion he had come by this ring illegally when it was sold by an unscrupulous Nazi soldier to his dealer. Kate recommended in her report that her client start the process of repatriation. It belonged—in her opinion and perhaps under international law—with the family of the Jewish collector who was the last known rightful owner.

As if she could read Kate's thoughts, Bella said, "So who's the rightful owner of Gertie's gold button? Where'd it come from?"

"Honestly? I don't know. Maybe the answer does lie with the Cheapside collection. But there would have been hundreds of almost-identical ones worn by wealthy merchants and their wives throughout Elizabethan London. We have no proof."

Bella, perhaps sensing Kate's hesitation, went back to the manila folder from which she'd taken the family tree and pulled out a sepia photo of a gaunt woman leaning against a spinning wheel. She was dressed in a thick woolen skirt, an apron, and worn boots. "This is Clementine Murphy. Our Irish great-great-grandmother."

"She looks like such a frail old woman. It was criminal how hard they made them work."

Bella's face clouded over. "Clementine was just over forty in this photo."

Kate felt like she'd just been slapped. She peered at the photo of Clementine Murphy. "That's just five years older than I am now."

"Be grateful you weren't born to the lower classes in Edwardian times, if that's what a booming economy, free education, and 'Rule Britannia' looked like . . . I can't imagine what it must have been like to watch your babies die."

As soon as she said it, Bella flushed a deep red and covered her face with both hands for a moment before removing them and looking Kate squarely in the eye.

Her look made Kate nauseated. She tugged at the curl sitting over her eyebrow and smoothed it behind her ear. She knew what would follow, and her head scrambled to find some words. A new topic. Anything to stave off the conversation to come.

But it was too late.

"I'm sorry," said Bella softly, her voice cracking with empathy as she reached out and put her hand over Kate's, covering the button. "There's no grief like the loss of a child."

All the grief and guilt that had been bundled together and buried for four years was suddenly uncovered and exposed. Kate thought of her baby's tiny pale face poking out from the swaddling, his head crowned with a mass of thick darks curls—her curls, Essie's curls. She recalled his heavenly newborn smell. Purple lips. Eyes that never opened.

The left side of Kate's torso started to ache. She had lain a whole night on this side in her hospital bed, clutching her newborn, pressing him close as if she could spirit some life into him.

Jonathan had sat in a chair in the corner, head between his knees, unable to speak. All his years of medical training had borne down on him, like a glacier of guilt. Kate knew she should have said something that night to console him, to assure him that none of this was his fault. To show how much she cherished him. But how could she? All her words had fled.

The midwife had understood. She had said nothing, yet sat beside Kate for hours with a hand on her shoulder as Kate shivered and shuddered until there were no more tears. Her simple gesture had kept Kate yoked to humanity on that blackest of nights.

Somehow, Kate now forced herself to lift her face to bask in the sun's last rays, forced herself to breathe in, to inhale the heady scent of summer. After a moment, she blinked back her tears.

It was a routine she'd perfected in the last four years. Blinking away her tears, pushing her sadness back into the bottle and screwing on the lid. Her grief would strike, with crippling force, in unexpected places. It was like being struck over the head and knocked out when you were merely strolling down the street. At other times, it felt like the gentle undertow of the ocean dragging her under. Her doctors and therapists said the grief would become tolerable with time. They said she had to move on with her life. That she mustn't blame herself.

But how to move on when so much had been lost?

How to be a mother with no child?

She thought of Essie. Perhaps Essie hadn't talked much about life in London because she too had been carrying some sadness. Why rake over all that pain and stir it up? It was hard enough just to wade through an ordinary day.

Kate swallowed to clear her throat, but still no words would come. She thought of the journal buried deep in her bag. She carried it everywhere, yet rarely opened it. She didn't need to.

The carefree person who had bought that diary to record her thoughts on pregnancy was a ghost. So, too, were the black-and-white shadows of the ultrasound images she had pasted on its pages for safekeeping.

"It's okay," said Bella, her warm hand still resting on Kate's.

Kate looked at the hand covering her own, and thought of Jonathan squeezing this same hand to console her when they had no words left, only tears or silence. He'd squeezed her hand again as he'd handed back the keys to the Louisburg Square house when he left for New Zealand, their marriage broken beyond repair.

Bella met Kate's eyes and Kate managed a weak smile.

"I'm so sorry you lost Noah."

And there it was. Their Noah. Their precious baby boy.

A waiter approached and ushered them to another table for dinner. Once they'd ordered, Bella asked softly, "Have you spoken to Molly lately?"

"We've texted."

"She's worried about you. Thinks you're holding her at arm's length."

"What? That's ridiculous. I've just been traveling so much . . . the projects just keep coming."

"That's what worries her. And me, to be honest. I mean, none of us are immune from being workaholics." She took a sip of her wine. "But are you working because you love it or because you don't want to sit still? Because both can be true. And as far as I can tell you haven't stopped traveling since Jonathan left."

Kate nodded and said softly, "I can't help it. It's selfish, but when I see Emma . . ."

Bella squeezed Kate's hand. "I understand. Of course it hurts; your babies were born only months apart. Each birthday must be a reminder."

"I love them so much. Jessica, too. It's just that when I look at their family I can't . . . I can't forget my own."

"No one expects you to forget. But you're part of Molly's family too. Don't forget that. Your sister loves you like crazy. Remember when she punched me in the nose when I was teasing you about . . . ?" Bella paused, screwing up her nose. "I don't even remember what for. I can only remember taunting you one minute, then lying spread-eagled on the sand the next. She was vicious."

"Still is. Don't mess with her girls."

They both laughed as a waiter arrived with their shared plates. The clatter of cutlery on tabletops offered a reprieve as dishes filled with fresh burrata and char-grilled scallops were placed in front of them.

Both women ate with gusto as they veered into more comfortable territory, swapping work stories and catching up on holiday plans. When the waiter came to clear some empty plates, Kate and Bella each ordered a glass of rosé and more focaccia to mop up the juices. Grief and focaccia went together quite well, Kate was discovering.

As the waiter withdrew, Bella scooped some squeaky burrata into her mouth.

"Mmm, this is heavenly. Trust the out-of-towner to know the best places to go. If it had been left to me we'd be at my local Italian. Which is good, but not *this* good."

She wiped some crumbs from her lips with her napkin and pushed the white cheese toward Kate. "Have some before I eat it all."

The waiter returned with their rosé.

Kate took a sip and felt herself growing calmer. She wasn't sure if it was the alcohol, or the courtyard brimming with greenery, good food, and twilight.

She sat still, trying to lasso her emotions within the walls of the courtyard. It was crushing to have the world look at you with pity. People meant well when they shook their heads and said sorrowfully, "I don't know how you get out of bed every morning."

The truth was, neither did Kate.

But she *did* get out of bed, day after day, and she had kept moving until she'd started to feel a little less numb. Since Noah's birth, Kate had sought out small things to make her smile. The perfect espresso. Sitting on her front stoop with the autumn sun on her face while Emma rolled around in the tiny golden leaves that covered Louisburg Square. Valrhona chocolate.

In time, Kate had also started to set herself small goals and take on some assignments. The uncovering of a lost watercolor sketch for a maharaja's emerald neckpiece in the Cartier archives—each stone measured, scaled, and placed just so. Unscrambling the annotations in the jewelry inventory of Anne of Denmark and working out which pieces had been reset or sold.

Now, trying to find out how a small gold button had made its way into her family—and if it could indeed be connected to the Cheapside buttons she'd seen at the Museum of London.

Uncovering history took her deep into tragedies. But sometimes tracing the line of a jewel, the light bouncing off a diamond, showed Kate that, just like jewels, people could be reset and have a different kind of life.

As if gauging the shift in Kate's thinking, Bella said, "I'm not sure where this button—or pendant—has come from, but that drawing of yours links us and our great-grandmothers. Your job is to trace heirlooms and origins of precious pieces, but it's hardly surprising this Cheapside mystery is more than a job for you. I see it all the time in my work. People will do anything to keep their families together. And when they fail, they need to find something to fill their hearts."

Bella paused and took another sip of her wine. When she spoke, it was in a voice as soft as cotton wool. "When everything has been lost, families ruined, it's not uncommon to cling to something that reminds you of happier times."

Kate thought of her pregnancy journal, then her sapphire earrings.

Bella gently took the necklace from Kate and held it up so the button pendant caught the light. "Gertie drew that sketch of the button, I'm sure of it. So she must have seen the button—or one like it—with the jewels intact."

Kate sat still, sipping on her wine, pondering the coincidence that these buttons were the same as the ones she'd seen at the museum earlier this week. If Bella's button was linked to the Cheapside collection, then, as a historian, Kate would be obliged to expose it. After all, she was writing a report for her Swiss client suggesting he repatriate his treasured ring. Bella would have to give up her heirloom, and it would join the other buttons at the museum.

It was a professional conundrum, but at the heart of it was a far more personal question: Had Essie stolen a button from the Cheapside collection? Was that why her great-grandmother had never returned to London? But Essie spent eighty years in Boston, and surely the chances of being caught had faded. No one was going to arrest an old woman for the theft of a button, were they?

Chapter 11

ESSIE

LONDON, 1912

The walk home from school was always slow. Essie dropped her metal bucket to one side of the railway track running alongside their street, then placed a boot on the steel to feel for the familiar rumble of oncoming locomotives. Flora and Maggie joined her, scavenging for pieces of coal to fill the bucket as if they were on a treasure hunt.

The twins bent low to peer between the sleepers and slipped their small hands underneath to be certain they didn't miss any chunks that had spilled from the coal car as it roared past. Down near the wharves along the Thames, dear Freddie would be doing the same—collecting sticks and stray bits of wood to keep the old stove and boiler running at home.

Once the bucket was full of coal, the girls wiped their filthy hands on the grass beside the tracks and started to walk home.

Essie looked into her bucket, and then thought of the rotting bucket filled with soil and jewelry Danny and Freddie had found

The Lost Jewels

over at Cheapside the day before. It was impossible to get the image of the clump of soil dotted with gemstones out of her mind. She'd wanted to stay for a closer look at this treasure, but Mr. Hepplestone had ordered everyone to put down their tools and step out of the cellar and sewerage lines onto the footpath. No one was to breathe a word about what they'd seen.

With every step she tried to rid herself of the picture in her head of the foreman's warm and open smile, the way he'd touched the brim of his hat and greeted her like a lady. She'd been drawn to him, a bit like Gertie staring at her gold button, as if she couldn't quite believe something so shiny and golden existed. Just like the button, the foreman wasn't meant for the likes of her.

And yet, he'd written after they met yesterday. His ivory calling card stamped with gold copperplate letters was tucked into her apron pocket. On the back was a hastily scrawled note.

Dear Miss Murphy,

I hope you don't think it impudent of me to write. Our conversation was somewhat interrupted today and I'm most sorry.

I would be delighted if you would agree to correspond with me, if not meet for tea with an appropriate chaperone of your choosing.

I'm hoping this note may find you by way of your brother.

Most sincerely,
Mr. E. Hepplestone

Freddie had been so caught up with the button game, and then trying to untangle himself from Flora and Maggie, that it was only

105

later in the evening that he'd remembered to deliver the card. He muttered, "He's a strange one, that Edward, Es. You'd better not tell him 'bout what I brought home . . ."

Essie touched her pocket and withdrew her hand as if it had been stung. She wasn't sure what to make of the foreman's card, so she decided to do nothing. Besides, she had enough on her plate caring for Ma, Freddie, and the girls. It wouldn't do to be all giddy over a gentleman she'd met briefly in a muddy ditch.

The coal bucket was heavy and Essie switched arms. As they passed by the back lane, smells of cooking escaped from kitchen windows and hung thick in the air. Essie pictured mothers divvying up loops of Cumberland sausages and mash to clean, ruddy-faced children, with some stewed rhubarb or perhaps a sliver of still-warm butter cake to finish.

The twins scampered along shoulder to shoulder with their noses in the air, inhaling the delectable scent of other people's suppers. Only bread and dripping awaited them at home, though they never complained.

Gertie dawdled behind Essie and the twins, running her hands across ivy-clad walls and admiring orange nasturtiums and purple pansies spilling out of window boxes. London was exploding with life and color as the days grew longer and warmer.

Every now and again Essie would find a hole in the fence and gaze at gardens with bright borders and lines of carrots, peas, and parsley in neat rows, imagining what it would be like to tend a large plot of her own instead of the few clumps of parsley and sage and the climbing beans that clung desperately to the fence.

Gertie paused to study a bush studded with creamy roses scrambling up a drainpipe, standing on her toes to reach the flowers with their faces opened up to the sun. She plucked at the petals as if she were trying to work out how all the pieces overlapped, and Essie marveled at her sister's insatiable curiosity. What would become of this open-faced child as she became a young woman?

Essie glanced down at her hand holding the bucket and winced at her filthy nails and protruding veins. Gertie's hands, though dirty, were still fine and unscarred. They were the hands of an artist. Hands made for turning the pages of books.

Last week, Essie had met with Father McGuire at the vestry without her mother's knowledge. The priest had given her short shrift and repeated the headmaster Mr. Morton's decree: there would be no allowance made to keep the three Murphy girls in school.

"We simply have no more funds available. It's been a difficult year for us all. Imagine if the church made this exception for every child in the parish," Father McGuire said at his desk as he tucked into a thick cut of steak covered with mushrooms and pillowed on a pile of creamy mashed potato. Essie's stomach growled with hunger as she tried to ignore the peppery, buttery scent. The priest didn't even look up as he dismissed her from his office with a fork.

Essie had left in despair.

Gertie was about to be consigned to a factory corner, pinning collars to shirts. Her fine hands would become raw and bloody from constant pinpricks.

Essie would do anything to stop it . . . she was determined to try to convince Ma to let Gertie do the entrance examinations for the school for clever girls Miss Barnes had mentioned. But how?

When they reached home, Essie entered their tiny kitchen and almost tripped on the copper tub they used for bathing. It sat full of dirty water slick with gray suds, cold in front of the unlit boiler. Ma had forgotten to empty it when she'd finally woken and bathed.

"Girls," she said over her shoulder to Gertie and the twins as they piled into the kitchen, "can you carry this outside to the lav and tip it out, please?"

She heard them sigh in unison behind her, but didn't dare turn to see their disappointed faces as they realized there was no Ma—and no supper—in the kitchen. Instead, she emptied lumps of coal into the boiler and struck a match so she could prepare supper and heat some water. Next, she lit the oil lamps, which bathed the floral wallpaper with warm light, but also highlighted the peeling, moldy corners.

The spinning wheel sat in the corner of the kitchen, but the balls of wool lay in the basket untouched.

Essie walked over to the mantelpiece and picked up her late father's tankard, giving it a shake to check for coins; this was where her mother's daily spinning takings were deposited.

It was empty. Ma must have nipped down to the Merry Cobbler on the corner with the navvies and treated herself to a pennyworth of porter. Then kept treating herself until there were no more coins left.

Essie slipped out the back door to the garden and found her mother lying faceup inside the chicken coop. Ma was cursing and half waving an arm in the air, trying to swat away the half-dozen filthy brown hens perched on her legs and running over her belly. The egg basket was tipped sideways and her dress was splattered with mud.

Essie sighed and her shoulders sank.

Returning to the kitchen she found Gertie scribbling away in her notebook when she was supposed to be emptying the tub.

"Gertie, put that away and run next door and fetch Mrs. Yarwood. Go!" She turned her head so her sister wouldn't see her tears.

Essie ran back outside, grabbed her mother under each arm, and dragged her from the coop. It was like lifting a deadweight, and her mother's head flopped from side to side.

"Essie, love." Her mother's words were slurred. "Sorry. I just came out to collect the eggs and I must have tripped."

"Ma . . ." But there was no point being angry—her mother was too far gone to take any notice. Instead, Essie shooed away the chickens that followed them out of the coop. But the stubborn hen nesting in her mother's wicker basket refused to budge.

"Off! Out!" Essie said as she tipped the basket to one side to be rid of the hen. She was dismayed to see that only one egg remained unbroken. They must have smashed when her mother tripped. These were the first eggs of the week, and now there'd be no eggs for supper tonight.

Essie turned back to her mother and noticed that her dress had rucked up to reveal a bloody knee.

"Does it hurt, Ma?" she asked, kneeling quickly and wiping the wound with her sleeve. "Here, let's see if we can get you to sit up."

Her mother waved an arm in protest but Essie squatted behind her and gently lifted her by the shoulders. Her mother fell back against Essie, hiccupping.

When her spell had finished, Ma turned and stared at Essie before raising an unsteady hand to tuck a strand of hair behind her daughter's ear.

"My Esther—you look so like him, you know," she slurred in her thick Irish accent.

"I know, Ma," said Essie sadly.

"You're kind like him too. You could always rely on Conrad. He did the right thing by me. We sailed to London because my parents threw me—"

"I know, Ma . . . I know," said Essie as she cradled her mother in her arms as if she were a baby. She brushed her mother's thick dark hair away from her face and wiped the mud and chicken shit from her left cheek.

"I miss Pa too," Essie whispered. "We all do."

"Seven bonnie bairns he gave me."

Essie sighed. She sometimes wondered about the two little babies that passed away either side of Gertie. Molly with measles, Deidre—Deedee—lost to whooping cough. Both taken before they could walk.

She looked at the chicken coop in one corner of the yard, the squalid outhouse in the other, and shivered. She could hear Flora coughing in the kitchen. She needed to do something about that, she thought wearily.

Ma shifted and stroked Essie's cheek. "You're almost grown now. Same age as me when I had Freddie. You'll be wantin' to find a good husband."

Essie started to protest: "Ma!"

How could she leave home when her mother couldn't even stand up? Who would care for the girls? No, she'd stay, and she'd work her fingers to the bone if that's what it took to ensure the girls would grow up to have a better life than this.

She thought of the women in white, marching by the Monument. She imagined Gertie among them, dreaming, planning . . .

Her mother grabbed Essie's chin with surprising force. "I'll tell you, though, Miss Esther Murphy, there'll be no trying before they buy for you. You hear me? You'll not bring shame upon your father's name. A lass with your pretty face and fine figure—"

"Ma!" Essie flinched. It was impossible to see how the Murphy name could be sullied any further. Everyone knew Clementine Murphy was a drunk. Even the priest, Father McGuire, had suggested that he make home visits on Sunday afternoons rather than have Clementine bring the family to communion. The last time they went to church, Essie's mother had tipped the entire contents of the communion cup down her gullet as she knelt, and the shocked priest had had to wrestle the silverware from her grip.

"I'll throw you out, Esther Murphy. The lot o' you will be in the workhouse as quick as I can blink. If you or any of my girls—"

Essie was saved from the usual tirade by the appearance of Mrs. Yarwood with Gertie.

"Well, Gertie. You put the kettle on and then take the little ones to your room. There's a girl. Essie, let's get your mother up."

Mrs. Yarwood smoothed her skirts and winked at Essie. Her neighbor had no children of her own, yet regularly swept in and took command of their household like she'd been doing it all her life.

"Clemmie, can you stand? Oh, you've hurt your knee? Righto, take my arm. Essie, you grab the other arm. Now, let's see if we can get you standing."

The two women lifted Essie's mother to her feet, and they helped her limp into the kitchen and sat her on a chair.

Mrs. Yarwood started to unbutton Ma's dress, while Ma slapped her hands away. "I'm fine," she mumbled. "Just tired."

"I know," Mrs. Yarwood said soothingly, not taking a jot of notice as she peeled the filthy layers of underskirts and tunic from Ma's skinny body.

Essie ran to and from the tap outside, filling pitchers of water and transferring them to the round copper tub. When the kettle had boiled, she added the hot water and then helped Mrs. Yarwood lift her naked mother into the bath.

Essie began to sponge her mother, just like she did the twins. As Essie washed the remaining chicken shit from her cheeks, her ma nuzzled into Essie's hands like a small child. But when Essie looked her ma in the face, there was no hiding the bloodshot eyes and purple rings. Essie would have given anything to wash away her mother's sorrow and shame.

Meanwhile, Mrs. Yarwood unbraided Clementine's hair and massaged it with a few drops of sarsaparilla.

When they were done, Mrs. Yarwood held the dozy Clementine while Essie dried her and slipped a crisp white calico nightie over her head.

"Let's get you settled into bed then, Clementine."

They walked upstairs with Essie's mother supported between them. Ma's brass bed took up the entire room—the only other furniture was Pa's desk, which stood like a shrine in the far corner.

It was all they had left of him. When they'd had to move to the Yarwoods' garden flat four years ago they had sold everything except the bed and his desk.

Mrs. Yarwood helped Essie finish drying Ma's hair and wind it into a side braid with rags.

"There, there. You'll feel better in the morning."

Essie studied the floral wallpaper and felt her chest tighten.

Things would be just the same in the morning . . .

Her mother went straight to sleep, her cheeks rosy, smelling of sarsaparilla, between white pillows and sheets.

Mrs. Yarwood turned and squeezed Essie's arm. "You're doing well, Essie. Your linen is as white as snow, there's not a scrap of grease in the kitchen. You wash and scrape this place and all that's in it every night. Clementine . . ." She stalled. Then, after a glance at Essie's red, raw hands, she pursed her lips. "You'll be coming over for supper at ours tonight."

"But—"

Mrs. Yarwood raised her hand. "No arguments, now. I have such a big pot of supper cooking, it would take Mr. Yarwood and me weeks to eat it. And he does like different dishes . . . So you see? You'd be doing us both quite the favor."

Essie started to cry. Mrs. Yarwood was so kind, and Essie was just so very tired. She wanted to crawl into bed with her mother and sleep. But she thought of the girls and their skinny legs . . .

"Thank you. I'll bathe the girls, and we'll be over."

"That's more like it." Mrs. Yarwood drew Essie into a hug and rubbed her back. "See you in an hour."

Chapter 12

Essie knocked at the door while the girls stood behind her in fresh dresses with pink cheeks.

Mrs. Yarwood flung open the door and gathered them all into a big hug. Flora started to cough and their host stepped back and studied the girl, quickly pressing the back of her hand to the child's forehead. Turning, she checked Maggie's forehead too before stepping back to let them in.

"Ladies, I hope you brought your usual appetites. Mr. Yarwood has already had his supper." She waved them inside and down the hall before shutting the front door.

The smell of roast beef wafted down the hallway, and they eagerly followed the scent.

As they walked past the front parlor, Essie spotted Mr. Yarwood sitting in his favorite leather chair, smoking a cigar and reading *The Times*.

Mr. Yarwood quickly lowered his paper and nodded at Essie and her sisters and gave them a warm smile as they passed.

"Hello, Miss Murphy. Hello, young ladies."

"Good evening, Mr. Yarwood," Essie replied as she ushered the girls down the hall and into Mrs. Yarwood's bright kitchen with its buttercup walls and floral curtains. Instead of the Murphys' dirt floor, the Yarwoods had gleaming floorboards polished with linseed oil.

They sat at a sweet round oak table, already set with soup-spoons and blue linen napkins. Essie unfolded her napkin and gestured at the girls to do the same. Maggie flicked her napkin with a flourish and giggled as she laid it across her lap, spine straight, as if she were dining at the Ritz.

Mrs. Yarwood busied herself ladling soup from a big tureen into blue bowls.

Flora leaned over to smell the soup, and Maggie shot Mrs. Yarwood a quizzical look, not daring to speak.

"Lentil with a few caraway seeds. I thought I'd make up a bit of soup using the cider stock I had left over from the ham," Mrs. Yarwood said, in answer to their strange looks.

"Well, it sounds delicious," said Essie, lifting her spoon and nodding at the girls to do the same.

"Wait! Just one more thing," said Mrs. Yarwood, and she bustled over to her cool box. She produced a jug from which she scooped a dollop of cream into each of the soup bowls and sprinkled them with parsley.

Essie lifted her spoon to her mouth. The soup was thin, slightly salty from the ham and sour from the cider, sweetened and softened by the lentils. The cream thickened the soup, and the caraway seeds left a warm hint of anise on her tongue.

"The caraway's gone to seed already in my garden." Mrs. Yarwood pointed to where the plants feathered among the neat lines of carrot tops and tomatoes in her backyard plot. "It's been so unseasonably warm . . . Here, have some more, Miss Maggie."

Mrs. Yarwood swooped on Maggie's empty bowl and refilled it, again adding cream and parsley.

Essie frowned a little at Maggie. "Careful, don't be greedy—"

"Nonsense! I'll have none of that. These girls have hollow legs that need filling. Don't you Gertie, dear?"

Gertie looked up from stirring her soup; she had been lost in a daze, studying the pattern of the cream melting into the broth. "Thank you, Mrs. Yarwood," she said. "This is better than anything King George is being dished up, I'm sure of it."

"Eat up, Gertie-girl. There's plenty more where that came from." She patted Gertie on the shoulder then leaned over to Essie and whispered, "I put a little extra pinch of the caraway on account of the girls. It'll warm their heads and their tummies and hopefully help to drive away those nasty coughs."

Mrs. Yarwood acted as the neighborhood's unofficial dispensary. Everyone knew that if you were going through hard times and couldn't afford to visit a doctor or hospital, you could send to Mrs. Yarwood for some thyme and myrrh powder to ease a sore tooth, a licorice and calendula liniment to ease a rash, or a bitter cough syrup sweetened with cinnamon so the little ones would swallow it by the spoonful. Sometimes Mrs. Yarwood would keep the child at her home for a day or two until a fever had passed.

Made lively by the hearty meal, the girls were chattering excitedly around the table. Gertie's cheeks were flushed as she recounted a ballroom scene from a play she was studying with Miss Barnes, describing the silk ball gown and billowing skirts of Juliet as she linked arms with a dashing intruder and danced at the grandest ball in Verona.

"Can't you just imagine a place where all the floors and walls are made of marble, and the women can wear silk gowns in any color they like?" she enthused.

"I'd choose a ruby red," Flora declared.

"I'd choose purple," said Maggie. "And Essie would choose blue. Bright blue."

"You know me too well," said Essie. "But don't forget my diamond earrings and gold buttons—" Essie stopped. Gertie's button. What had she done with it? More importantly, what *could* they do with it? Freddie had mentioned a pawnbroker who did the rounds of the building sites. Stony someone, that was his name. She made a note to ask Freddie as a plan started to form in her mind. It might not lead to silk dresses, but it was a start.

"I'd choose white, with green and purple ribbons," said Gertie with a set jaw, making Mrs. Yarwood chuckle.

"I'm sure you would, Gertie-girl!"

When they'd had their fill of soup, Mrs. Yarwood carved thick slices of beef and served it with roast potatoes and fresh peas and carrots from her garden. She put another plate aside and covered it with a cloth.

"For you to take home for Freddie. Poor fellow . . . all those long hours he works."

"Thank you. You spoil us, Mrs. Yarwood," said Essie, grateful that her brother would not miss out on this delicious treat.

The girls devoured their meals with gusto. When they were done, Essie stood to help clear the plates, but Mrs. Yarwood gently pushed her back into her chair.

"Just you rest your feet now. I'll take care of this washing-up when you've left; it will give me something to occupy myself. Mr. Yarwood will be halfway through his newspaper and won't thank me for interrupting him before he's finished!"

Mrs. Yarwood smiled fondly as she gestured up the hallway, and in that moment, she was the same dreamy bride whose likeness graced a silver frame on the wall near the entrance to the kitchen. Mrs. Yarwood caught Essie studying the picture and flushed slightly.

"Thirty years next month. Posting a letter, he was. Right near the Victoria station. We both reached toward the postbox at the same time and, gentleman that he is, Mr. Yarwood stepped back and allowed me to post my letter first. Our eyes locked and, well . . ." Her face was as red as a beet now, and she wiped her hands on her apron.

Flora giggled and Maggie looked up at Mrs. Yarwood from under her long lashes. Mrs. Yarwood reached out and tickled Maggie under her chin.

"It's not much of a story, I know. Silly, isn't it? Meeting at a postbox. But I could tell right in that moment that Mr. Yarwood was a good man. A kind man. He came for tea at my parents' house the following Wednesday. He then came every Wednesday, before he went to his night accounting class. We went on like that for months. Sometimes on a Saturday we'd go out for a walk around the Serpentine, followed by an ice cream. Vanilla. Or strawberry . . ."

Mrs. Yarwood stood and picked up her plate.

"I'm carrying on. We're no Romeo and Juliet, but we've been happy enough. Saved our pennies for a year until we could marry. Made a down payment on this little place, then the garden flat where you rent. We didn't need all the rooms in the end, since we weren't blessed with children. So we are pleased enough to see a good family in it."

Essie would be forever grateful the Yarwoods had rented their garden flat to the Murphys, otherwise they'd be with the rest of their kind in the slums over the lane—or, worse, the workhouse. Both families lived in an old row house, divided into two. The Yarwoods had the bigger half, with the majority of the garden, and the Murphys had the smaller flat with a garden just big enough for a chicken shed and a few rows of vegetables. The sun's last rays were beaming through the window, bathing the kitchen in golden light. Essie sighed and ran her hands over the neatly pressed tablecloth. Leaning back in her chair, she imagined eating all her meals at a table like this, surrounded by the girls and Freddie. And Ma, of course—when she was sober.

In the mellow light she thought of Edward Hepplestone, the man with the green eyes. The wrinkles around his eyes when he smiled. His full lips. There had been something in the look between them . . . Should she respond to his note?

She was still pondering this question when Mrs. Yarwood placed the last of the dirty plates in the sink with a clatter and turned back to face her guests. "Now, I wonder if you little mites have a bit of room in your tummies for cake?"

Maggie's eyes widened and she looked to Essie to see if this was a trick.

"I have here a little left over from Mr. Yarwood's afternoon tea: apple cake. His favorite."

She cut four thick wedges and transferred them onto pretty blue plates with scalloped edges.

As Flora reached for two plates to pass them along, Mrs. Yarwood cried, "Wait!"

The little girl withdrew her hands smartly as if they'd been smacked.

Mrs. Yarwood smiled and produced a small bowl. "You don't want to be missing the best part. Clotted cream! This won't keep until tomorrow so you'd best all have a double scoop."

Essie suspected Mr. Yarwood had been dispatched down to the corner store the minute Mrs. Yarwood walked back in her front door having issued her dinner invitation.

"This will put a little meat on those bones," she said with just the faintest furrow of her brow. "And one for you, Miss Essie."

Mrs. Yarwood placed the biggest slice of cake in front of Essie. She wasn't sure whether she could eat anything more. Her stomach had shrunk along with their circumstances. Still, she didn't want to appear rude, so she lifted her fork and began to eat, savoring the caramelized apple with just a hint of brandy.

She frowned as Flora pushed a too-big chunk onto her fork with her fingers and wobbled it to her mouth before stuffing it in.

Not to be outdone, Maggie ran her finger over her already-empty plate and lifted it to her lips to lick so as not to waste a drop of the heavenly thick cream.

"Flora! Maggie! Manners!" hissed Essie, remembering back to when her mother used to let her lick the spoon when she was baking. She can't have been more than eight. Her mother's belly had been as round and ripe as the Kerry Pippin apples that fell from the tree in their backyard. In fact, Clementine's belly had been so big that Essie had had to help her tie the apron strings. Oh, how she'd loved it when her mother made apple pie . . . It had been such a long time since she had. Not since Da had died. It seemed to Essie that the Murphy children had lost more than their father to the war; they had lost their mother too. But she was determined that the twins, at least, wouldn't feel Ma's absence the way their older siblings did.

Essie sat in the rocking chair in the corner of their tiny bedroom sewing, oil lamp burning beside her. She was hemming a pair of pants for Freddie that she'd fashioned from an old woolen blanket Mrs. Ruben had folded into her basket when no one was looking. If she steamed the trousers in the morning—and no one studied the stitching too closely—they should be a sturdy enough pair for work.

Essie hadn't failed to notice Freddie's foreman's pristine suit and pressed shirt. What would it be like to wake up to fresh linen every day? She'd noticed his strong hands, too, and she slowed her needlework just for a second as she imagined what it would be like to have one of those hands caress her cheek.

She could feel herself blushing. Had she been trying to impress him just a little yesterday afternoon in Cheapside when she'd lifted her chin and behaved as demurely as a true lady might? She'd been desperate for him to see her not just as a factory worker—a navvy's sister—but instead as someone at home in a foyer with gilded ceilings, oil paintings, and wide hallways.

She imagined he might have a sister or a mother among the throngs at the Monument in their white dresses.

Her eyes strained as she stitched the last of the hem. She sighed and folded the pants before standing and placing them on the chair. Then she carried the lamp over to her bedside table and climbed into bed beside Gertie. Under her sister's hand lay the ledger book Mr. Yarwood had given her. Essie prized the notebook from beneath the girl's hand and placed it on the table beside the lamp.

Essie knew she should turn the lamp off, but she was restless and couldn't sleep.

On the far side of the bed, the twins lay curled together, arms entwined atop the blanket. She sat up a little and watched their chests rise and fall, observed the dark shadows under their eyes. They were not even a decade old, and yet they wore the weariness of the elderly.

Outside there were shouts and whistles as the public house closed. Irish accents boomed down the narrow streets as their owners staggered to their homes reeking of beer. Essie thought of her mother's torn stockings. Had she stumbled home just like these men, swaying and sad? Knowing that the morn would bring a day just as miserable as the last? And on that cheery note, she turned off the lamp, pulled the thin blanket up to her chin, and went to sleep.

Chapter 13

KATE

HYDERABAD, INDIA, PRESENT DAY

Kate bounced around in the back seat of the taxi as it bumped over potholes, watching a purple plastic god Shiva bob and rock on the dashboard as Lady Gaga blasted from the stereo. Even the diva's soaring notes failed to block the constant screech of horns and thrum of engines as the Hyderabad traffic crawled toward the ancient mosque of Charminar. Marcus sat in the front seat with the window down, camera poised. Scooters and motorcycles weaved across the lanes of the road and onto the footpaths, and thick exhaust fumes mixed with tantalizing cooking smells.

They stopped at a traffic light and a knot of skinny children banged against the doors of the taxi and thrust their upturned palms through the window even as Kate started to roll it up. The kids remained brazenly optimistic, running alongside the car laughing, teasing, as the lights changed and the driver moved off. They were desperate, but not angry.

Hyderabad was seething with life. Kate had never experienced such chaos. But, then, she'd never been to India before.

Marcus looked over his shoulder and grinned. "It's a lot to take in."

Kate shook her head in wonder. "It's like . . . it's like life has exploded."

Even though she'd been told her first moment in India would be unlike any other travel experience, she'd smugly dismissed it. But outside, women in bright saris and shawls carried baskets with gold bangles layered all the way up their arms. Stately Shi'a women in black burqas and hijabs walked alongside men in open shirts, shorts, and flip-flops, while hawkers in *salwar* suits peddled their wares on every corner. Lanky youths sporting Coldplay and ripped i h a t e t r ump T-shirts sipped chai at tables set on footpaths.

They continued past rows of crumbling concrete buildings, teeming with peddlers and strung with colored tarpaulins as the Charminar appeared on the skyline.

Marcus's phone rang. As he held it up to see who was calling, Kate saw the name a a a o l i v i a on the screen.

Kate wondered what o l i v i a had done to merit the priority a a a that would lift her to the top of his contacts list. She thought about when she'd last seen Marcus—at the Tiffany anniversary celebrations in New York a couple of months back. The striking woman on his arm dressed in Dolce & Gabbana had definitely *not* been a a a o l i v i a. Kate tried to recall the woman's name: Natalya? Natalie? She'd had the steel-blue eyes and straw-colored hair of a Russian supermodel, top of her class from Wharton Business School, and a new top-floor office at J.P. Morgan.

Marcus turned slightly for privacy, speaking in a hushed voice. "Liv, I promise! I'm only here a couple of days, so you can still meet me in Galle . . . Okay, I'll call you tomorrow. " He turned and caught Kate's eye. "Love you too," he said casually before ending the call and tucking the phone into his shirt pocket.

Kate swallowed, a little thrown. Marcus had spoken the words so lightly—so tenderly—that it had shocked her.

She wasn't indignant on behalf of the Russian goddess. Natalya/Natalie had looked like she could lead a revolution as she'd outlined her new job overseeing collections and special acquisitions to Kate. She imagined there was a long queue of men vying for a permanent position on that golden arm.

Marcus adjusted the scuffed camera bag on his knees and a lock of hair fell across his face. He briefly lifted his left hand and rubbed his chin, as if he was struggling with a decision. His hands were large, calloused, and weathered by the sun, a far cry from the fine-boned pale hands of conservators and curators—or Jonathan's surgeon's hands.

Kate's own phone beeped with a message from her sister: *Lunch next Friday when you are back in Boston? Just us. Jess working, Em at kinder. Let's go fancy.*

She quickly typed in a response: *Sure! Ditch kinder and bring Emma. Can't wait. xx*

Bella was right. Kate considered her cousin's button and the linked sketches and replayed the words she'd been turning over in her head ever since their dinner the night before: *The most precious things in life can't be bought or replaced.*

She missed seeing Molly, Jessica, and Emma every week. When Jonathan had first moved out, she'd spent several days a week curled up on their sofa with Emma, watching *The Wiggles* DVDs, both of them gazing wide-eyed at the people dancing in colored sweatshirts, and clapping along to "Fruit Salad," "Yummy Yummy," and "Big Red Car." Jessica cooked comfort food—spaghetti and meatballs, *coq au vin*, and lasagna—while Molly managed Kate's divorce settlement and helped her organize her receipts into color-coded piles before curling up beside her on the sofa and resting her head on Kate's shoulder, just as she had when they were children.

"Your curls are going up my nose again," she'd complain as the handsome Red Wiggle shook his index fingers in the air and gyrated his hips.

The four minarets of the Charminar rose from an ocean of cars and taxis, almost an apparition in the heat and haze. The traffic had all but stalled, so Marcus paid the driver, grabbed his camera bag, and said, "Let's go," as he opened his door and stepped out into the maelstrom.

"It's beautiful," Kate said, standing stock-still as she admired the peaked arches and Islamic patterns dancing around the corners of the mosque.

Marcus grabbed her hand and pulled her close as they weaved through honking rickshaws and scooters to dart down a lane.

"We need to go straight to the bazaar," yelled Kate above the noise. "I can't wait to see the traders—"

"Before we do anything else, we need to eat."

"Where?" Kate eyed a man bundling samosas into brown paper bags at a roadside stall.

"Laad Bazaar." Marcus pointed to where the crowds were funneling into narrow alleys.

But Kate was too hungry to wait. "Hold on," she said, and she approached the man and bought a samosa for each of them, fumbling the unfamiliar coins as she paid.

"*Keema samosa*," said Marcus as he tore his in half, releasing spice-scented steam. "Hyderabad food is different to the rest of India. The whole city is a mix of Arab and Turkish cultures."

Kate devoured her samosa, licking the drips of garlicky minced lamb and yogurt from her fingers. "These are incredible. Maybe I should get more?"

"Trust me, you'll want to leave room . . ."

Marcus led her into a maze of alleys, past stalls selling spools of bright cotton, endless rows of golden bangles studded with gemstones, earthenware pots, and bags of spices in every hue. Soon they came to a central alley, where the aromas of spices, roasting meats, and piquant curry sauces blotted out the diesel and smog.

They reached a tiny hole-in-the-wall and Marcus stopped. An old woman in a pink sari with gold bangles tinkling up her arm seated them on wooden crates at an outdoor table covered with a checked cloth. They asked for a beer each, and Kate pressed the bottle to her cheek to cool herself.

"You order, please," she said. "I eat everything."

"Great." Marcus grinned. There were beads of sweat at his brow, and his linen shirt was already damp and creased, but he looked so at ease sitting there in a crowded alley among the shrieking hawkers and crush of shoppers.

"How many times have you been here?" Kate asked.

"Four times. Once as a backpacker at eighteen, then three times for work."

"Work?" Kate thought of the glossy fashion spreads and jewelry catalogs he was booked for years in advance, then his cover for *National Geographic* she'd spotted at Heathrow.

"Don't look so surprised. You think I just do fashion and jewelry? I enjoy the fashion—it's edgy and the people are fun. But it's the *people*, not the fashion, that I find fascinating . . ."

"I didn't mean . . ." Her ears started to burn.

"I know." He waved his hand and smiled. "I like to explore, to try to capture what makes this world tick. Do you know how many war photographers do weddings?"

"Really?"

"True! Light and shade, Kate. You can't just focus on the dark stuff; it'll tear you apart." Marcus paused, his jaw tensed, and Kate caught a glimpse again of the shadows that had crept across his face in the museum. He opened his mouth, about to say something else, when a parade of green plastic plates arrived piled with food.

"Heaven!"

Marcus talked her through the dishes. "Start with the buttermilk *vada*." He pointed. "The fritters are made with fennel and spices, and the sauce is buttermilk with curry leaves, finished with a scoop of yogurt and some coriander leaves on top."

Kate obediently scooped some onto her plate and began to eat.

"I've never tasted Indian food like this," she said.

"These days people come to Hyderabad for the food, just like people in past centuries came for the diamonds and gemstones."

"You're not taking any pictures?"

Marcus shrugged. "Not of my food. Not my thing. I like to just . . . eat, you know? Enjoy the moment, savor the company."

Kate lifted a napkin to her lips to hide the blush she felt creeping onto her cheeks. What was wrong with her? Maybe the heat and jetlag were catching up with her.

Next up was a lentil dal made zestier with tamarind; kebabs marinated in chili and coriander (so tender they melted in her mouth); and a creamy *malai korma* with potato and paneer dumplings. Kate's favorite, though, was the *dum biryani*—basmati rice cooked with turmeric and other spices, then piled high with marinated meats, served with green chilies mixed in a peanut masala.

As she tore a piece of roti and dipped it in the leftover masala sauce, Kate studied the curves of the Charminar just visible at the end of the alley. Beside them was a stall dripping with strands of pearls. It wasn't a stretch to imagine a similar scene centuries ago as diamond dealers and silk merchants loaded up oxen and braved narrow tracks on mountain passes as they traveled the silk route between here and Persia. She pulled out her notebook and recorded her impressions before tucking it away again to eat.

When they'd finished eating, the old woman cleared their plates and poured them cups of chai, which was accompanied by crescent-shaped biscuits that tasted of coconut and saffron.

As Kate bit into her second biscuit, she said, "There're millions of stalls here. How'd you know to come to this one?"

"My guide introduced me last time. Aarav. You'll meet him this afternoon when he takes us to meet a couple of gem dealers."

Marcus smiled at the old woman and raised his hands together in thanks. "That was incredible."

It struck Kate how easygoing Marcus was with women. When she'd first met him she'd expected him to be what Sophie would call "a bit of a lad," but he'd always been a polite and attentive colleague. They'd worked well together in London, as always. He'd solicited opinions from Saanvi and Gayle and peppered them with questions about each piece as he shot. It wasn't so much that he was charming—for he certainly was—but that he was genuinely interested in the curators' expertise. Kate was ashamed to think that she'd dismissed his rugged good looks and charm as part of a standard playboy fashion photographer package.

Marcus paid the old woman for lunch, and she beamed. "Thank you, sir. You come back. India is in your heart."

Kate and Marcus wandered back out into the bazaar. She didn't mind the dusty kids swarming about her, or peddlers poking at her shoulders and shouting at her to buy beautiful emeralds, beautiful gold bracelets, a golden sari. Women grabbed her hands and promised to make her beautiful with henna tattoos, others draped strands of pearls down their swanlike necks and swayed to Hindi pop music.

Kate stopped and bought a beautiful blue cashmere shawl for Molly and a burgundy one for Jessica. She also bought a handful of green glass bangles.

"For Emma—my niece."

"Who needs an emerald watch?" Marcus chuckled as he handed over money for a magnificent sheer turquoise cashmere shawl. He offered no explanation as to whom he was buying it for, but he asked that it be gift wrapped. "They don't have the exact green I was after. But this is lovely."

Kate nodded. "It sure is," she said as he tucked the gift into his camera bag.

They kept walking, Marcus with his camera in hand, discreetly taking photos as they walked among the crowds. He was so respectful of the people around him, never training his lens on someone's face, instead taking a detail of a painted tile, the line of a copper pot, or a plate of grilled lamb kebabs steaming with coriander, cumin, and garlic.

They stopped to watch a spice merchant pull trays of spices from an old brick oven at the back of his stall and then grind them up to make garam masala. Kate bought a bag for Molly, who loved curry perhaps more than any other food.

"I'll have a bag too, please," said Marcus. "Though I'm not sure I could replicate any of the dishes we just had. Still, I might try my hand at that *biryani*. You could come and taste it for me, tell me if I get it right."

"Where's home for you when you're not traveling?" Kate realized she'd never asked. They'd been acquaintances and occasional colleagues for years, but she had no idea where he was based.

"Sydney, mostly. Plus I have a shoebox apartment and studio in New York. Paris for the shows."

She rolled her eyes. "Right, then it should be easy for me to make it from Boston for dinner . . ." As soon as she said it, Kate had a yearning to be curled up with a hot chocolate and a good book on her velvet sofa at home in Louisburg Square. She touched Essie's sapphires at her ears as if they were Dorothy's red shoes

131

and could transport her home. She'd landed in a supersize Oz and it was both exhilarating and baffling.

Marcus checked his watch. "We have a bit of time before the first appointment Aarav has arranged. He'll meet us at the diamond dealer—over on the far alley where you can see the Charminar. Very discreet. Eighth-generation dealer."

"Should have some interesting stories from the past."

"Definitely! I'm also really glad that you scheduled a trip to see some mining in Sri Lanka. The mines up near Ratnapura are something else. I think we can do something amazing with the pics—and your article—linking in this bazaar, then the mines, to give people a sense of the journey of a gemstone."

"Hope so." Kate grinned.

Marcus went still. "After Golconda Fort tomorrow, I'm going to Galle for five days for a beach break before I meet you up in the mountains. You should come. I know you planned to stay at the hotel here and do some writing, but who doesn't love a few days by the sea?"

"Marcus . . ." Kate felt flustered as they stepped out of the shop and warm bodies bumped into her, pressing silk and sweaty cotton against her sticky skin. "Aren't you . . . meeting someone? I heard you on the phone . . ." Kate ducked her head. She didn't want Marcus to see how embarrassed she was at being caught eavesdropping on his phone call to a a a ol iv i a.

"Yes, I plan on having a few days' break with Liv." Marcus hesitated for a moment. "She's my daughter."

Later that afternoon, as the light faded and the call to prayer rang out across the city, they walked among the surging crowds. Kate's shoulders were knocked and she was almost forced against the wall as the street heaved with bodies. Never had she seen so many people. Marcus stopped at a shop selling vintage framed photos. Kate pulled out her notebook and wrote about the line of jewelers across from them, each with flashing lights in the windows, and samples of gold chains and pastel gems arranged on velvet pedestals. Hawkers were out the front, each louder than the last.

A man with no teeth grabbed Kate's arm and tugged her inside to where Marcus stood. "Come see."

The hunched shop owner pulled out a black-and-white photo of a striking Miss World winner from 1966. Her poise, long glossy hair, and licorice eyes suited the diamond crown and scepter. But it was a reproduction painting that caught Kate's eye—it could have been a scene straight out of Bollywood, with a white man lounging on a red velvet seat dressed as a Hyderabadi businessman in a burgundy-and-gold *qaba* skirt, fur-lined gold robe, and a silk cream turban studded with rubies and diamonds. Kate instantly recognized the figure as one of the most famous early foreign diamond merchants.

"Who's that?" asked Marcus, narrowing his eyes to read the caption.

Kate smiled. She'd seen this face in many of her history books. "Jean-Baptiste Tavernier. He wrote volumes about his travels in Golconda. He came six times from Europe in the seventeenth century. But there were other European diamond buyers from

Britain, France, Holland, and Belgium. The East India Company had their own British gem traders on the ground."

She thought of the Golconda diamond that had caught her eye at the museum. There was every chance the diamond rough would have been sold in a market just like the one she now stood in. But where did it go next? How did *that* Golconda rough end up in a champlevé ring abandoned in a London cellar?

Marcus asked the shopkeeper the price and paid for the painting without haggling.

Kate raised an eyebrow. "You could probably have bought the original oil painting for that!"

Marcus shrugged and held it out. "We flew here business class, caught an air-conditioned taxi, and checked into a hotel that used to be a palace. Men like these guys would have come by ship, risking shipwreck, pirates, or scurvy. Or come overland, risking disease, robbery, and murder. Also, can you just imagine the heat?"

"Not in those robes, I can't." Kate tapped the picture. "But I agree, that's the lure of gemstones." She thought of George saying he wouldn't necessarily sell to the highest bidder. "It sets something afire in our soul when we touch a beautiful gem," she whispered, almost to herself.

THE BAZAAR

Ekmel stood at the edge of the bazaar setting up his stall. Just steps away the creamy minarets of the Charminar stood like sentinels, ghostly in the morning mist, as the hum and bustle of the markets started to rise.

The gem merchant unfurled a roll of hide across his table, but left the gemstones and jewels tucked under his turban. He preferred to stick to the edges of the market, staying well clear of the carpet peddlers, beggars, and loudmouthed diamond dealers who screeched and bickered across the middle aisles until the market closed before evening prayers.

Women draped in black dresses and veils weaved among the vendors, prodding at fish and chickens in cages, buying bagfuls of dried fruit and nuts, loading beans and rice into baskets on their backs. The smell of roasting kebabs, cardamom, and stewing apricots filled the crisp air, mingling with the sweat of horses and oxen and the pungent hair of goats corralled in a pen at the southern end.

Ekmel had just finished arranging some gems in a wooden box when he noticed a young man standing still and silent among the chaos. The youth met his gaze with a raised chin, a pride out of kilter with his gaunt face and filthy bare feet. Ekmel closed the box and locked it as the youth pressed through the crowds and made his way toward him.

As the youth approached, Ekmel rested a hand on the dagger at his belt. He wanted this beggar—or slave—gone before his customers arrived.

"I have something I wish you to sell for me."

The man sighed. Every day skinny boys and youths just like this one streamed over the mountains from Golconda Fort and beyond, walking barefoot for days just to sell stolen slips of silk, dusty surcoats, or stolen gemstones at the market. He shooed them all away, just as he should shoo this youth away—however, there was a dignity about this youth that he couldn't explain.

"What is your name, boy?" he asked.

"Sachin."

"Show me what you have," Ekmel said with a sigh.

The boy reached under his turban and removed a filthy cloth. He untied the string and tipped a rough into his palm.

Without hesitation, Ekmel lifted the diamond rough up between thumb and forefinger and reached for his eyepiece. The stone was of the clearest water. He stood with the boy and whispered in a low voice, "Golconda."

The youth nodded.

Ekmel glanced around the market to see if any of the king's men were nearby. They'd been known in recent months to raid the market stalls and throw any traders who bought stolen diamonds from slaves into the dungeons—or worse. Still, he felt sorry for this weary youth.

Ekmel said, "I have a foreigner meeting me here this morning to look at diamonds."

"Can you sell him this one?"

"Perhaps." Ekmel shrugged. "But my commission will be higher given the circumstances . . ."

The youth's expression remained unchanged.

"I'll take half."

The boy pursed his lips, but nodded.

"Go!" Ekmel urged. "Eat some food and return here in one hour."

Sachin nodded, his ribs rippling through his dusty skin.

Muttering to himself that his wife would wring his neck if she found out, Ekmel tucked his wooden box under his arm for safekeeping, took a coin from his purse, and walked the boy across to the food stalls. In his native tongue, Ekmel ordered a plate piled with steaming yellow rice topped with a spicy lentil stew.

Instructing the boy to keep out of sight, Ekmel turned to go back to his stall.

"Please . . ."

Ekmel turned back.

"You will sell the diamond for a fair price, won't you? My brother died and we need to make an offering. My family . . ." His voice faded, as if he'd run out of breath and was too tired to speak.

Ekmel nodded curtly. "I will see what I can do."

The foreigner arrived at the agreed time, but instead of the usual dark waistcoat and pants he'd worn to the bazaar these past months he was dressed in the Persian style, with a qaba *skirt in red silk and a matching burgundy robe. On his head was a golden silk turban with a ruby the size of an eye sewn at the center.*

Taking this adoption of local dress as a sign of goodwill, Ekmel spread the diamonds he'd removed from his own turban into the wooden box lined with silk, allowing the foreigner to take his time as he picked through the gemstones. Finally, Ekmel slipped the diamond from the youth into the box, and held his breath as the foreigner picked up the youth's rough and turned it over in his hand.

"We can have it cut for you, sir," Ekmel offered, gesturing toward the cutters and polishers huddled over stone wheels at the far end of the bazaar.

The foreigner shook his head. "My buyer prefers to cut and polish his own. I'll take this diamond today, with those pink sapphires."

Ekmel nodded and named his price. As he expected, the foreigner bargained hard. He was about to settle on a figure, when he glanced up and saw Sachin watching. The boy had said he wanted a fair price for his family.

So, against his better judgment, Ekmel held firm. "This diamond, sir, is from Golconda. You can tell . . . the purest water."

Eventually, the deal was done, gold exchanged.

"Prepare the stones for travel," demanded the foreigner.

"Certainly." Ekmel placed the diamond rough with the three sapphires in a small leather bag, then placed it in a wooden box

and wrapped the box in a square of white cotton cloth. Finally, he sealed the parcel with red wax and pressed his merchant's seal into the wax with his ring.

Ekmel handed the box to the foreigner. "If I may be so bold as to ask, sir, where are you from?"

"Antwerp," the man replied. "But these stones will travel with me to Bandar Abbas." The foreigner leaned in conspiratorially, buoyed perhaps by the excellent deal and the smell of sweet chai and simmering stew teasing from across the alley. He whispered, "I have a letter of introduction to a Dutch jeweler—Polman—who has a reputation for buying the best stones. Prefers to cut them himself."

The foreigner wiped droplets of sweat from his pink cheeks and waved the sealed box in the air. "See you on my next trip. Good day, sir."

Chapter 14

ESSIE

LONDON, 1912

Essie tugged on the twins' hands as they walked up West Hill in Wandsworth with Gertie, Freddie, and his friend Danny on Saturday morning. Freddie had convinced them all it would be well worth their while to visit old Stony Jack, the pawnbroker who regularly popped by the Golden Fleece at quitting time to have a pint with the lads.

They'd been walking since breakfast. The streets of terraces curved uphill, topped with endless rows of chimney pots spewing black smoke.

But the warm days had brought cheer to the streets. Flower boxes overflowed with ferns, periwinkles, petunias, and fuchsia. Ivy smothered walls. As they crossed a lane, Essie paused to take in the sweetness of star jasmine spilling over a fence and imagined herself in that backyard in the evening, lying on a blanket and the air thick with perfume as she read Miss Barnes's copy of *The Wind in the Willows* to Flora, Maggie, and Gertie. She picked a sprig to pop in a jar of water to grow some roots and plant in their own barren plot.

The twins skipped ahead, swinging off lampposts and weaving between men in long coats wheeling barrows loaded with salt blocks. They pressed their foreheads against the sweetshop window and gaped at jars full of colored sweets and toffees and the long braids of licorice that dangled from string near the ceiling. Essie wished she had a penny to buy her sisters a bag of aniseed balls or lemon sherbets.

"One day I'll buy you a bagful of each. You'll have so much toffee you'll be sick of it," said Gertie.

"Not likely," scoffed Maggie.

"Never!" said Flora.

Essie's heart sank. Perhaps she could manage an extra loaf this afternoon. The girls had walked without a word of complaint, despite splitting yesterday's crusts before they set off. There was nothing else to offer them. Not even eggs.

As they moved up the street, the twins took turns counting down the house numbers.

"Eleven."

"Nine."

"Seven," squealed Maggie as she hopped up and down pointing at the blue door, almost tripping over her boots.

Essie studied the name stenciled in neat letters above the front door:

G. F. Lawrence
Antiquarian

Underneath, swinging in the wind, was the strangest sight: a small Egyptian statue.

Gertie stared, transfixed.

Essie pulled her shawl tight about her shoulders and put her hand on Freddie's arm to stop him from entering.

"I thought you said his name was Stony Jack and that he was a pawnbroker?"

"He is!" said Freddie. "The lads at the Golden Fleece say he's always good for a pint—"

"—even if what we find in the muck is worth nothin'," said Danny.

"We'll see, won't we?" said Freddie, patting his coat pocket. "I reckon he'll pay a pretty penny for what I have 'ere."

Essie thought of the foreman whose green eyes matched the green gemstones in the hard clay ball. Edward Hepplestone. He'd called to the men to halt their work and keep the discovery in the air where he could see it, but by the time he'd climbed into the cellar, most of the navvies would have thrust their hands into the clay and debris and pulled a handful into their pockets, quickly secreting it in their drawers or boots as soon as they were able—just as Freddie had.

Danny and Freddie had somehow managed to hide a lump of dry clay the size of a football on-site, and they'd brought it home after work. Not straight home, of course. There'd been several rounds at the Golden Fleece on Thursday night. Freddie was careful with the drink . . . but who could blame him for having a beef-and-Guinness pie washed down with a couple of pints with his friends every now and again? It beat coming home to stale bread and a drafty bedroom.

She paused. Freddie and Danny would most likely lose their jobs—or go to jail even—if anyone found out that they had pilfered some of the jewels. Essie had seen the notices in the papers about stealing from worksites around London. She'd unpeeled one from their kippers just days ago:

In the event of any goods or precious materials being retained by the finder—or handed over to another—instead of being passed in to London police, the finder will be liable to prosecution.

Then again, Freddie said there were so many, who would miss just a few . . .

She thought of the necklaces so fine they looked like flowers threaded with gold. Colored gemstones in green, blue, and red pressed into the dirt when the treasure was discovered at Cheapside.

Essie felt like she was squeezed into a too-tight coat she couldn't undo. She didn't like the idea of Freddie and Danny taking something that clearly didn't belong to them. But she thought of Flora and Maggie coughing away. Flora's hollow chest rubbed with camphor oil and wrapped in brown paper. Their poky kitchen lined with dirt, broken crockery, and rats that pounced from the fireplace. She thought of the unopened letters from Miss Barnes that Ma refused to read.

Then she thought of what she could do if only she had more money. Three meals a day. They might be able to move somewhere with a little more room—perhaps even with an indoor flushing lav. Ma could stop her spinning and her hands would heal. (And if Ma felt better, surely she'd give up the drink?) The girls could finish school. She glanced at Gertie, standing with her notebook tucked under her arm. She didn't go anywhere without it. She could buy Gertie a new notebook of her own.

Freddie would be able to offer a home to a sweetheart. He'd been out twice with young Rosie Jones from the greengrocer, but Essie couldn't help noticing the furrow of Mr. Jones's brow when she'd gone to the store with the twins to buy salt and flour last week, his eyes running over their thin dresses as he handed over their purchases. His pursed lips said it all.

"I promise you, Essie," Freddie was saying now, "Stony Jack'll take care of us."

Essie very much doubted that was true. No one who was even *supposed* to care for her family had managed to. Not Ma or Pa, not Mr. Morton at the school, nor Father McGuire and his parish. Freddie was doing his very best, she thought with a sigh. But her older brother was an optimist, a dreamer. Unfortunately, dreaming didn't fill empty bellies at night. It was up to her. But she looked at her brother's wide eyes and hopeful expression and thought of how the future might look. Then she pushed open the door and entered the pawnshop.

Sitting at a large oak desk was a stocky man with neatly combed white hair and a thick gray mustache. He wore a smart blue wool suit, stiff collar, and a black silk tie, much like Essie made every week in the Rubens' factory. This was Mr. Lawrence, she presumed.

His desk was messy, overlaid with scraps of paper and lit with a brass lamp. Random objects dotted the surface: terracotta vases, a carved wooden hand, cigar boxes, and some mottled iron arrowheads. His walls were covered with mirrors and tapestries.

Bookshelves were lined with leather-bound volumes leaning against marble busts, stone axes, and yet more terracotta vessels.

He looked up from his paperwork and studied Essie and her companions through round wire-framed glasses as they all piled into the shop. "Come in, come in." He put down his pen as they entered and crowded around the desk. "Be a good girl and lean on the door to close it, won't you?" he said to Gertie. "Otherwise that blasted bell will jangle all afternoon." He smiled an apology.

Gertie closed the door and wandered across to the bookshelf, running her fingers down gold-embossed spines as if to imprint each title in her brain. Flora gazed openmouthed at a small marble statue of a topless woman, while Maggie giggled at the fig leaf a man wore on the shelf right at the level of her nose.

"Good morning, gentlemen." Mr. Lawrence beamed at Freddie and Danny, then nodded at Essie in the corner. "Miss." The antiquarian gave them a bemused look. "So, to what do I owe the pleasure?"

Danny stepped forward and put a parcel on the table as tenderly as if it were a newborn, then Freddie unwrapped it and held up a ball of clay under Mr. Lawrence's lamp, revealing glittering gold necklaces, some colored stones, and some buttons stuck in the clump.

Mr. Lawrence peered at it. "What do we have here, then?"

"I think we found something special, sir," said Danny.

"Is that so?" replied Mr. Lawrence.

"Some of the lads said you might have a bit of coin—" Freddie began.

"Or a pint," interrupted Danny.

Essie shot him a furious look. She'd come along to ensure her impressionable brother wasn't persuaded by Danny to spend some of the money on a few rounds of pints at the pub with the lads. She wanted at least enough money for a few weeks of school and to give Ma's raw hands a break from the spinning. Freddie had agreed, but who could blame him for wanting to spend time with lads his own age having a laugh, or taking Rosie Jones to the moving pictures and perhaps a bit of afternoon tea?

"What do you think?" asked Freddie anxiously.

The antiquarian pushed his glasses up his nose and sat up straighter. Without saying a word, he picked up the ball and turned it over, revealing traces of gleaming gold and blue stones.

When he spoke, his tone was measured, but warm. "I'm not sure," he murmured. "Where did you say this came from?" He peered at the young men over the tops of his glasses.

The pair shifted uncomfortably, and Danny's ears started to redden.

"Which worksite were you on?" he probed.

Danny and Freddie looked at each other, and Freddie shook his head in warning.

Mr. Lawrence's eyes narrowed, and in that instant Essie saw he understood.

"No matter, we can discuss that later. In the meantime, I'll need to inspect this mess more closely so I can give you a good price."

He poked at the clay and five gold buttons fell onto the desk with a clatter. The largest was the prettiest of all, with a line of blue stones threading through the petals. The curve of the petal looked so lifelike it might bend with the breeze.

Mr. Lawrence picked up the large button and held it up to the light between his thumb and forefinger, turning it over so the jewels caught the light.

"I wonder . . ." he said thoughtfully. "I wonder who wore this button."

He gestured to a print of Queen Elizabeth on the wall behind him. "Look! See the gold buttons sewn into her white frilly neck ruff and sleeves, the gold chains draped around her body, the bejeweled cross at her neck and rings on every finger? Her ships were crossing the oceans; traders brought jewels back to London from across the seas. This city was the center of the world . . ."

Essie blanched, thinking of where her own waistband had been turned inside out and restitched.

"Why so many buttons?" whispered Maggie as she poked at one.

"Well, lass," Mr. Lawrence continued, "I agree it's a decadent way to hold a coat together." He chuckled and patted his own belly, then leaned in conspiratorially. "Especially when there's a chance that you might pop one off after too much grouse and port."

Maggie stared openmouthed at Mr. Lawrence's waistcoat, as if she expected it to burst right in front of her. Essie remembered the button Gertie had sketched and wondered if her sister had returned it to Freddie.

Mr. Lawrence touched the ball of clay. "Perhaps I can deliver your payment in person, maybe meet you for a pint. What do you say, gents—Friday after work?"

Essie's stomach sank as Danny said, "Golden Fleece?"

"Right you are."

"Done."

The men shook hands, then Danny and Freddie made for the door, clearly reluctant to spend any more time in this strange shop filled with stuffed animals and ghosts of the past.

Essie turned to leave, but Gertie was still standing at the bookshelf, frowning and trying to piece together a terracotta vase with a relief, as if it were a jigsaw.

"Ah, I've almost given up on this Roman beauty. A boy not older than you brought this in from near the Bourse, where they've been digging up the banks of the old Walbrook." The antiquarian waved at a shelf of terracotta pots. The one Gertie was holding had the fine features of a deer, its antlers broken.

"I patch them back together with red ocher and beeswax. Just picture old Londinium, a bustling city between two hills with red-tiled roofs and a marketplace at the center. I like to think of a Roman girl using this to collect water from the Thames just here."

He took the deer vase from Gertie, who seemed to have forgotten entirely that they were here on business and was treating the shop like some kind of museum.

"A girl just your age could have lived with her family on a tiny alley, just off the Walbrook. Pigs and chickens in the backyard."

Essie could imagine herself in such a yard.

"The girl would have spent most of her days at the markets, helping her parents and siblings. Perhaps they were leatherworkers, weaving sandals like this."

He lifted a blackened sandal.

"Or perhaps they painted mosaic tiles, or had a kiln for making pottery." He waved at the array of terracotta pots. "Whatever their craft, at the end of the day they'd come home. The girl would perhaps sew or do some mending, the boys would fetch water and wash. The mother would cook a stew in a shallow terracotta pot, perhaps with hare and wheat. There would be spice merchants at the market, so if they could afford spices from the Orient there might be pepper, cinnamon, or ginger. Or maybe a hot sauce for the meat made from dates, prunes, and damsons."

Essie felt her stomach rumble, and Flora leaned against her.

Life in Roman times sounded far more delicious than now.

"In the corner of their central room they might have had clay urns filled with olive oil, red wine, or garum."

"What's garum?" asked Maggie.

"Rotten fish sauce," replied Mr. Lawrence as Maggie looked faintly nauseated. Somewhere behind her, Essie heard Danny snicker.

"And this"—he held up Gertie's piece of clay—"would have been essential to their life. Think how many hands have held this vessel. Then yet more feet passed over it as it lay in the London bog." He pointed to the clump of mud and jewels on his desk before continuing, "Each piece that comes here tells me a little more about life in London. But it's not just the story of our city, child; each piece is the story of a person. How did they come to own it? How did they use it? What did it mean to them—how did it change their life?"

Essie smiled and looked over to where the sun was sneaking through the windows and felt it warm her arms.

"You are all very welcome to come back and visit me anytime. I'm always here on Saturdays."

Chapter 15

The following Saturday was the day of the school excursion trip to the Greenwich Observatory parklands. The children were dressed in their Sunday best and lined up on the dock in jittery pairs to board the ferry from Southwark: a motley line of children with sarsaparilla-scented braids, mismatched boots, and too-thin dresses. Once aboard, the children stood on the foredeck with open mouths and shivered in the thick fog and filthy smog all the way to Greenwich, exclaiming at every landmark.

"Tower Bridge!"

"Westminster!" whooped Flora between coughs.

Gertie sat with her back against the cabin with her precious notebook, drawing the line of the city among a haze of industrial smog. Somehow it looked more cloudlike, more whimsical, on the page. Essie wondered what it would be like to sail right along the Thames, beyond London, out into the ocean and into different ports. Different cities, different worlds.

Arriving at Greenwich pier, they stepped from the ferry steamer onto the docks and were ushered past a shrimp seller with a sizzling pan atop a wine barrel. The children looked forlorn, leaning toward the enticing smells as Miss Barnes ushered them off the pier, past the gates of the naval college, and into the park. Mr. Morton clipped the back of the littlest boy's head as he accepted a shrimp from the ruddy-faced merchant and gobbled it in one bite.

"You children continue up the path to the park with Miss Barnes. Father McGuire and I have an appointment, but if we catch an inkling that any of you are misbehaving . . ." He eyed the impish boy.

The children drew a collective breath. No one wanted to be struck with a ruler—or the belt—today.

Miss Barnes flipped a pocket watch from her coat and gathered Gertie and Essie together by the elbows as she addressed the children.

"Come, quickly. I've something to show you."

Essie grabbed the twins' hands and followed Miss Barnes as she took off up the path to the Royal Observatory. The hill was steep and planted with pockets of oak and linden trees. Only when the path took a sharp turn could everyone catch a glimpse of the famous dome and the red time ball perched on a turret above the grand Flamsteed House.

Miss Barnes checked her watch again. "Hurry. Stand here, class." The teacher shepherded them against a tall wall and Essie could feel the summer heat on the stones through her pinafore.

"Now, watch," said Miss Barnes as she pointed to the giant red ball and they watched it rise slowly up the mast before dropping suddenly to the bottom.

Maggie and Flora gave a cheer, and Miss Barnes looked at her watch. "One p.m. Greenwich Mean Time. I come every year just to check that this old thing works."

Essie turned to look back down the hill and across to the Thames, thinking of all the Londoners, boatmen, and sailors who were checking their own watches against the red ball. Everyone moving around the boroughs doing their daily business and all those who came ashore to bring goods from countries far away were threaded together by this instant. She gazed back up the hill to the towering Flamsteed House and the giant red ball and imagined lines from this point stretched out to distant lands across the globe like black threads. Meridian lines spread around the globe from this very spot.

She thought again about the rivers of jewels she'd seen in Cheapside. Emeralds, pearls, and gold necklaces. Gertie's button. When were they buried deep in that cellar? Who would bury such treasures and never return? Essie recalled the words of kindly Mr. Lawrence: *Each piece is the story of a person. How did they come to own it? How did they use it? What did it mean to them—how did it change their life?*

The Thames to her right was obscured by a park, beyond which a power station with towering chimney stacks spewed smoke into the sky. If she followed the line of the river back toward London, the far side was dotted with so many chimney stacks that they looked like matchsticks disappearing into the haze.

Directly in front of her was the naval college built in a neat grid. The park they stood in was a gradual green slope running up from the shore to the Observatory. Men in top hats promenaded with women in long fitted silk jackets and matching hats. Essie looked at the twins, studying their sallow skin and sunken eyes, and was grateful their shriveled legs didn't stop them playing a game of hide-and-seek among the trees with a handful of their classmates.

Essie, Miss Barnes, and Gertie unfolded blankets and unpacked sandwiches for the children.

"Cheese and pickles—what a treat!" said Gertie. "Food!" she yelled, and the children came running, plucking at sandwiches and pushing them into their mouths before running back into the woods to resume their game.

"There's not a bit of crust left for the gulls," said Miss Barnes. "I should have brought more sandwiches . . ." She looked disappointed, and Essie realized that lunch had been provided thanks to the generosity of Miss Barnes, not the school.

When the children had tired of hide-and-seek and had returned to lie on the grass and blankets with their faces turned up to the sun, Essie and Miss Barnes wandered down the hill arm in arm with Gertie.

"Miss Murphy!" Essie turned at the sound of her name and, to her surprise, recognized the striking young foreman with green eyes whom she had met at Cheapside nine days before.

Shocked, she blinked twice to check it was indeed him, and quickly started to smooth her skirts as her legs trembled a little. She'd thought of him every day since that meeting. She hadn't replied to his note, of course. What would she have said?

He jogged up the path to meet her, panting, then removed his boater hat as a greeting.

"Miss Murphy, I knew it was you at once. And this must be your sister—you could be twins!"

"Not likely," Gertie said as she blushed and elbowed Essie in the ribs. The corners of her mouth tucked into a shy smile, and Essie gave him her hand to shake.

"This is my sister Gertrude," said Essie. "And her teacher, Miss Barnes. Meet Mr. Hepplestone."

She paused, fishing for things to say. "We've just been for a look at the Observatory."

"I'm sorry I missed you. I was on the way up myself. Who accompanied you?"

"The school." Essie tugged her skirt lower to cover her shoes.

"An annual outing," Miss Barnes explained. "We like our students to experience the Observatory."

Mr. Hepplestone gestured to where a black motor vehicle was parked on the edge of the lawn. "I thought it was a lovely day to take my new toy for a spin. Test the engine." He looked proudly over his shoulder at the gleaming vehicle before he started to walk down the hill with them. Essie's stomach sank as she realized that a drive with Mr. Hepplestone was even less likely than attending a women's march at the Monument.

The twins came running up, wrapping themselves around Essie's skirt. Maggie's ribbons were undone, and Flora's dress had grass stains right down her back. Both their little cheeks were so pink with the sun and activity, Essie wished she could race back up to the top of the Observatory and stop time—to hold this moment forever.

"Who are you?" asked Flora, while Maggie stood back and coughed from the exertion of her run.

The foreman removed his hat and gave a little bow, dipping his head. "I'm Mr. Hepplestone. I work with your brother, Freddie."

"He's not here," said Flora brashly.

"Flora!" said Essie.

Before Essie could continue scolding, a fiddler started to play and they were surrounded by a troupe of juggling clowns. Bright red noses matched the ball at the top of the Observatory, and the little girls started to spin to the music.

The tallest clown stepped forward and pulled a chestnut from behind Flora's ear. Maggie's mouth fell open as she tugged on her own ear in a frantic search for a treat.

The same clown reached for the ground as if bending to tie Maggie's laces, and produced a coin from the hem of her skirt. Maggie jumped up and down, clapping her hands as the clown tucked the penny away into his vest pocket.

The clowns moved on, trailed by clowns on stilts playing accordions, and others cartwheeling and doing backflips across the smooth grass.

Essie and Mr. Hepplestone soon found themselves separated from the others as clowns stomped and juggled between them.

"May I be honest with you, Miss Murphy?" said Mr. Hepplestone as he stopped walking and turned to face her.

"Of course," said Essie. She was moving into unfamiliar territory, and she wasn't sure how to proceed.

"I was hoping to bump into you. I overheard Freddie and Danny talking about you helping with the children at Greenwich Observatory today, and so I thought . . ." He'd turned a little pink in the sun. He cocked his head sideways, green eyes twinkling and teasing.

Essie's heart quickened. Could it be true? Had he really motored out to Greenwich just so he could bump into her? More likely it was a coincidence and he was just trying to flatter her . . . But when she looked from under the brim of her hat, he was still gazing right at her.

They walked down the path, the sun on her face and butterflies floating with the breeze. At the bottom of the hill stood a black Clydesdale, twitching his tail in the sun and eyeing the world from under drooping eyelids. Attached to the horse was a wooden ice-cream cart manned by a smiling fellow with thick black curls, a mustache, and a pink candy-striped vest and matching boater.

"Please?" said Flora running toward them with a cheeky smile. Maggie was two steps behind. Miss Barnes finished watching the clowns and came to join them.

"Please?" echoed Maggie.

Essie knew she should take home the two spare pennies she kept in her handkerchief for an emergency—they would buy enough vegetables for soup for a week. But the closeness of a handsome man standing within reach was a heady distraction. For a moment she almost convinced herself that she could afford to part with her pennies.

Mr. Hepplestone said, "Actually, I quite fancy one myself. You must let me treat you. I insist."

The girls rushed ahead to the cart, shrieking, "Ice cream!"

"We have vanilla or strawberry left—no more chocolate," the ice-cream seller informed them in a thick Italian accent.

"Oh, strawberry, please!" Maggie clapped her hands together.

"Strawberry it is," Mr. Hepplestone declared. "One cone for each of us, please."

"Our own cones?" Flora looked at Maggie, her eyes wide. Essie thought if the girls' smiles were any broader their faces might burst.

With their cones in hand, they walked to stand in the shade of a tree. The twins ate their ice cream in a kind of trance, then clambered back up the hill to join their classmates.

Meanwhile, Essie, Gertie, Miss Barnes, and Mr. Hepplestone all sat with their backs against a huge oak tree, taking their time. Essie allowed herself to relax as they spoke about time and astronomy, chance and circumstance, and the changing streets of London. Mr. Hepplestone commended Wren on the splendid job he did redesigning St. Paul's and the streets around London after the Great Fire. He prayed the new buildings he was supervising would likewise stand the test of time. As Gertie sketched the skyline, Miss Barnes chatted about the curriculum at her new school and the women who had recently started at St. Hilda's in Oxford. One had decided to study mathematics, another law, and a third astronomy. The latter girl had been inspired after an excursion just like this.

Essie eyed the dome of the Observatory, glinting like a jewel in the sunlight.

Miss Barnes stood up and said, "If you'll excuse us, I'd like to take Miss Gertrude here on a tour of the Observatory while the other teacher watches the children."

"Do you think they'll let me look through a telescope?" asked Gertie eagerly as she leaped to her feet and brushed the grass from her skirt.

"We'll see. There's also a pinhead view of London . . ." Miss Barnes threaded her arm through Gertie's and led her back up the hill toward the red ball.

As Mr. Hepplestone chatted amiably, Essie realized that he was not, in fact, a foreman for the building contractors that employed Freddie. Rather, Edward Hepplestone was a nephew of the firm's owner, brought in to help manage all the demolition and rebuilding that was taking place across the city.

He made no mention of the treasure they'd unearthed at Cheapside, though Essie knew he had seen it. Instead, he talked about his uncle's house in Mayfair and the dinners of roast beef with all the trimmings that were a regular Sunday repast. Essie admired the cut of his linen suit—French, judging by the snug lines fitted to his broad shoulders and slim hips. They cut them a little squarer at the Rubens' factory. Essie tucked her hands under her skirts. Sitting here in the park it was almost as if she and Edward had everything in common, but then the cut of his suit and her work-roughened hands reminded her otherwise.

Time seemed to drift with the haze of the afternoon, and Essie was surprised when Miss Barnes, returning with a flushed Gertie, pulled her pocket watch from her coat and exclaimed, "Goodness! We've been gone for two hours. Hopefully Mr. Morton and Father McGuire have enjoyed their annual lunch at the naval barracks and won't have noticed us missing."

Essie realized from Miss Barnes's tone that the outing to Greenwich wasn't about the headmaster and priest spending time with the children in their care. The excursion gave them the respectable veneer of doing their charitable duty.

Essie looked up to where some of the older girls were packing blankets into wicker hampers as the children—Flora and Maggie included—rolled and tumbled down the steep hill behind them.

"We were told to meet them at the pier at half past four. We'd best be moving." Miss Barnes shot Essie an apologetic look. "Come, Gertie. Help me gather the children and pack up the last of the things." She ushered Gertie up the hill and out of earshot.

"I'm sorry—I've kept you all afternoon," said Mr. Hepplestone. But the glint in his eye suggested he was anything but sorry. Or was she imagining it?

Essie had an image of her mother lying with her face covered in mud, chickens clucking on her belly, desperately warning Essie against handsome men like this Mr. Hepplestone. His immaculate suit and carefree smile should be causes for suspicion. But Essie was intrigued. She envied his ease in the world.

She and Mr. Hepplestone walked the same streets of London, but it felt as if they existed in different times, different meridians. He could not imagine the dirt floor and copper tub she went home to, but Essie had snatched a glimpse of his world; it was there in the Fortnum & Mason window, in the expensive suits and shirts she sewed every day, in the glimpse of a French heel under silk skirts as it disappeared into a leather-lined automobile or marched among the crowd of women at the Monument. She folded these images into her heart, hoping that one day things might be different for her own family.

Mr. Hepplestone pulled a gold watch from his jacket, and she thought of the jewels and gemstones unearthed at Cheapside. Emeralds the very color of Mr. Hepplestone's eyes.

"I must get back," he said. "I promised my family I'd dine with them."

Essie imagined him in a white dinner coat and vest, and shivered. Did he share her reluctance to part company?

"If I wasn't already committed, I would offer to drive you and your sisters home," he added.

Essie was touched by his sentiment. But the thought of letting this lovely man see where she lived made her feel queasy. She was ashamed of their garden flat. But what made her feel worse was this shame. As if her family were a dirty secret to be hidden.

And yet, Essie thought, Mr. Hepplestone must have some idea of their circumstances. Freddie was a navvy, after all. And still he had sought her out. Hope bloomed in her heart, like the first tender shoots of spring. Essie was filled with an urge to reach for Mr. Hepplestone's hand and hold him there for just a few minutes longer and pepper him with questions. She wanted to ask him about the jewels that were dug up . . . Did he know whom they belonged to? About the younger sister he'd mentioned who was finishing her schooling in Switzerland. She wanted to know whether he had ever sailed down the Thames and out to sea, or if he ever dreamed of going?

He stood up and brushed some grass from his pants. Then he held out a hand to help Essie to her feet. His grip was warm and strong and she felt a little dizzy suddenly. It was probably just the heat of the day, she told herself. Or the unaccustomed sweetness of the ice cream.

"I would like to continue this conversation, Miss Murphy. May I take you to tea next week?"

Essie could think of nothing else but Mr. Hepplestone's invitation as she and Miss Barnes ushered the children onto the steamer ferry. They all sat on slatted seats on the afterdeck, wind whipping their hair around their faces. The children were quieter on the return journey, tired and sunburned.

"What a coincidence to see your friend at the Observatory," Miss Barnes remarked.

"He's not my friend," Essie replied. "He's the foreman on the site where my brother works. They're demolishing buildings over Cheapside way."

"Well, he seemed happy enough to see you today," the teacher teased as she gave Essie a nudge with her shoulder.

As the ferry dipped with the tide, and the dome of the Observatory glinted in the late sun, Essie tipped her head back and enjoyed the last rays. For the first time, she felt excited about what the next week might hold.

Chapter 16

Essie spent the following weeks moving between the factory and home with a lightness she'd never felt before. Mr. Lawrence had made good on his word and delivered some money to the boys at the Golden Fleece.

Unfortunately, Freddie hadn't been able to stop Danny from treating the bar to three rounds before he escaped with his share. He came home and sheepishly presented Essie with the remainder. She had gone straight to Mr. Morton and paid the outstanding amount for the girls' school, before visiting the fishmonger and Mr. Jones at the general store to settle their debts. She had just enough left over for food for the next few months, if she was careful and hid the money from Ma.

Freddie told Essie he'd been asked to do another job with Danny and the lads outside London, and he had not been home since last Friday. Father McGuire delighted in telling her that he'd heard a handful of navvies had gone to Gravesend for a lark. Essie tried to ignore the flush she could feel spreading to her cheeks. She knew the priest lumped Freddie in with other ne'er-do-well navvies in their neighborhood and assumed he was a drunkard like their ma. Essie couldn't deny Freddie enjoyed the odd night out with the lads, but he always handed over most of his salary every week to Essie to run the household. If there was a little extra missing sometimes, it was carelessness. Or a wishful gambling bet. There was not a mean bone in Freddie's skinny body.

The priest had made a point of speaking with Essie after his weekly home visit with her ma. Over the top of his glasses, Father McGuire snapped, "I wondered where those funds might have come from. I did hear, Miss Murphy, that all your family's debts at the school have been paid." His eyes had lingered a little too long at her breasts as he spoke, as if to imply that the source of their windfall might perhaps lie there. "My confession box is always open in the afternoons . . ."

Essie was furious, but of course she couldn't tell him where the money had actually come from. She endured Father McGuire's hints in silence; she had nothing to confess to him—though she promised herself this would be the week she confessed to Ma that she'd been stepping out with Edward, as he now insisted she call him.

For the last few weeks she had not been working an extra shift in the factory, as she'd claimed. Instead, she and Edward visited the moving pictures, where they saw *The French Spy* and she permitted Edward to hold her hand. They spent afternoons lounging on striped deck chairs in Hyde Park eating ice creams or warm muffins that broke apart and spilled runny fruit into her lap.

Occasionally, Edward would tip his hat at an acquaintance in the street, or usher her past an elegant couple in furs he'd exchanged greetings with outside a teahouse. These were the kind of women in French heels who marched at the Monument—perhaps she and Gertie could join them. It was just a matter of time before Edward introduced her to his circle, his family, but every time she thought to ask, the words stuck in her throat.

They roamed the Victoria & Albert Museum, and took tea and scones in the darkest corner of the grand hall filled with chandeliers. Essie wished she could smuggle some treats home for the girls in her handkerchief. Once, they'd visited the Natural History Museum and Edward had walked her past giant roughs of sapphires, emeralds, and diamonds, peering closely at each one without saying a word. She thought of the football of dirt, studded with jewels, that Freddie had held above his head. So many had made their way to Stony Jack. Had others also held on to a keepsake of this magic?

She wondered who was missing their treasure. The piles of gemstones, buttons, neckpieces, and rings on Mr. Lawrence's desk had been so immense that it was improbable to think no one would come looking . . .

Just as quickly as the thought arrived, she pushed it away. Her family were thieves. Any one of them could go to jail if Mr. Lawrence turned them in! Her stomach churned at the thought, but in her heart she felt Mr. Lawrence was a kind soul. Still, she remembered the notice from London's town clerk in the newspaper wrapped around her kippers weeks ago.

When Essie returned home from her Saturday jaunts roaming the curved tree-lined streets and glossy front doors on the way to the Serpentine with Edward, she always made sure to slip a small bag of aniseed drops to the twins when Ma wasn't looking. The Saturday before, she'd told Edward that Gertie had a fondness for reading, and as they passed a bookseller along Piccadilly Circus, he'd bought an illustrated copy of *The Secret Garden*.

"It's my sister's favorite book," he told Essie.

"You shouldn't. It's too—"

"You said Gertie was quite the artist; I thought she'd like it," he said simply as he pressed it into Essie's basket.

When Ma had eyed her suspiciously as Essie presented the book wrapped up in brown paper and twine, Essie had lied, saying it was a gift from Mrs. Ruben.

"For me?" Gertie's face puckered with confusion as she turned the stiff new pages. "A *new* book," she said dreamily. "Can you imagine a garden filled with overgrown vines and a wall so high that you could hide from the world? And from Ma!" she added in an undertone as she traced her fingers over watercolor leaves. "She'd never find me. Too hard for a drunk to—"

"Gertie," snapped Essie. "Enough!"

"Why do you always stick up for her? How can you stand it?" Gertie looked at their mother, whose papery hands were shaking as she tried to unscrew the lid of her bottle.

"Never heard of a Jew that liked giving presents," muttered Ma as she took a swig from the bottle and sank into the threadbare armchair.

Essie let her mother's hurtful comments pass. If it wasn't the Jews it was the Italians. The Poles. Whoever had failed to extend the credit and hand over a bottle of liquor that week. She didn't discriminate with her bitterness, and there was nothing to be gained by laboring the point when her mother could barely stand upright and would not remember a word she'd said in the morning.

Mrs. Yarwood was happy enough to look after the girls on a Saturday. In fact, she insisted on it, though just last week her eyes had narrowed a little as she quipped: "There's a rosy flush about you of late, Miss Essie. It's lovely to see you smiling." She took a breath before her voice dropped and she whispered, "You deserve an occasional afternoon off, but be careful, lass." She patted Essie's hand and said nothing about Essie wearing her Sunday best to work on a Saturday.

The trio of younger sisters enjoyed their Saturdays with Mrs. Yarwood, walking to the Borough Markets to buy soft loaves of bread and hard cheese. Sometimes they'd picnic on the bank of the Thames; other days they'd spend all afternoon in the cheery yellow kitchen preparing fancy meals from a secondhand cookbook Mrs. Yarwood had picked up at a local fair—slow-cooked beef cheeks in red wine and buttery mashed potatoes, pork chops in apple cider with strawberry *trifle*. Essie would arrive to collect her sisters and be forced to stay for a two-course feast they'd cooked, aprons tied around their waists and flour smeared across their cheeks and little noses.

Gertie would write down the recipes for ham cooked in cider followed by a tart gooseberry jelly. One evening, when their lips were stained purple, she wrote down recipes for blackberry curd and blackberry jam.

Today, Essie had arrived at the Yarwoods' a little earlier and the kitchen was filled with steam and the tangy scent of lemon.

As Mrs. Yarwood dictated, Gertie was writing out the recipe for a cough mixture:

2 spoons honey
pinch of thyme leaves
ground peppercorns
squeeze of lemon (fresh)
(Add to boiling tea, or water)

Essie closed her eyes and pressed her hand to the cheek Edward had kissed as he bid her farewell. It had been only the briefest of pecks, but as he leaned close the scent of his soap and freshly laundered shirt had mingled with the muskier smell of his skin. She'd wanted to trace the tip of her finger across his red lips, then across the top of his collar before touching the ribbons of muscle she imagined ran down his back.

"I'm sorry, Essie. You're blushing . . ." he'd said as he stepped back.

But Essie wanted him to stay close, and it took all her willpower to ignore the beating in her ribs and the strange heat that rose under her dress.

She yearned for more time with Edward. The first few times they'd met Essie had worried that it might be imprudent to see him without a chaperone. But Edward was always so respectful that her mother's slurred words of warning as she lay smeared in chicken shit and mud started to resonate a little less. This was different. Her mother couldn't possibly understand. Bad luck and bad choices had curdled Clementine until she was sour.

Essie looked at the last of the afternoon light streaming in through the kitchen window, then across at Mrs. Yarwood bent over the kitchen table, reciting recipes to Gertie and rubbing the twins' backs as she spoke with a voice as smooth as honey. The Yarwoods' home had an easiness; there was a gentle rhythm to life there. The patterns of their days were unchanging. It was a steady home filled with love, laughter, and endless cakes and jams.

The kind of loving home Essie dreamed of making for herself. The more she saw Edward, the more she craved his company.

That night, as Gertie slept, Essie eased the notebook out from underneath her sister's elbow and turned to a blank page at the back where she permitted herself to write:

Mrs. Edward Hepplestone

Mr. Edward and Mrs. Esther Rose Hepplestone

As soon as she wrote it, Essie ripped the page out and used a match to burn it, holding the tip of the corner so as not to scorch her fingers, and watched the ash flutter to the floor.

Chapter 17

KATE

GALLE, SRI LANKA, PRESENT DAY

To: kkirby@outnet.com
From: sophie.shaw@shawandsons.co.uk
Subject: YOU OWE ME

The subject line made Kate smile; it was typical Sophie.

Kate was sitting at her hotel room desk making a start on her Cheapside article after an afternoon stroll around Galle. Her walk had taken her along potholed streets crammed with crumbling Portuguese churches, elegant Dutch villas, and British warehouses smothered with bougainvillea that offered glimpses back to the days when ships sailed into port, gathering precious spices, dyes, ebony, rubies, and sapphires.

She glanced at her own sapphires, sitting on the bedside table . . .

Marcus had booked separate suites for them on opposite sides of the hotel. Kate's looked over an infinity pool to the Indian Ocean, and she preferred to write with the plantation shutters open. The humid air that crept into her air-conditioned room was infused with the scents of salt water, sambal, and antique teak furniture.

She took a sip of her tea and looked out the window to where Olivia and Marcus were sharing an oversize deck chair. Liv shared Marcus's athletic gait, surfer's shiny, tousled hair, and easy smile. The eighteen-year-old seemed delightfully untroubled by her father's introduction of a colleague into their father-daughter getaway at the airport that morning. Perhaps she was used to it.

"Pleased to meet you, Kate. Dad told me you're a historian." Olivia had smiled as she shook Kate's hand, a little shyer now. "I've got exams coming up. I wish I had your ease with old texts— Shakespeare and Austen are *killing* me. Seriously!"

"We could chat about them sometime. Which Shakespeare?"

"*Taming of the Shrew.*"

"Feisty!"

"Is there any other kind of Kate?" chipped in Marcus, amused, as he grabbed Olivia's backpack from the luggage carousel.

Now, Liv's coltish leg was draped over her father's foot, jittering as she excitedly explained something, hands gesturing wildly to the sky. Kate wished she could bottle the Australian's exuberance.

On the plane from Hyderabad, Marcus had explained before watching a movie that Liv's mother, Julia—his ex-wife—had remarried an athletic auditor fifteen years ago. Liv had ten-year-old twin half brothers, Jack and Harry, whom she adored.

"I was always traveling for work, leaving Jules in Sydney with a colicky toddler. I didn't realize . . . I was young and naive."

He grimaced ruefully. "It was hard on her. Unfair. I thought the work would give us stability, a future . . ." He sighed. "So stupid! I should have been there. Helped more. The irony is, once we split I spent way more time with Liv. Taught her to ride a bike and sail. I spend at least two months in Sydney every year over summer. When I'm away we Skype a few times a week. The past couple of years we've tried to squeeze a trip in at least once a year. It's harder to find the time, though, now that her life is so busy! Musical rehearsals, rowing camps, exams, a party, weekends with friends. Boys!" He shook his head in mock horror. "Dad has dropped *waaay* down the list."

"Sounds like a normal teenager. And Julia? Are you . . ." Kate stopped. It was none of her business whether or not Marcus was on good terms with his ex.

"Jules and I are good. Andrew's a great guy. He's kind, and really supportive of Liv. They live in an old sandstone cottage with a wide veranda overlooking the harbor. Jules teaches yoga at a studio she can walk to. She got the life she deserves." Marcus had shrugged resignedly as he tapped the screen to choose a movie, conversation over.

Kate watched Marcus throw back his head and laugh at something his daughter had said. He was lucky to have maintained such a close bond with Olivia, she thought.

She smiled as she clicked open Sophie's email.

Kate,

Hope you enjoyed the party!

That image of the Colombian emerald with the Swiss watch inside, then your Golconda diamond, got me thinking . . .

Remember the visiting tutor who mentioned this watch in his lecture about emeralds from Muzo, Colombia?

Kate looked up to see that Marcus and Liv were in the pool now, laughing as they tried to dunk each other. Liv's skin was brown and smooth—like Julia's, according to Marcus—but father and daughter shared a high forehead, square jaw, and easy laugh.

Marcus glanced up at Kate's window and waved. "You coming for a dip?"

"In a bit," she called back. "Sophie Shaw from Shaw & Sons got a lead on one of the pieces. I'll finish reading her email then come out."

"You're missing out," said Olivia as she dived under the turquoise water.

Kate smiled and went back to Sophie's email, which was as scattershot as when her friend told a story over a beer.

Anyway, there was a big trial with the East India Company. (You were too hungover to pay attention to this last bit, if I recall.)

I spent the afternoon at the Parliamentary Archives scrolling through rolls of transcribed legal documents. The original depositions are on thirty rolls of skins which they won't let me near, which is a shame. I asked to copy a couple of bits, which I've attached. There're also a whole bunch of logbooks and diaries of the East India Company at the British Library. I went and copied some pages, if you're interested . . . and have half a year to read them!

You're welcome.

Soph xx

P.S. Don't be all work in Sri Lanka.

Kate clicked on the attachment. Sophie had sent the official complaint summarized for the London court.

28 April 1637

Gerhard Polman, gem merchant and jeweller, after traversing many countries in search of precious stones . . . in the year 1631 put himself on board an English East Indiaman in Persia on his way home. He had with him a large collection of gems and precious stones, collected during the previous thirty years.

On the homeward voyage Polman was poisoned by Abraham Porter, surgeon of the East Indiaman, and his goods were divided among the crew of the ship. The crime becoming known, parts of his estate ultimately came into the hands of the East India Company . . .

Kate scrolled through the transcripts Sophie had sent. It appeared the ship's crew had killed Polman a couple of weeks out of Mauritius, tore his clothes off and tossed the naked body overboard. They had then helped themselves to bagfuls of jewels and gemstones and snuck ashore at Gravesend before the *Discovery* reached London. But why was Sophie sure there was a connection to the collection in the Museum of London?

She continued reading through an inventory of Polman's chest and cross-checked it with Saanvi's precise catalog from the museum. There were leather pouches packed with the clearest diamonds, turquoise, and natural pearls from Persia—pawned and resold along Cheapside. Kate found herself flipping between the testimonies, her notebook, and Saanvi's catalog. So many of the rings and gemstones sounded similar to those in the Polman trial. The East India Company had ended up retrieving some of the jewels.

But nobody could be certain *all* the precious pieces that circulated through the hands of the gem cutters and jewelers along Goldsmiths' Row in Cheapside were ever retrieved.

Kate trawled through the list until she hit a description that made her heart beat a little faster: *a greene rough stone or emerald three inches long and three inches in compass.* She did a quick calculation in her head and looked at the dimensions of the watch in her notebook. To achieve all the facets of a hexagon, the rough would have had to have been this size. Emeralds were notoriously full of flaws, and often crumbled at the first cut by a lapidary—it was unusual for an emerald so large to survive such an intense transformation. Her admiration for the artisans who crafted the watch swelled.

Kate sat back and read over the trial testimonies . . . a man murdered for a green stone.

She replied:

Thanks, Soph, amazing work. IOU big time. Love to see any diary entries of the *Discovery* crew.

K x

Then she clicked back to her own document and moved her cursor down to the section on the emerald watch and added in a couple of sentences. When she was done, Kate took a sip from the teacup that sat by her right hand. Though now cold, the white tea was delicious and tangy. As she refilled her cup from the rapidly cooling pot, another email from Sophie arrived. Her friend was a machine.

To: kkirby@outnet.com
From: sophie.shaw@shawandsons.co.uk
Subject: Diary of Robert Parker, SS *Discovery*, 1631

She scanned the facsimiles of the diary pages, seeking any personal clues that might link Gerhard Polman's emerald with the watch in London.

20 April 1631

I've been long enough in the bowels of a ship to know what I am supposed to yearn for on land. And it is true enough. I can't think of the last time I touched skin, except on the receiving end of a slap across the cheek from the surgeon, or a kick from the carpenter.

It's my job to deliver a draught of beer and plate of salted meat and cheese to the Dutchman's cabin every night. The look on his face tells me he misses the jewelled yellow rice covered with pomegranate seeds and chunks of grilled meats as much as I do.

I'm the only one he permits in his cabin. He sits at his desk all day polishing blue, red, and clear stones, setting them into rings and buttons. Yesterday his desk had twenty score pouches of pearls and cloth bags filled with gemstones that I thought his cabin was afire!

He unwrapped the large emerald and allowed me to touch the green stone. It felt eerie, both a blessing and a curse.

Afterward, the Dutchman pulled a clear rough from a leather pouch hanging around his neck and held it under the lamplight.

His voice was soft, reverent. As if the rough he held was magic.
I felt it too. For though the stone was unpolished, when I looked
inside it glowed warm with the lamplight. He whispered that this
diamond rough was from Golconda . . .

As her fingers ran over the museum catalog, tracing Robert Parker's shaky script, she went back to the article she was writing and wrote a new line. When she'd finished, she sent the last paragraph off to Sophie for comment before her thoughts returned to the black-and-white ring. It was entirely possible the Golconda diamond had traveled from India to Persia then on to London in one of Polman's leather pouches.

Outside, she saw that Marcus had climbed out of the pool and now stood toweling himself under the shade of a palm. He called out something to Liv about having a shower before dinner, but she ignored him and kicked underwater to the end of the pool. As he bent over, Kate noticed a thick pink scar slicing his back and continuing over his shoulder blade. It disappeared as soon as he straightened.

Oblivious to her gaze, Marcus was watching Olivia, a proud smile on his face. Kate worried a dark knot in the grain of her desk with her forefinger. The tenderness of his look unspooled a hurt deep in her stomach, but also threads of something else. Something . . . happier.

Kate's computer pinged. It was a reply from Sophie.

Nice work! Now go get yourself a martini by the pool.

Kate snapped her laptop closed and walked outside.

Kate and Marcus sat beside the pool. They'd finished the last of the sour fish curry and had resumed work on their laptops. Liv had joined them for dinner but had disappeared to study an hour ago.

"Another beer?" asked Marcus as he signaled to the waiter.

Kate leaned back in her chair and stretched languorously. "Why not?" she replied as she plucked her tank top from her damp skin at the shoulders and tucked some escapee curls back into her ponytail. Her thick Irish curls were not compatible with the humidity. She wiped her forehead and took a moment to admire the silvery moonlight reflected on the ocean.

The beers arrived and she pressed hers to her neck, savoring the coolness of the glass against her skin. The heavy air was sweetened with frangipani.

"Boston's going to be a hard sell after this," she joked. But even as she said it, it felt like the waves were tugging at her to come home. She missed her family.

When Kate looked back at Marcus, his eyes met hers over the top of his screen. But his face no longer wore an easy smile; instead, his expression was darkened by shadows, eyes filled with despair.

"What's wrong?" asked Kate, concerned.

"I'm editing the photos I took before I met you in London— from a diamond mine I visited in Ghana."

Kate recalled his gaunt face and rumpled clothes when they'd met at the museum. She'd dismissed it as jetlag mixed with a touch of laziness. She'd never thought to ask where Marcus had flown in from. The surfboard must have been intended for this holiday with Olivia.

She got up from the table and moved around behind him to look at the screen.

A little boy in bare feet and ragged clothing stared boldly at the camera, droplets of water gathered on his face and chest. "He can't be more than four," she gasped. She thought of Emma safely curled up on a Persian rug at home, no doubt demolishing a Lego car Molly had painstakingly put together.

"This boy's one of the lucky ones."

Marcus clicked to the next image and Kate was reminded of all those images of soldiers sinking into muddy trenches in the First World War. Men were covered in clay, bent over knee-deep and elbow-deep at the bottom of a pit. Women too, some with babies strapped to their backs. Even children were hard at work, yellow mud coating their skin.

In the next frame, a group of young men dressed in orange high-visibility vests kneeled on a concrete pad in prayer, surrounded by red desert.

Marcus kept clicking through his photo folder as he said, "I'll pitch it to *National Geographic*. But wait—I haven't finished!"

He continued to click through photos, telling Kate the stories behind the pictures he'd taken in gem mines around the world. A man dangling from a rope inside a cave in Colombia with just a headlamp and a pick, eyes bloodshot and inflamed from black dust as he chipped for emeralds. Another pushing a wheelbarrow through snow six thousand feet up in the Karakoram mountain range in northern Pakistan.

"This dude's hoping for some rubies, quartz, or aquamarine. Maybe a bit of topaz."

The last image was of a man in a turquoise sea, with a net wrapped around his neck and a wooden peg fastened to his nose.

"Pearl diver," said Kate.

Marcus sighed and closed his computer. Kate placed her hands on his shoulders to steady herself, images whirring in her head. They both remained still, soothed by the rhythm of the waves lapping at the sand.

Then Marcus reached up to place his hands on hers. After a few moments he began to stroke them with his thumbs. The only sound was the waves and their breath.

Her impulse was to leave. To go back to her suite and try to sleep, try to forget these images. To forget Marcus.

She should pull her hands away, go back to her room, and close the door.

But Marcus had not just touched her hands: his warmth had stirred her heart.

Kate thought of the Colombian boy with ebony eyes and green emerald roughs in his hands. The delight in his face that made her heart sing. A mother cradling her child inside a filthy trench, eyes locked on the baby's face, its tiny hand clutched in hers.

Pockets of love and hope. Marcus managed to find moments that transcended their horrific circumstances.

Kate thought back to that museum basement in London and mentally traced a line of people and gemstones that started deep underground and atop mountains, carried on ship's decks over many seas. She thought of the work-roughened hands that shaped rings and cut diamonds—to celebrate love and commemorate loss. She thought of black forget-me-nots and pansies intertwined on a tiny diamond ring.

"I'm sorry." Kate withdrew her hands. She was truly sorry for the injustices that were happening around the globe, that had happened throughout time. Sorry for the little Ghanaian boy and the Colombian boy, for Essie and the secret Kate suspected kept her great-grandmother from returning to London, and also for herself.

She was sorry, too, for Marcus's obvious heartbreak. Kate looked at the shadows under Marcus's eyes and understood that he carried his own layers of grief—his regret and mistakes—under that smooth golden skin and sunny demeanor. What were the words he'd used? *Light and shade.*

Kate studied Marcus's strong shoulders and the line of his back. She admired his strength, his purpose. He captured on camera the trivial, the beautiful, and the cruel, yet still carried hope and generosity in his bones. He dived into the messy tangle of life, wasn't content to study it at arm's length.

To think that she'd once thought of him as frivolous. She'd been so wrong about Marcus.

Kate lifted her hand and ran it through his curls. He held her hand against his cheek, before swiveling to face her, a question in the tilt of his head.

Kate's heart fluttered, then beat harder. Somewhere, a shutter slammed closed against a window as the breeze picked up.

In the ensuing quiet, she looked at him with her own questions, brushing away the gnawing doubt, whispering that she didn't deserve this moment of bliss. *Does Marcus feel the same way? Is this just for now, or . . .*

He had an almost-adult daughter, she reminded herself. Who lived in Sydney.

But something stronger tugged at her. There was a stirring in her stomach, then lower. She wanted to push her sorrow to one side and embrace this moment. To press against Marcus and run her hands down his back, over his scar. Desire flooded her veins and she realized it was insane to fight it. She needed to connect . . .

Kate leaned down and kissed Marcus. His lips were soft and tasted a little of coconut. When she pulled away, he grabbed the back of her head and gently pulled her back down for a longer, hungrier kiss.

Slowly, maintaining eye contact, Marcus stood. Then together they walked into her room, which was dark other than the flickering of a candle that must have been lit when the staff entered to perform the turndown service.

Without a word, they moved straight to the bed and stretched out across the sheets.

Marcus pressed against her and the beating of his heart in his chest matched the beat of her own. His breath was a little louder now, deeper. Kate felt any hesitation slip away as she drew the spices into her lungs and reached for him.

He shifted his weight so that Kate now lay tucked beside him, running her hand under his T-shirt. As she pulled it off, she traced her fingers over the scar on his shoulder.

"How?" She kissed it.

"I slipped on a mountain pass in Pakistan and gouged my shoulder open on a rock. They had to medevac me out and I had surgery in Islamabad." He smiled slightly, embarrassed. "I know it looks like I was a marine or something, but I was no hero.

The guide in front was carrying the equivalent of his own body weight with all my camera gear, and the one behind had all the food. I just had my camera slung around my neck and slipped on some pebbles when I leaned over to tie my shoelaces. The poor guys had to carry me down the mountain between them as well as all the gear."

She slowly kissed the scar and breathed in his sweat. As she breathed out, she said, "Maybe we shouldn't. Liv—"

"—is fast asleep in her room on the other side of the hotel. I banned Netflix. Opening her physics workbook seemed to induce severe jetlag."

He kissed her neck and then her shoulder, and began to kiss his way down her shirtfront. He started to unbutton it, then stopped midway and looked up, amused. "Any more questions?"

Kate had millions. Most significant of all: Was this a good idea? But instead she bit her bottom lip and arched her back, and any doubt rolled away with the rhythm of the sea.

Chapter 18

Over the coming days, Kate, Marcus, and Liv settled easily into a holiday and work routine. Their trip up to the mines in the mountains was scheduled for their last day in Sri Lanka. Kate was surprised at how much she craved the companionship. How great it felt to laugh, eat, and move with people she cared about by her side.

Sophie was right: it felt good to let the light stream in.

Each morning started with a surf at sunrise. "Didn't know you surfed," Marcus said with a laugh as Kate joined him on the beach with a board she'd rented from the hotel.

"College in California. Surfing was basically my major!" she'd replied as they ran out into the shallows and plunged into the waves.

After a surf came yoga by the pool. Marcus was underwhelmed at the prospect, but after some cajoling from Liv decided it was easier to join in than to resist. For Kate, it was nonnegotiable. Since Noah died, her morning exercise—even if it was just a lazy stroll around her Louisburg block—was as crucial as breathing. It was Molly who'd downloaded the YogaDay app onto her phone. "Fifteen minutes. I promise it'll help." Though it pained her to admit, it had turned out that decent amounts of sleep, exercise, and nutritious food—not her original diet of buckets of chocolate, peanut butter toast, and chardonnay (who knew?)—helped to allay the grief and anger that knocked around in her chest.

And it turned out that sex helped too.

For the first time in years, Kate found herself grinning like a giddy schoolgirl at the thought of a man. She yearned to be touched. Whenever she and Marcus were together, even if it was just working at the desk, her skin felt like it was on fire.

This was unexpected. Molly had set her up on a couple of dates last year—one with a scatterbrained violinist, and another with a recently divorced partner in her law firm—but Kate had known pretty much after the first glass of champagne that they were not for her.

She had not expected to feel the steam train of lust that accompanied the delicate first moments of a relationship ever again.

She paused. Was that what this was? A *relationship*?

Marcus sat beside Liv, squeezing lime juice over cheeks of fresh mango. "Here, I saved you some food. Liv was about to eat all the pancakes."

"Dad!"

"I'll just have one, Liv, promise." She winked.

"Trust me—once you've tried them, you'll want them all!"

Kate sat down and helped herself to a crunchy hopper—a light pancake that looked like fried pressed spaghetti but tasted like rice. She topped it with freshly shredded coconut mixed into a sambal with chili, tamarind, and onion. The savory dishes were accompanied by a colorful platter of fresh jackfruit, mango, and Kate's favorite, the sweet-and-sour rambutan.

Two espressos were delivered, and the smell of fresh coffee made her smile. For the past few days Marcus had been casually attentive. He'd noticed that she preferred her coffee short and black, that she liked to take her white tea with a drop of cold water so it didn't burn her tongue while she worked. He offered advice as she worked on her Cheapside piece and sought her advice on some of the watch and pomander images. They'd always had an easy banter as colleagues, and she was pleased that, rather than it being awkward when it came to her choice of images, it was a delight to share the work with someone who cared as much as she did.

After breakfast, Marcus took a chopper into the mountains, while Liv drank green smoothies and ate glutinous acai bowls between study and swims. Kate worked on the memento mori project for her Swiss client, and continued writing the Cheapside article.

In the evening, they went for a long walk along the beach and admired the lit-up Galle Fort, then headed back to the hotel before the evening winds whipped sand and sea mist into their faces.

After their walk, Liv excused herself to go study. "Time to hit the books. Can't wait until this year is *done*."

"Do you think she knows?" asked Kate on the third night, as they sprawled naked under white cotton sheets in her room.

"Knows what?" Marcus teased as he ran a finger down her thigh.

Kate propped herself up on her elbow. "I'm serious."

He reached up and kissed her forehead. "I'm sure she's onto us. She's just turned eighteen—she's pretty much a grown-up."

Kate must have looked as embarrassed as she felt, because Marcus went on, "Look, she's concentrating on her final exams, then her gap year. She's not that interested in what her old dad is getting up to. Besides, she likes you."

Then he leaned over and kissed her while tracing the curve of her hip, before clenching her tight. Kate couldn't get enough of his strong arms around her body or the taste of his salty skin.

Afterward, as they lay sweating in a tangle of sheets, they shared random snippets of their lives back home. Marcus described his hikes into Western Australia's Kimberley Ranges, where the red dust settled into every crevice of your body and backpack, and the best vantage point from which to take in the New Year's Eve fireworks on Sydney Harbour. Kate told him about her autumn walks through Boston and her love of Essie's Louisburg house, creaky with history—how one of her favorite places in the world was Essie's sunny buttercup-yellow kitchen with matching curtains, always filled with baking smells.

Inevitably, as always, their talk turned to the Cheapside story.

"That first day, you had a drawing of a button that matched the ones in the Cheapside cache. What's the connection?"

"I'm not sure." Kate tried to match Marcus's carefree tone. "I found it with my great-grandmother's papers. She was originally from London. And it turns out my cousin Bella wears the same button on a chain around her neck. The one in the sketch has jewels, though, and Bella's doesn't."

"Now *that's* a story. Are you going to include it?"

"Not until I have evidence. My great-grandmother didn't speak much about her childhood. Her family were poor Irish immigrants. I asked her once when I was eighteen . . ." Kate shrugged. "I asked her why she never went back to London, but she wouldn't tell me. I still have no idea . . ." She now understood that Essie had probably kept her complex feelings—particularly hurt, loss, and disappointment—bundled up and tucked deep inside her heart. She pushed the image of the envelope with the silver fern lying on her desk at home from her mind.

"Mostly Essie just talked about everyday stuff—fish on Fridays, collecting coal pieces from train tracks, the suffragette protests. Kids playing soccer down cobbled lanes."

"She sounds like a storyteller. Must run in the family."

"Maybe. I prefer to stick to jewelry. More tangible."

"So what are you going to do?"

"I don't know . . ." She half pulled a pillow over her head in frustration. "I mean, what if Essie—or someone close to her—stole the jewels? How else would a poor family come by Bella's button?"

If her great-grandmother was a thief, Kate wasn't sure if she could write about it. *Should* she? Her great-grandmother had created a great legacy in Boston, championed many worthy causes. Why ruin Essie's reputation?

Kate winced. "I'm not sure *that's* a story I want to tell."

Marcus pulled the pillow from between them as he leaned on one elbow. "Well, you don't have to decide now. There're so many gray areas."

"Marcus, I'm preparing a report for a collector demanding that a ring be repatriated to the Dutch Jewish family it belonged to before they fled the Nazis in 1940. If *I* don't fess up, that would make me a total hypocrite as a historian. Bella's button belongs with the others at the museum."

"Not . . . exactly."

"Why?"

"Well, for starters, none of the jewelry in the collection was owned by the Museum of London. The museum didn't even exist in the 1600s."

"Sure, but—"

"So who buried the collection? I mean we don't know who owned the jewels, right? Also, how did your relatives stumble across these pieces hundreds of years later?"

"Essie had an older brother, Freddie. He was a navvy—a construction laborer—who died on a worksite near Cheapside. It's possible he saw the jewels when they were recovered in 1912 . . . or found some." Kate couldn't quite bring herself to say, *or stole some*. But from the expression on Marcus's face, he understood.

Kate continued, "Essie used to tell us a fairy tale about a big box of treasure being pulled out of the ground—pouches of pearls, handfuls of gold chains, and rings for every finger and toe. It was guarded by a man with eyes the color of emeralds. He cast a spell on her."

"What kind of spell?"

"She didn't say."

"Sounds like a typical Irish fairy tale to me."

"This was different."

"She transferred it to her life in London. So, was this mystery man a leprechaun? Leprechauns are known for making mischief. Did she capture him?"

Kate eyed him and gently pushed his shoulder. "I'm serious!"

Marcus brushed a strand of hair from her face and said, "Kate, folktales are made up. But at their heart they're stories about the messy business of being human. Rage, jealousy . . . lust." He ran a finger across her stomach.

Kate and Marcus stared at each other and the only sound came from the blades of the fan beating overhead. All those years behind the lens had taught him where to focus.

"Now, about Bella's gold button . . . one sister had the drawing in Boston, the other sister kept the button in London. Both match the buttons in the museum. Surely the button must be the key to what you're looking for?" Marcus said.

"I don't know." She shrugged. "But I'm worried it's somehow tied up with the reason Essie left London and never returned."

"Perhaps you'd better answer that first."

Marcus had a point. She needed to widen her parameters.

Kate rolled over to grab her glass of water from the bedside table and caught a glimpse of herself in the mirror lit up by the moon. Her face was scattered with freckles—no doubt brought out by the tropical sun. Her curls were a knotty jumble from humidity and salt water. But her face looked softer, more relaxed. Gone was her tightly clenched jaw. Grief and guilt would always be a part of Kate, tucked deep within like organs. But as the moon highlighted her crooked nose and slightly sunburned cheeks, she recognized something quieter, something happier . . .

Beyond the Sparkle: Behind the Scenes at the Museum of London (draft)

BY DR. KATE KIRBY

Photography by Marcus Holt

For over a century, academics and historians have been trying to unravel the mystery of who buried a priceless collection of over five hundred jewels and gemstones in a Cheapside London cellar, and why. But the journey of the jewels from the roughs in the ground to painstaking creation is every bit as intriguing.

A jewel never lies. It expresses the very best of humanity—beauty, devotion, loyalty, adventure, and hope. It can be a commitment to love, or a reminder of a loved one in death. However, underneath the polishing and soldering often lies trauma, terror, guilt, and greed.

One of the oldest pieces in the collection is a Byzantine white sapphire carved with the image of Jesus presenting his nail-punctured hands to a doubting St. Thomas on one side and backed with an exquisite enamel flower on the other . . .

(Insert pics)
(Caption: L–R) Enamel necklaces; a Byzantine white sapphire cameo; an exquisite pomander to be filled with scented oils; timepiece inset in Colombian emerald; salamander emerald hat pin (tbc); champlevé ring with diamond from Golconda.

Chapter 19

On their final day in Galle, Marcus asked Liv to come with them in the chopper up to Ratnapura.

"Don't pull that face, Liv. Physics, chemistry, and the Bard can wait."

Liv smiled at her father, then Kate, and said, "Okay."

Was Kate imagining the slightest knowing smile on the teenager's face?

Marcus turned to look at Kate, who felt naked under his gaze. Every time their hands brushed at dinner it was electric. When he'd helped Kate return their dinner plates into her hotel room the night before, he'd pressed her up against the wall hidden from Liv, kissing her neck slowly and pushing his groin against hers. Her thighs throbbed with the memory.

It was as if Kate and Marcus were naughty lust-struck teenagers, and Liv the parent they had to hide their holiday trysts from.

They snuck between bedrooms when they suspected Liv was long asleep, then set phone alarms before dawn so they could start the day in their own rooms. Kate put her unusual behavior down to the tropical air.

Marcus read her early paragraphs of the Cheapside piece, and they edited the photos of the emerald watch, the salamander, the pomander, and the white sapphire St. Thomas pendant together.

"What about the champlevé ring—did you get any close-ups? I'd really like to have a look at the enamel. It'd be great to feature that detail."

"I haven't finished processing them all, but I'll send the images through for you to have a look at when I'm done. Give me a week."

The one topic they avoided was what would happen when she flew back to London to finish her research and then returned home to Boston.

Instead, in the dark of night Kate pressed her cheek to Marcus's skin and memorized the whorl where his skin puckered with the scar—as severe and beautiful as the star in any sapphire.

They spent the morning flying over the coast, past fishermen crouched on stilts sticking up out of the ocean, before heading inland over dense tropical rainforests and up over mountains ribboned with tea plantations.

Eventually they landed on an alluvial plain beside a river, not far from a large cluster of open huts with steeply pitched thatched roofs. Marcus grabbed his camera bag and said, "C'mon. These are the mines."

The trio crunched their way over river pebbles toward the huts.

"Those are *mines*?" asked Liv, pointing to the holes secured with bamboo scaffolding to prevent them from collapsing.

"Sure are! The roof is just to keep the sun off. They can only mine here in the dry season, as these river flats swell when the rains come." Marcus had put his bag down and was screwing his wide lens onto his camera.

The area in which they stood was cleared, but it looked like the vines and thick foliage of the rainforest a hundred yards away were creeping back in to swallow the valley. Gemstone roughs were only discovered in this region after they'd been dislodged and washed into the waterways. Streams, rivers, and creeks ran through the mountains, leaving deposits of blue, pink, and yellow sapphires and pink rubies, cat's-eyes, and garnets, as well as a long list of other colored gemstones—more gemstones than in any other place in the world.

"Ratnapura: city of gems," said Marcus.

Kate looked up into the mountains and marveled that the exact deposits of all these magical stones still remained a mystery. For reasons she couldn't explain, this cheered Kate. She loved that Mother Nature didn't reveal all her secrets.

Marcus ushered them over to a pit, where workers in white shorts hoisted buckets of gravel out with a series of pulleys. Their muscles strained at their necks and backs, their skin was shiny with sweat. Marcus approached the foreman, who was expecting them, and introduced Kate and Liv. With the workers' permission, Marcus started to take photos.

Liv spoke first. "I wasn't expecting it to be so, so . . . hand-driven. I thought mining was mostly done by machine these days?"

"Open-cut mines are forbidden," said the foreman. "At the end of the dry season, all these pits are dismantled and the holes filled in. Revegetated. The government keeps a close watch too, regulating pay and conditions."

Kate nodded and moved across to a small dam where a handful of men were winnowing gravel and water through straw baskets, sifting for gemstones.

The men stopped and struck poses for Marcus as he clicked. A few waved shyly at Liv, and she waved back as she started to fiddle with the lens of her own camera. Marcus had given it to her yesterday. "For traveling when you're done with school. I know it's cumbersome, but this is the smallest, and you've got a great eye, so . . ."

Liv had given her father the biggest hug. "You really didn't need to. I'm already so grateful for this trip. Beats studying in Sydney with my brothers kicking balls against my door all afternoon!"

"Pleasure. And I promise I won't tell your mother how much you're missing Jacko and Harry." He grinned. "Can't fool me, kiddo."

Marcus dropped to one knee beside Liv to show her how to get a better angle to shoot the pits. He was patient and gave clear instructions, even when Liv started to thrust her camera under his nose in frustration because a light was blinking or the shutter wasn't working.

"Try again. You'll get the hang of it."

He glanced up at Kate and smiled, cocking his head on a slight angle with just the hint of a raised eyebrow. Kate would miss this look when they flew out on different planes tomorrow.

While she had been wrapping up her final day's writing in Galle yesterday, an email had appeared in her inbox from an executive at Cartier asking if Kate were perhaps free to meet with their master enameler, Madame Parsons, at one of their workshops later this week in Paris. There was a private commission they wished to record for their archives, some sketches they'd like her to see—with the utmost discretion, of course. Kate realized that this brief meeting would give her an opportunity to talk with a master enameler about the champlevé ring. Perhaps get a different angle for her magazine article—Jane would be thrilled!

Kate would go to Paris, then return to London, before she could finally head home to Boston.

She'd asked Marcus on a whim last night to join her in Paris, but he had to fly back to New York for Fashion Week, and then to Colombia. He was going on from there to Sydney for Liv's end-of-school celebrations that kicked off in a few weeks.

"I promised Liv and Jules I'd be there. I missed those precious early moments—I'll be damned if I'm going to miss this!" His voice softened. "I'm sorry. If I'd known . . ." Marcus's dark eyes had bored into hers.

"I get it," she said with burning cheeks. And she did understand. Marcus dived deep into every moment and held it steady. This was the end of their moment . . .

She wasn't surprised. Marcus had shaken something awake in her and for that she was grateful. If she was embarrassed, it was because her mind had overshot into thoughts of the future, and the past few years had taught her how dangerous that could be.

As Kate stepped forward to peer into the pit, she studied the layers of sediment and rock and the shadows on sinewy arms heaving up buckets of gravel. Behind her, the scratching sound of winnowing baskets settled into a rhythm as the mist rolled down the mountains.

Beside her, one of the miners plucked at his basket of gravel like he was picking flowers. So many hands passed over a jewel from the moment it was removed from the gravel. Each time, a life was altered.

Kate thought of the tiny black-and-white ring with the diamond from Golconda. Though it was probably mined in the 1600s, it was likely the pit mines had looked a little like this. She reflected on its journey from the mines, perhaps passing through the thick walls of the Golconda Fort she'd walked with Marcus in India, then being traded in Hyderabad's bazaar with the call to prayer ringing out from the Charminar across the city. The diamond rough would have been wrapped up in silk or cotton, no doubt, then marched on the back of a bullock chain overland to Bandar Abbas, where perhaps this mysterious Polman bought it, along with other precious gems. He'd attempted to bring them to England on a ship, risking pirates and shipwreck, and had been murdered for his efforts. Somehow the diamond had made it into the hands of an artisan jeweler, who crafted the exquisite champlevé band. Such a beautiful diamond, such a hazardous journey. Kate was following the same journey, with the comfort and convenience of a plane. What both journeys shared was the quest for beauty, for truth.

THE SHIP

BANDAR ABBAS, PERSIA, 1631

Robbie Parker moved along the boom checking folds in the sails, ignoring the steady rocking of the ship. All around him the crew worked to load, roll, and store barrels full of tobacco, Shiraz, and fresh water below deck.

Behind him, the Discovery's captain was murmuring with the surgeon about a new passenger.

"His name's Polman—Gerhard Polman," said the captain as he waved the transport papers.

"Dutch?" asked the surgeon.

"Indeed. But he's been here for decades. Paid the East India Company a hundred pounds for safe passage to London. Trouble is he's poorly . . . and not from the drink."

Robbie whistled. One hundred pounds was a king's ransom. Why was this passenger paying so much?

The captain caught Robbie's eye and gave him a stern look before barking, "Help, boy!" He pointed to the longboat knocking at the prow, where the passenger lay on a stretcher, pale and sweating.

The sailors winched him up to the deck very slowly, careful not to knock him on the rail.

"Almost aboard," coaxed the surgeon as the crew brought the stretcher to rest on the deck. The passenger yelped and clutched at his belly.

The Dutchman's head tipped to one side and his white shirt caught in the breeze, billowing open at the neck. Beneath the shirt he wore a leather pouch on a string. He moaned and tucked it away, buttoning up his shirt with shaky hands.

The boy looked around to see if anyone else had noticed, but the rest of the crew were busy hoisting aboard the passenger's luggage: several heavy trunks as well as smaller wooden caskets.

The ship groaned and shifted with the breeze. Polman shuddered.

"Easy, easy." Robbie touched the passenger on the shoulder in a bid to calm him and studied the shoreline.

He thought of the girl at his favorite dining room swathed in black silk, her dark eyes traced with kohl. Bands of gold encircling her arms, chains around her belly. The tinkle as her hips swayed when she served him mint tea and plates of steaming yellow rice. How he'd longed to put a hand on each hip and sink his head into the soft strip of flesh above her skirt.

He glanced at the sun over the mountains behind the city and wondered when he'd visit these shores again. Would he remember where to find the girl? Would her father let Robbie visit after their table's bawdiness last night as they filled their gullets with Shiraz?

He didn't even think to ask her name . . . Robbie's chest ached with shame.

"Carry this gentleman to his cabin," instructed the surgeon.

"One. Two—"

"Wait!" cried the patient, lifting his hand.

The surgeon shushed the Dutchman as if he were a fussing toddler. "Sir! It will be far more comfortable for you in your cabin. I insist."

The passenger ignored the surgeon and looked over to where the last of his trunks was being hoisted aboard.

A burly sailor yanked hard on the rope, then accidentally released his grip. The trunk spun out of control through the pulleys, creating an unnerving whistle. The sailor cursed under his breath and rubbed his burning hand on his thigh.

The Dutchman twisted his head to where the trunk had hit the deck. The carpenter was righting the chest and repacking the tools that had spilled from it. Robbie turned to follow the Dutchman's gaze.

In among the pile of tools was a rough green stone about the size of Robbie's fist. He'd been ashore in Bandar Abbas long enough to recognize an emerald. Beside it was a leather sack that had fallen open, and a trickle of clear stones spilled out like running water.

Among them was a diamond rough that shone a little brighter than all the others, with the slightest hint of gold. He stepped forward to pick it up but was pushed aside by one of the deckhands, who grabbed the diamond along with all the others, placed it in the chest, and slammed the lid shut.

Chapter 20

ESSIE

LONDON, 1912

"What's happened?"

Mrs. Yarwood had greeted Essie at the Yarwoods' front door with a distraught expression.

"It's Flora."

Essie had arrived home a little later than usual this Saturday evening, having lost track of time as she enjoyed her first silver service Devonshire tea at Fortnum & Mason with Edward.

"I'm so sorry, love . . ." Her neighbor choked on her words.

Essie bolted down the hallway to find Flora and Maggie on a mattress, chests wrapped in brown paper, hair lank around their pale faces. The room smelled of pine oil and fear.

Ma was kneeling beside the twins, rubbing Flora's chest with Mrs. Yarwood's oil before reaching for each of their hands and pressing them to her heart.

Gertie entered the room carrying a bowl of hot water, while Mrs. Yarwood draped a woolen blanket over both girls. Flora's skin was gray and her rib cage shuddered with each breath. Maggie started to cough, her head lolling to the side when the attack had subsided. She found Essie's eyes, and the edges of her lips moved a fraction.

"I've sent Mr. Yarwood off to fetch the doctor," Mrs. Yarwood told her.

But the words barely registered as Essie ran to the twins.

Mrs. Yarwood had hardly spoken when they heard the front door open. Essie's stomach flipped with relief, and she squeezed Maggie's tiny cold hand.

"You'll be right soon enough," she whispered as Gertie stared at her across the steaming bowl of water.

But the man Mr. Yarwood ushered into the room was no doctor; Essie looked up to see Father McGuire, draped in his black robes. He smelled of cigarettes and scorn.

"It's the croup, Father. Their little lungs are so weak—bless their souls," sobbed Ma. "Please!"

Essie looked at Flora and Maggie, who were straining to breathe.

Gertie rolled her eyes and muttered through gritted teeth, "The girls need a doctor."

Essie doubted there was a prayer in the world that could save these two, but without so much as a glance at the sweaty, sallow faces of Flora and Maggie, nor a word of solace to their mother or sisters, the priest began to recite the Hail Mary.

Essie dug her nails deep into her palms and tried to swallow, tried to find words to protest as the walls started to close in.

"Holy Mary, mother of God, pray for us now, and at the hour of our death . . ."

When Gertie was tucked up in bed each night, Essie lit the oil lamp, tiptoed upstairs, and lifted Gertie's notebook from the side table. She sat in the rocking chair with the ledger in her lap and opened to the page with the lost twins. She studied the fine line of Maggie's limbs, the bow-tie birthmark on Flora's neck. Ran her fingers over their loose braids and kissed their freckles, as if she could breathe life onto the page.

This was the room where she'd rocked the twins to sleep in a shared cradle through long winter nights. When they were sick, she'd rubbed Russian tallow or goose fat into their sunken chests, wrapped them in brown paper, and held them close to keep them warm.

It had taken just two days from the Saturday when they had fallen ill for Flora and Maggie to draw their last breaths. Inseparable till the last, Flora had clung to Maggie's limp form as they both faded away.

The church sent a horse and dray filled with coffins, and the twins were carried out and loaded into the smallest two.

The funeral had been almost a week ago now, but the day of the funeral remained stark and vivid in her mind.

As the dray clattered over the cobblestones, the coffins slid around and Essie wished she could shout to the driver to take a little more care. She knew the girls couldn't feel the bumps, but all the same . . .

Essie walked beside Gertie, clutching her hand.

Ma stepped gingerly behind, half carried by Freddie. Essie's brother had turned up on the night the girls took their last breaths, filthy, broke, and ashamed. When he'd seen the state of the twins, his wretched face reflected the grief and regret of them all.

The funeral in the stone church was attended by a handful of local Irish families, and a line of coffins blessed in a batch. It was a service that could have just as easily been presided over by the tax collector, it was so devoid of emotion.

A line of coffins, a litany of prayers. An unconvincing homily. It finished with a burial in the paupers' yard up the road.

Gertie muttered to Essie as the priest gave a righteous sermon denouncing sin and asking for forgiveness, "It's a little late for prayer now."

"He's praying for their souls," hissed Essie with a sharp look to quell her sister. "Now, hush, otherwise he might stop. The twins' poor souls will be stuck in this freezing church forever."

Essie didn't blame Gertie—she shared her anger. Eyeing the stained-glass windows filled with lightning bolts, crosses, and other reminders of God's wrath, Essie wished she had a rock to shatter them. What business did such a vengeful God have with Maggie and Flora?

Father McGuire glared at Essie from the pulpit. Gertie squeezed her hand. Mrs. Yarwood pressed her handkerchief into each eye, and Mr. Yarwood leaned forward with his head bowed. Ma sat sniffing, tattered skirts pooled around her hips.

It was the worst day of Essie's life.

Chapter 21

Essie met Edward at their usual meeting spot at the corner of Hyde Park, as they had arranged the previous Saturday. Essie had wanted to send a letter to cancel. Her heart was too broken. She missed the twins, and her head was churning with rage. What could she do for Gertie to make things better? How could Gertie finish school so her life wasn't wasted too? She'd thought about forging Ma's signature on the permission papers to take the entry exams for Miss Barnes, but she couldn't just sneak her sister into a different school.

It had been Gertie who had put her hand on Essie's wrist and insisted she go. "I know you've not been going to Mrs. Ruben's on Saturdays."

Essie looked up, surprised. Her cheeks started to burn.

"For one thing, nobody sings because they are going to work for an extra day."

"And?"

"And . . . there's always a glow to your cheeks when you get home. And no factory smell on your skin. Last time you smelled of cut grass and strawberries." Gertie gave her a knowing look. "I don't s'pose there's either of those in the factory. I guess I'll find out soon enough when I start work there."

"Stop! I won't let that happen."

"Es, you need to stop trying to fix us all." She reached out and took Essie's hand and whispered sadly, "There's no point . . ."

"Stop saying that! I couldn't save Flora and Maggie"—bile started to burn the back of her throat as her stomach roiled—"but it's still possible for—"

Gertie pulled away abruptly and covered her face with her hands. Her body shuddered as she started to sob.

Essie touched Gertie's shoulder. Their grief for the twins sat heavy in their bones. If Essie let it, it would drag them both under. She looked at Ma, snoring in their only good sitting chair—sleeping off last night's bottle of whisky. Freddie had only just arrived home this morning. They had not seen him since the funeral earlier in the week.

"I've been meeting Mr. Hepplestone—Edward"—she blushed—"since our excursion to the Observatory. We walk in Hyde Park, go to the pictures. Sometimes we even have tea . . ."

Gertie's mouth twitched and she half smiled. "I'm pleased for you, Es." She grabbed her older sister's hand. "You deserve more." She shook her head at their ma, still asleep slumped in the chair.

"Edward's bought a flat in Mayfair," blurted Essie. "He wants to show me. We're going there this afternoon, straight after our usual walk in Hyde Park." She stopped, guilt stuck like a stone in her throat.

She'd imagined, *hoped*, that maybe if Edward was as sweet on her as he seemed that there might be a future for them. A future with fresh sheets smelling of lavender, their own bedrooms with a desk for Gertie, and a yellow kitchen full of slow-roasting beef and apple pie, just like the Yarwoods'. And surely it meant something that he was taking her to see his new flat. Perhaps he, too, was imagining that one day they might live in it together . . .

Edward closed the heavy wooden door to his apartment, and Essie's heart skipped a beat. They were alone for the first time that day.

Freddie had insisted on accompanying Essie.

Just as she'd been about to leave, Freddie had come in from the yard, where he'd been fixing the chicken coop, and said, "Wait, I'll be coming with you, Es." His eyes softened as he touched Essie on the shoulder. "I know you've been walking out a bit with Edward Hepplestone. Danny told me he'd seen you around." His dark eyes shone with hurt. "He was worried I wasn't looking out for you, what with all that's happened and me being . . . away."

Yet as soon as they reached the grand wooden door of Edward's apartment building, Freddie looked down at his hand-stitched felt pants and dusty shoes and quickly excused himself. "Gotta go meet some of the lads down the road," he muttered.

So Essie and Edward would be alone in Edward's new apartment for as long as it took Freddie to drink his pint down the road—and maybe a second and third, if darts went his way. She couldn't blame her brother for his reluctance to step into his boss's fancy new digs. He dreamed of getting his own two-up two-down with Rosie Jones one day . . . but his loyalty to Ma, Essie, and the girls meant there was nothing put aside for savings.

Edward pulled the security chain across the door and tucked the key into his waistcoat. Then he took Essie by the hand and led her down the wide hall and into a large empty room with duck-egg blue silk wallpaper. A chandelier dangled from a golden ceiling rose, and she gasped.

"It's beautiful," she said. "This blue is my favorite."

"I know. I remember." He smiled and held her gaze for a beat. "What do you think of the view?"

She stepped across to the bay window and saw London outside—but not the London she was used to. This was a London of sleek black motorcars, of elegant women in stylish coats with fur cuffs and men in bowler hats.

Essie's stomach fluttered, and for the first time since the twins had died she felt aglow with happiness. Was it possible that she could live in this London—and bring her family with her? Though she still hadn't met Edward's family, she recalled. She wanted to ask when his sister would be home from Switzerland, and when she might be introduced to his parents, but she didn't know how to without seeming pushy or forward.

Edward, meanwhile, was eager to continue the tour, leading her through the master bedroom and a luxuriously appointed bathroom with claw-foot bath, gold taps, and hot running water, before pointing out the two smaller bedrooms at the back.

"I plan to move in a couple of months," he said proudly. He put his arms around her and gave her a squeeze. "But before I do, there are some opportunities in Boston for my family's company. I'm sailing over for business. I could even end up living there someday."

"You mean you might be *moving* to Boston?" Essie's chest tightened and her cheeks started to burn—it had been silly of her to imagine they had a future together. Ludicrous.

"In time, perhaps." He shrugged. "We'll see."

"When do you sail?"

"Tomorrow. But before I go, I have something for you—so you don't forget me while I'm gone." Then he added softly, "I'll be coming back for you, I promise."

Edward reached into his pocket and pulled out his purse. Hooked onto its end, like a shepherd's crook, was a tiny silver hairpin studded with turquoise stones at the top of the hook.

As Edward unhooked it, she moved forward for a closer look.

"It's a bodkin!" she exclaimed. "I've seen ladies who come to the factory wearing them in their hair. Mrs. Ruben's best customer has one with diamonds. She let me hold it last week." Her eyes widened. "Can you imagine?"

"Well . . ."

Essie stilled. Edward had been responsible for the Cheapside site. Freddie had said there was an unspoken agreement between the lads to divvy some of the spoils between them, instead of handing them over to Edward. But what if Edward also kept some jewels? She eyed the bodkin. Did he pay for this apartment with his wages, an inheritance, or with stolen jewelry? Essie shook the shadows of uncertainty from her head, telling herself the Hepplestones were people of means. Respectable. She chided herself for thinking otherwise as she ran her hands across the wall and felt the ripple of silk . . .

"This is for you."

He stepped closer now and slid the hairpin into her hair. "It's beautiful," he said. "Like you." He tipped his head to the side, those green eyes asking only one question.

Essie knew she shouldn't, but against her better judgment she stood on her toes and kissed him. His lips tasted of cherry syrup. They drew away from each other for a beat, and then kissed again with greater confidence. He wrapped his arms around her and lifted her onto the table. Her heart raced and her breath was ragged as his fingers caressed her cheeks, her hair, her neck.

Slowly, Edward unlaced her boots and let them each drop to the floor with a thunk. Then he stood and placed both hands on her shoulders, eyes burning into hers.

He promised.

Her throat was dry. Her heart thumped, and she longed to lift her legs and wrap them around Edward's waist, to lose herself in this strange sensation of heat and desire that made her limbs ache. But she wasn't sure what to do.

So she did nothing except sit a little stiffly atop the table, knees primly together.

Edward started to unbutton her dress quickly, slipping it down so her shoulders were laid bare and creamy in the twilight. He kissed her skin, and his fingers lingered on her shoulders before he traced the line of them.

"Oh, Essie," he whispered as he started to feather his fingers down her spine. "You're so beautiful . . . this skin," he sighed, and he trailed kisses down her back until her dress was bunched at her waist. Linen scratched against her soft stomach.

Edward stepped in front of her now, and cupped her breasts with both hands, groaning. Her back arched involuntarily, and suddenly she found herself pulling off his jacket, fumbling with the buttons of his waistcoat. He took over, stripping off his waistcoat and shirt and flinging them to the floor.

They pressed together skin to skin, breathing ragged. She'd opened her legs so he stood between them, and she could feel him pressing into her through the cloth of his trousers.

She hesitated. What if Freddie . . .

Edward leaned forward and kissed her deeply. More than anything she wanted him. All of him. She wanted to feel his flesh pressed against her skin . . . to feel alive. Essie was so very tired of feeling lost, sad, and ashamed. Was it so wrong to snatch a moment of joy?

"Edward . . ." She seized his hand and led it to the warm spot under her skirts, between her legs. He gasped, then fell to his knees, slowly slipping off her drawers. He then slid his tongue up the inside of her thigh, moving higher and higher until he reached the point where her thighs met.

After that, it all seemed to happen so quickly. She lay down on the table as he unbuckled his belt and unfastened his pants. He leaned into her, feeling first with his fingers, then he thrust himself into her. She bit hard into her hand as the warm sensation she'd been feeling was pricked with sharp pain.

He stopped, sensing her discomfort. "Sorry . . . I'll stop. We'll wait until—"

But Essie pulled him by the shoulders so his full weight was pressed against her groin and adjusted her hips. The burning sensation softened.

Essie didn't want him to stop. Not ever.

As they moved together she was aware of the light falling across the room, shadows shifting against the crystal chandeliers. Her brown curls rippled across the table like an ocean. Edward buried his nose in her hair and pressed faster and faster until Essie thought she couldn't stop.

She sighed. Edward shuddered, then stilled.

Edward rolled to the side, groaning. "Essie Murphy," he whispered. "Thank you." Then he reached across and clasped her hand. They lay together like that for a moment, her head on his chest and his arm wrapped tight around her. He whispered again, so softly that she almost missed it, "I wish you were coming with me to Boston. One day I'll take you."

Another promise. Her heart filled.

She kissed his chest. "That would be wonderful," she said. "But what about Gertie? I couldn't leave her."

"Shh." He kissed her forehead. "I'll take care of it." And he kissed her again before gently helping her back into her dress.

"We'd best—"

"Of course, before Freddie . . ."

They spoke shyly, glancing at each other and blushing like schoolchildren.

Essie turned away to pull on her drawers and lace her boots while Edward refastened his shirt, waistcoat, and jacket. She'd just finished fixing her hair when the doorbell rang.

"It's Freddie!"

Edward kissed the top of Essie's head and gave her hand a reassuring squeeze before he walked down the hallway to answer the door.

"Well, hello, Freddie. Any luck?" Essie could hear Edward's voice carry down the corridor. It was only when she smoothed her skirt and tucked a curl behind her ear that she realized her lovely hairpin was missing. She quickly checked under the table and scanned the floor.

Nothing.

Edward must have removed it from her hair and tucked it away for safekeeping.

She felt the heat rising to her cheeks as she recalled what had just happened between them.

No matter, he would return it to her when they saw each other again on his return from Boston. It was only to be a short trip, and then he would be coming back to her, just as he had promised . . .

The door whipped open and Essie's mother stood framed in the doorway, holding a candle.

She pulled her shoulders back and stood as if she were a queen. Her hair was neatly swept into a bun, and her green shawl was wrapped around her shoulders to hide her filthy tunic. But the dark rings under her eyes and the spider's web of red veins across her pasty cheeks and nose betrayed her.

Essie cringed as Edward held open the door of his motorcar for her to climb out. Freddie had hurried inside some minutes ago, leaving Essie and Edward alone to say goodbye.

It was kind of Edward to offer to drive her and Freddie home at this late hour. He'd insisted—said he was driving out anyway for a late supper with friends at a new restaurant before he set sail tomorrow. Essie felt threads of hope and confusion twist in her stomach as she pictured him drinking and dining in a posh restaurant with his well-dressed friends. How would she ever fit into that world?

Essie met her mother's icy gaze as she stood on the doorstep and brushed her nerves aside. She needed to move quickly to shoo away her mother before she spoke—or, worse, invited Edward inside.

Her chest tightened with embarrassment and shame. What would her beau think of her if he saw how she lived? Would it make him realize that she didn't belong with him in his Mayfair flat?

"You shouldn't have waited up, Ma."

"Well, when your brother came inside alone, I got to wondering what could be keeping you." Ma narrowed her eyes as she took in Edward's bespoke striped suit, front-creased trousers, and pale shoes. "And now I see."

"Ma'am." Edward removed his cream Panama hat to reveal a neat part and stepped forward under a streetlamp with his hand outstretched. "Edward Hepplestone. I'm pleased to meet you." He beamed with the easy confidence of someone who was welcomed wherever he went.

"Mrs. Murphy," Ma grunted stiffly. "It's after ten thirty. And I'll thank you not to be keeping my daughter outside." Clementine reached forward and wrapped her fingers around Essie's wrist, squeezing tightly. "Good evening, Mr. Hepplestone." She nodded haughtily.

"Evening, ma'am." He tipped his hat in farewell. "Esther. I'll see you—"

But Essie didn't get to hear where and when he would next see her, because Ma had whipped her inside and slammed the door.

"Ma! That was so rude. I didn't get to say goodbye."

"Now you listen here, miss." Ma stepped close, and Essie could smell the gin on her warm breath. "That pretty man with his striped suits and sharp shoes is not for the likes of you."

Essie felt her neck growing hot. "But—"

"Those green eyes will get you into trouble." She poked Essie's shoulder. "Are you understandin' me?"

"But, Ma, he loves—"

"He *loves* what's on offer beneath your skirts, Essie." She tugged at her daughter's dress before reaching into her own apron and pulling out a tiny bottle. She removed the lid with shaking hands and took a sip, then sighed with relief.

When she spoke again, her voice was soft. "Don't be daft, child. You know what they say: *A sea wind changes less often than the mind of a weak man.* And weak he is, lass. Those shiny eyes and new suit will be gone as quick as you give him what he's asking."

Essie felt her cheeks redden with rage and humiliation. Her mother was wrong. Tonight was . . .

She closed her eyes and remembered Edward's fingertips tracing along the top of her bare shoulders, peeling off her bodice, kissing her back as he unbuttoned her dress.

She shivered. What she and Edward had was special.

How could her mother understand? Poverty had made the once-fair Clementine Murphy bruised and broken. But Essie would show her ma it was possible for fortunes to change. For hope to triumph.

Chapter 22

KATE

PARIS, PRESENT DAY

Kate stood in Cartier's workshop at the top of a Haussmann building in Rue de la Paix, Paris. The sun streamed through the giant sash windows as she gazed out. Luxury jewelers and fashion boutiques lined the street below, their elegant awnings billowing in the light breeze. Above, identical window boxes spilling over with red and pink flowers were attached to every balcony.

She smiled, and her stomach grumbled. She'd peeled apart a flaky croissant from a paper bag during her dash from the Opéra metro, but now she wished she'd arrived a little earlier to sit at one of the marble-topped café tables below. She'd have sipped mediocre Parisian coffee while trying to decide between a plain buttery croissant with raspberry jam, or a more decadent almond croissant filled with gooey frangipane.

The Cartier workshop smelled of leather, metal, and ever so faintly of smoke. Kate made a point to visit once a year; it was a way of absorbing the inspiration and passion that drove the world's finest jewelers, and to be reminded of all the skilled hands that passed over a jewel or a gemstone. Each time she was struck anew by the care and precision, but also by the sheer audacity of what a bit of imagination and dreaming could accomplish.

Color palettes and vials of colored crystals were arranged along walls. A dozen men and women leaned over microscopes, working with paintbrushes that were so fine they could be used to paint a grain of rice. Desks were scattered with loupes, tiny hammers, and anvils, and traditional suede catches were draped across the desks and laps to collect the slightest sliver of silver, gold, or platinum. Engravers used tiny diamond-tipped shafts to carve patterns into gold bands and watch faces, enamelist apprentices pounded glass into a fine powder in a mortar and pestle before adding water to blend up the enamel paste.

"Dr. Kirby, lovely to see you again." Madame Parsons, a master enameler, greeted her warmly.

"It's always a pleasure to visit your workshop," replied Kate, wishing that she'd blow-dried her mop of curls before meeting this Gallic Anna Wintour with her severe bob, silk blouse, and fitted pencil skirt.

"I have the illustrations here," the enamelist continued. "We sent you the photos that will be printed in the catalog to accompany your essay, but I'm glad you've found a moment in your schedule to see these sketches. The line of the hand is so important. It begins with one person's dream."

They spent the next thirty minutes poring over the designs of an elaborate colored-diamond necklace painted with gouache. There were detailed sketches of the necklace from every angle, showing how each diamond sat at the collarbone and caught the light.

"These should be in a gallery!"

"There are over three thousand diamonds in this neckpiece. More than the Maharaja of Patiala's 1928 commission."

Kate estimated it would take four years to complete all the cutting, framework, setting, and polishing. "Four years for a single necklace!"

"And it will never be worn in public, most likely." The enamelist's eyes sparkled, but she would never be so indiscreet as to disclose whom the necklace was intended for. Kate couldn't help but speculate . . . was it a Middle Eastern sheik, a French mistress, or a dot-com bazillionaire?

"I wondered if you might have a few minutes to look at these images from the Cheapside collection?" Kate said. She pulled out her phone and scrolled through Marcus's photos, showing an entranced Madame Parsons the enamel necklaces and buttons.

"Ah." Her face softened. "I have wanted to see these since I was a little girl tidying up and mixing paints in my papa's workshop."

Kate showed her the close-ups of the emerald watch and the pomander before coming to the salamander hat pin. "Look at this salamander—studded with emeralds up the back, but with an enamel underbelly that looks like fur."

"This salamander"—she tapped the screen—"it is begging you to tell its story. You paint the different-colored enamel—crushed glass—on in different sections, making a distinct pattern . . . like this fur. But there is nothing to separate the edges. It's trial by fire. We pop it into the kiln at fifteen hundred degrees, but we really don't know how it will turn out. It's a risk." She pursed her lips together and shrugged.

"Ironic, considering that in old legends it was believed that the salamander could survive fire."

"Exactly! And think of all the people this very salamander has outlived due to civil war, plague, and the Great Fire. London herself has been torn down, burned, and bombed. See how the enamel has rubbed away at the feet? I think it would not have survived four hundred years above the ground. The gold would have been melted down, the gemstones removed and made into something else, *non*?"

"Perhaps." Kate wished she had one of Marcus's details of the black-and-white champlevé ring to show Madame Parsons. Instead she tried to describe it, and showed the enamelist the rough sketch she'd done in her notebook.

"Remember, enameling is a language. Forget-me-nots and pansies. This champlevé ring is a work of love. To paint that pattern would take infinite time and patience. And then it goes in the kiln and perhaps . . . pfft!" She flung up her hands to indicate disaster.

"So, love then. Romantic? It couldn't be a mourning ring?"

"Black and white. Love and death. Even the rings made for death were meant to remind the living of loved ones. This is what I *adore* about enamel: it is the most expressive, the most human of the jewelry crafts. It is uncertain—like life itself, *non*?" She shrugged again and smiled.

Kate smiled back and nodded. "It sure is."

"This champlevé ring will have a transparency to it, a lightness. *That* I know for certain because it is made from molten glass. Also, if you look closely, the ring will reveal itself. The black and white will overlap . . . will penetrate one another, if you like? With champlevé, you have to let time take its course."

Madame Parsons was right. The mystery of the champlevé ring may just be unraveled if Kate could uncover the symbolism—the language—of the black-and-white flowers and how they might have come to be paired with this magnificent diamond.

Later that evening, Kate sat at her favorite table at Chez Georges, doodling in her notebook and flipping back to the floral patterns of the diamond ring, the words of Madame Parsons ringing in her ears.

Black and white. Love and death. Even the rings made for death were meant to remind the living of loved ones. This is what I adore about enamel: it is the most expressive, the most human of the jewelry crafts. It is uncertain—like life itself, non?

The waiter arrived, and she ordered the duck confit and a huge glass of Chambolle-Musigny. French comfort food—there was nothing uncertain about that!

As Kate waited for her wine, she traced the line of black forget-me-nots, running over her conversation with Madame Parsons. The master enameler's words reminded her of Essie's gift on her eighteenth birthday back in the study in Louisburg Square, and the last words she ever uttered to Kate: *I think you are perhaps starting to see that not everything in life is black and white.*

Like champlevé, life could be challenging and uncertain. Humans were capable of producing great beauty—to commemorate both love and loss. Kate agreed with Madame Parsons, the two were knotted together. The desire to be loved, to connect and to be remembered, carried through jewels and gemstones as they were set and reset. Forgotten and rediscovered. The history of a jewel really had no end. Often, it was a story of second, third, and fourth creations . . .

The pinot arrived and she took a sip, allowing the red wine to warm her throat.

She checked her watch. It was 1 p.m. in New York, and Marcus would be in the middle of a show. His phone would be switched off.

Just to hear his voice, she dialed his number anyway.

As expected, the call went straight to voicemail. *"Hey, Marcus here. Or not here. Anyway, leave a message . . ."*

She hung up without saying anything and put her phone on silent. Then she reached for a slice of baguette and slathered it with salty butter, took a gulp of pinot, and cursed herself for wishing Marcus were in Paris with her.

THE GOLDSMITH

Aurelia sat alongside her father at his workbench as he tinkered with a gold ring at his anvil. Above her head, long gold necklaces cascaded from hooks like falling leaves in the morning light, and a velvet bag of pearls sat half open. Ignoring the ting of his tiny hammer, she peered through the shutters across the Cheape Side, watching the street fill with horses and carriages loaded with rotting bodies headed for the pits.

She stretched her arms out and tugged on the shutter to let in the soft summer light. Papa frowned. As a foreigner, her father was forbidden from opening the shutters of his shopfront.

To their left, a trio of blazing red rubies sat above the door frame, guarding against the pestilence that had overtaken London. The workshop air was sharp and sweet. Each day Mama sprinkled the room with lemon water to stop the stink from the street creeping in. *Mama wanted Papa to close his workshop altogether until this sickness had passed, but Papa insisted on working. What else would he do with his time? Besides, Papa kept his doors open for trade despite the fact that so many Londoners had closed theirs.*

"How will I earn the money to feed us, my love, if I do not work?"

Aurelia watched Papa's eyes light up as he moved the gold ring about on the anvil until he was satisfied. She craned her head toward the sun like a cat, felt her left cheek become warm, and was grateful for these tiny pockets of contentment in their days.

Mama's steps had slowed since last summer. It had taken less than a week for her brothers David and George to die of the pestilence. She closed her eyes now, recalling the sight of their small bodies wrapped in linen shrouds.

That had been a year ago. Inspectors had since removed the cross from above their door that warned people to stay away. But they still had few visitors.

Papa looked up from his anvil and slid along the bench to where two pieces sat waiting for his attention.

Aurelia picked up the first, an emerald the size of a baby's fist, and turned it over in her hands, the angles of the green stone icy in her palm.

As she handed it to Papa he pointed to the hinge as he lifted the top piece to reveal an exquisite gold watch face. "I need to be careful. One slip of my rasp could shatter the stone."

She passed him the leather pouch containing the second item: a perfume bottle hanging from a gold chain tumbled onto the length of leather, and droplets of oil spilled onto the fabric.

Aurelia recognized the tang of the lemon oil and the woody rosemary oil they dabbed on their temples and wrists every morn.

Half dreaming, she dipped her fingers in the oil, lifted them to her nose, and picked up faint traces of lavender, rose, and cinnamon alongside the more powerful and earthy ambergris.

Papa turned the scent bottle in his hand. The white opals caught the light, as if the bottle were covered with the lightest of feathers. "Look at the enamel work." He pointed at the bunches of tiny flowers painted between rubies and diamonds.

"Champlevé, perhaps?" he said to himself, turning the pomander between his thumb and forefinger so the gemstones sparkled with the light. He placed it carefully on the leather.

"I have an idea . . ."

He reached into a locked wooden box on his workbench and produced a faded leather pouch. He unfastened the ties and used a pair of tweezers to lift a clear stone up to the light, turning it from side to side as if he wanted to study it from each angle.

"I'd bet my teeth this one's Golconda . . . it has the clearest water, see?"

Aurelia leaned in and caught the golden hue as he turned each facet up to the light. "It's beautiful."

"I bought it for a pretty penny long before you were born. Old Mr. Shaw bought a bagful of gemstones for a song from a ship's deckhand after the poor lad found himself in a spot of trouble after returning from Bandar Abbas. He'd done a stint in prison for theft from a passenger. Lost himself to the drink and gambling when he got out. Couldn't pay his debts. Old Shaw sat on the stones until the whispers had died down along Cheape Side. Luckily, the old man was always so busy he never wanted for extra stock."

Aurelia pictured the workshop just three shops down from theirs, but five times the size of her papa's and brimming with twenty lapidaries, cutters, polishers, and jewelers hunched over their benches.

"Who's it for, Papa?"

He placed the diamond onto the piece of leather spread in front of him and said, "Why, darling, it's for you. I plan to make it a wedding gift, for when you wed Jacob. Would you not expect a goldsmith to save his finest work for his only daughter?"

He went to the anvil and took the slim gold band off the point. "See how I have already shaped the gold? But I need to measure it on your finger."

As his daughter tried on the ring that would one day become her wedding band, her father sighed. "I'll not be able to hallmark or be given assay and touch until I am a master."

Papa looked down at the pomander with the broken chain glittering on his workbench, turned it over to study the enameling. "I need to make my masterpiece," he said. "Only then will I have freedom in this land."

Amsterdam, September 1665

Dear Aurelia,

My Wanderjahr *continues to delight! I cannot believe it has been six weeks since Berg de Jong—the finest jeweler and goldsmith in Amsterdam—has taken myself and my apprentice Dirk Jenk into his workshop overlooking the canal. Each day we sit at a long table under a window, leather catch trays affixed to the desk and resting in our laps, just like at home.*

Outside our third-floor window barges float up the canal loaded with tulip bulbs, cheese, and herring. Also, bags of spices and gemstones shipped from the Dutch East Indies and Ceylon. Cinnamon scrolls from the bakery next door mingle with the smell of metal and soldering.

How I miss your mother's kitchen, filled with the scent of warm appeltaart and fresh bread.

Every morning, two artists tutor us so that we may indeed be worthy of the title "Master Goldsmith." Currently we are learning to sketch flowers. Yesterday I drew some pansies, starting with the petals and keeping the heel of my hand on the paper until my lines felt confident and unbroken. The flowers reminded me of you with their modest charm and prettiness. Then I added a line of forget-me-nots, in remembrance of those we loved and lost.

I hope you and your mama are keeping well. I know I can rely on you to take care of her and the child she is expecting.

Until next week,
Papa

Chapter 23

ESSIE

LONDON, 1912

Essie stopped hanging out the washing on a line above the oven to dry, then reached behind and loosened her apron strings. She lifted a damp cloth to her face and took a seat at the kitchen table. She was dizzy—tired in a way she couldn't fathom.

She still had clothes in the boiler on the stove, but was grateful for the spare minutes of soaking she had until they needed to be hung out. Gertie was reading upstairs, Ma was asleep in the front room, and Freddie . . . Well, who knew when Freddie would be home?

Essie leaned down to unlace her boots and felt blood rush to her head. She sat up quickly and eyed the washing, making some quick calculations in her head.

Two months.

Two months since she'd bled.

Essie's first instinct was to run to Ma and lay her head in her mother's lap. But there would be no soothing words on the end of her mother's tongue. No comforting hands through her hair. Only ridicule and shame. Ma would throw her out as soon as she knew her eldest daughter was with child—hadn't she said as much many times?

Essie sat taller now, and ran her hands across her belly. Was Essie imagining it, or could she feel a flutter? Certainly her heart fluttered with excitement and her mind filled with thoughts of Edward: his broad hands, the blue corridor in his Mayfair flat, walks in Hyde Park.

She hadn't heard from him since he sailed for Boston. She'd hoped Edward would write, but understood that he would be preoccupied with work as he was away for such a short time. But if his words were true—and hadn't they always been—then he was due to be back in London any day now.

She tiptoed to Ma's room, stole a sheet of paper from Pa's old dresser. As she walked past her ma—gray-faced, snoring, and slumped in her chair—Essie froze. Her feet tingled with fear.

Was this what lay ahead?

Essie swallowed her fears, ignored the sinking feeling in her stomach, and stepped past her slumbering mother. When she stepped into the kitchen, she penned a letter to her sweetheart.

Dear Edward,

I hope your visit to Boston was rewarding.

When we last met, you promised you would return shortly, and I have been counting down the days.

I need to meet with you soonest. I am with child.

It has been somewhat of a shock, but I am certain of it. I know you would want to hear this news from me directly.

I look forward to seeing you soonest . . .

She hesitated before finishing:

. . . so we can make plans together.

E

Essie tucked the letter into an envelope and sealed it with wax from a candle. After she'd written the address, she paused and with a shaking hand wrote one last word underlined across the front:

PRIVATE

Chapter 24

Meet me outside Fortnum & Mason at 6:30 p.m.
E

"He's taking me to supper," Essie confided with a whisper of pride as she read the last line of Edward's letter to Mrs. Yarwood. She'd previously only permitted herself a glance in the windows at the tearooms with white tablecloths and silver trays piled with cucumber sandwiches, French pastries, and scones loaded with jam and clotted cream. Or perhaps they'd have chicken and mushroom soup, ladled from gold tureens and served with pillowy warm bread rolls and fresh butter. Her mouth started to water . . .

"He said it was important!" She inhaled to steady her jittery breath. "I haven't seen him since he left for Boston. I wrote to him last week, as soon as he was due to return." Her voice sounded steadier than she felt. She was giddy at the thought of seeing him. Finally, they would be able to make some plans.

"Then you'd best be borrowing my coat. The one with the fur collar. And some gloves. Return them to me when you get a chance. No rush, love," said Mrs. Yarwood. The older woman's voice was soft, but cautious. There was the slightest pinch to her lips.

"Please don't tell Ma. She doesn't approve . . ."

Mrs. Yarwood placed a gentle hand on Essie's shoulder. "Your mother cares for you, Essie. She only wants the best . . ."

A tear leaked from Essie's eye, and she wiped it away with the back of her hand.

"I mean it. You've all lost so much. Her grief . . ."

"I've told Gertie to meet you and Mr. Yarwood near Piccadilly Circus Station after school. It's so kind of you to take her to supper. I'm so grateful to you for having her in the afternoons and evenings while I do extra shifts. It's meant that she could finish this term at school."

Well, the extra shifts and *the money from the jewels,* though of course she didn't mention those.

Mrs. Yarwood squeezed Essie's hand. "It's been our pleasure to look after Gertie. We love her like she's our own."

As she pulled the coat across Essie's shoulders and started to help button it, she paused, and pressed a hand to Essie's cheek. "You look a picture," she said softly.

Essie stood underneath the awning at Fortnum & Mason, pressing close to the windows to avoid mud being splashed onto her skirts. An endless parade of motorcars and open-topped buses advertising Dewar's whisky and *The Evening News* honked and crawled around the fountain at the heart of Piccadilly Circus.

The chaos and confusion at the junction was matched by the churning in her stomach.

I have to see you . . .

Edward's words were tucked in her pocket, and she traced the outline of the envelope. He longed to see Essie as much as she did him.

Meet me outside Fortnum & Mason at 6:30 p.m.

The tight strokes of his penmanship were urgent. Fierce and passionate. He wrote with the same sure hand that had unbuttoned her bodice and guided her onto the table. Strong hands that steadied the oars when they went boating on the Serpentine.

Hands that had enveloped her own as she grieved in the week after the twins died.

She shivered as the icy evening breeze picked up and stung her cheeks and ears. Tried to slow her beating heart by imagining Edward pressing his cheek against hers as he greeted her, his sweet breath warming her neck.

Impatient, she turned her back to the wind and studied the fountain. Normally, Essie would not permit herself a glimpse of the naked statue of Eros set to stride across London. But this evening Essie studied the Greek god of love and remembered blushing when reading Greek myths late into the night by candlelight when Gertie had borrowed some books from Miss Barnes.

The stories had created the same stirring and tickling sensation along her limbs that she felt this very evening as she took in the line of the statue's arms, the tensed muscle in his bronze legs as he stood poised to leap, bow and arrow tipped to fire.

Eros had Essie in his sights.

Essie's head swam with emotion. Edward obviously had something urgent to tell her—to ask her.

I wish to discuss the arrangements in person . . .

Edward had apologized in the same note for the lack of contact, explaining it had been impossible to find a moment to write since his return from Boston. The flurry of building across Westminster and London were keeping Edward fully occupied. Also, Ma had been watching Essie like a hawk, sending Gertie or Freddie with her on errands as simple as fetching a bottle of peppermint oil.

It didn't matter: Edward was on his way right now to meet her. Alone.

Dusk fell and the electric streetlights flickered awake.

Essie glanced back at Fortnum & Mason. Inside, wicker hampers overflowing with boxes of tea, cheese, chocolates, and sweets were arranged between vases of pink and white lilies. Essie wondered if these were the same type of hampers the shop had famously sent to the suffragettes in prison who'd smashed these very windows a couple of years back. It had been all over the newspaper front pages at the time.

She wandered from the window to stand beneath a lamppost. Her feet were sore from the walk across the bridge, but she needed to shake the nerves—and excitement—from her legs, otherwise she'd be twitching at the table all evening.

Out of the evening mist an image of her twins appeared. Two smiling faces, dimpled and filthy. One slightly fuller in the cheeks than the other.

She sighed, and her chest tightened. She would give anything for a swift kick in the shins from Maggie as her skinny little legs twitched under the kitchen table while she mopped up her bread and dripping. Closing her eyes, she imagined leaning over Flora and pressing her nose into her curls smelling of sarsaparilla and soap as she sectioned the child's wayward hair into braids.

A sharp honk from a passing car startled Essie from her daydream. The giggling twins faded into the mist, leaving Essie's heart cleaved and aching.

She never knew when grief would show its hand—or if grief would ever leave. Even in moments of happiness, sadness always seemed to lurk in the shadows just a couple of paces away. Essie closed her eyes, taking the damp London air deep into her lungs. With each breath, her chest loosened a little and her breathing eased.

Edward would be here soon and all would be well.

Better than well: it would be perfect.

Hearing a brisk footfall behind her, she turned, and couldn't help breaking into a smile when she saw that it was Edward striding toward her.

He was wearing a new three-piece suit and a bowler hat, but underneath a dark curl had escaped and was stuck to his forehead. He pulled up abruptly two paces short of Essie, and clicked his heels together. His shoes were glossy with nary a scuff.

Had he worn this new suit to impress her? She wasn't one whose head was turned by a new outfit. All the same, she felt flattered by the gesture.

"Edward." She nodded with what she hoped was a demure smile. She lifted her gaze from his new shoes to his dark eyes. But the brim of his hat cast a shadow over his face. Her eyes searched for his in vain.

Edward tipped his hat back and looked her up and down, pausing for a beat, before shifting his weight and straightening his shoulders.

"Hello. Essie, I . . ."

He took a nervous step toward her and she could almost hear the thud of his heartbeat. His shoulders were pulled tight, and Essie felt her stomach flip when she thought of the smooth skin underneath his shirt, the strong contours of his back. How safe she had felt when wrapped in his arms.

A familiar stirring started along her limbs, but she shook it off, not wanting to appear distracted.

Edward's face was flushed.

She glanced inside the tearooms, glowing with warmth, and wondered why they hadn't gone straight inside. But Edward made no move to thread her arm through his—or even to kiss her or take her hand.

"Thank you for meeting me at such short notice," he said.

Essie beamed up at his tanned face, too embarrassed to admit she had waited daily for the note that signaled he was home from Boston, until she could wait no more and wrote herself.

"I—I have something for you." Edward thrust his hand into his waistcoat.

She took a step toward him and held her breath.

"Can you . . . can you hold out your hand?" he mumbled, a little shyer now.

Essie removed Mrs. Yarwood's silk glove, then produced her left hand. Her pale skin looked golden under the lamplight. She felt too shy to speak.

Beads of sweat dotted Edward's brow as he said awkwardly, "This . . . this is for you."

Edward grabbed Essie's hand and flipped it over. Her hand shook as he dropped something hard and cool into her palm.

She closed her hand around the object, not trusting herself to look. The curve pressed into the fleshy part of her palm, and her fingers traced the gemstone.

A ring.

Essie hardly dared to breathe.

Slowly, she held her hand up to the lamplight and unfurled her fingers one by one. Using her right hand, she lifted the ring from the palm of her left. It was painted white on the outside with a string of dainty black flowers and sprigs that danced their way up to a large square clear stone that glinted in the light.

"A diamond!" she whispered, and she looked at Edward, her heart full.

It was happening: Edward was proposing. All the tension drained from her body as she realized his gruffness had been nothing more than nervous jitters—the same as her.

Ma was wrong. Essie wasn't making a mistake. Edward wasn't a bit like other men.

Edward had looked beyond her stained hems, scuffed shoes, and rough voice, and seen something special. He loved her—he'd shown her that afternoon in his flat just how much—and now they were going to be a proper family. He'd even called her his rough diamond once, hadn't he?

But there was nothing rough about the ring she held in her hand.

"Oh, Edward!" Essie pictured the lace in the window at Harrods in Knightsbridge that she might be able to fashion into a bonnet for their bonnie boy. A boy—she was certain—with Edward's wide forehead and ruddy cheeks, dressed in britches and shiny new boots, just like his father. What a pretty sight they would make parading through Cheapside with a baby carriage—a rabbit pie and an apple underneath to deliver to Edward for his lunch. She glanced at the church dome at the end of the street, blue in the moonlight, and imagined stepping inside with clean boots and her baby in new woolen swaddling. Edward standing proudly at her side as they attended mass.

"It's beautiful," she whispered. She extended her left hand toward Edward, the ring still resting on her palm, and let it hover in the space between them.

Edward still stood red-faced and glued to the spot. Silent.

Realizing her beau was feeling a bit awkward—and perhaps a little exposed, standing under the shopfront awning—Essie considered slipping her engagement ring onto her left hand herself. Smiling, she noted he'd done well to find such a small band to fit her slender fingers.

So thoughtful. He was going to make a fine husband.

Shifting his weight and clearing his throat, Edward's hand dived into the inside pocket of his suit and he pulled out a stiff cream envelope.

He looked almost sad as he handed it to her.

"This . . . this is also for you."

"Thank you!" She quickly slid a finger along the tongue of the envelope and slipped out the piece of paper inside. She held it up to catch the lamplight and strained to read it.

Edward rocked back and forth on his heels, but stepped no closer. "It's a steamer ticket to Boston," he explained.

Essie's heart almost exploded. He had been thinking of her the whole time he was away, and now they were going to try their luck in America—together!

She looked again at the ticket in her hand, then raised her eyes to his, confused. "But there's only one ticket." She began to tremble. What did this mean? "So when . . . when will you come? And Gertie?" The Cheapside job was finished; Freddie had told her so just last week. Had Edward taken on another job?

"It's all arranged. I spoke with your mother just before I came to meet you."

She exhaled with relief as her heart sang and burst with sunshine. Finally, Ma would be proud of her. She tried to imagine him stooped in the front room, folded into their only sitting chair while her mother stood opposite smelling of sour brew, her tight puckered mouth stretching into an involuntary smile. How Essie wished she'd been present when Edward had asked Ma for her hand in marriage.

"You leave for Boston next week."

"But . . ." She didn't want to start their new life—this adventure—alone. And why must she leave so soon?

"What about Gertie?" she asked, suddenly agitated. "I can't leave her behind . . ."

She pictured Edward in his Mayfair flat as he straddled her body. He had leaned low and lost himself in her breasts, cupping them with both hands and kissing them all over, groaning. Tickling her nipples with his tongue before sliding down to her stomach and—

Her face burned as her body thrummed with desire.

Nice girls shouldn't think such things. But she'd never forget the sweet, sticky tenderness as they had lain together afterward, her head on his chest and him stroking her arm as he promised that one day they would be together.

Essie looked again at the steamer ticket, at the diamond ring in her palm. "But where will we have the wedding? And when?" A tiny part of her was giddy at the thought of Ma seeing her eldest daughter walk up the aisle and wed this fine young man.

"The ring—it's not for that; it's for the child."

Essie leaned against the lamppost to steady herself as her breath shortened. "You're . . . you're not coming to Boston with me?" She took a step back, confused. As she gripped the ring it suddenly felt like ice.

"My parents, they'd never . . . they'd cut me off." He was looking at his shoes now, unable to meet her eyes. "From the business . . . everything . . . I'm sorry."

"But what about Greenwich? You said you came looking for me! And the afternoons in Hyde Park and . . . and in your *apartment*. What happened between us was special. I felt it. You did too, surely if you explained to them—"

"I've tried," he said softly. "I'm sorry, Essie, but they've made it quite clear: if I marry you, then I lose everything."

"We could move to Boston, no one knows us there."

He shook his head. "That wouldn't work; people do know me in Boston."

"Somewhere else then. Anywhere . . ." She was begging now.

"I'd be cut off," he repeated. "Left with nothing. Do you understand?"

Essie stiffened and dropped her hands to her side. She did understand how awful it was to have nothing. Edward had only to look at her—and poor skinny Freddie—and see exactly what his life would look like if he were to cut himself off from his wealthy family. And he wasn't prepared to make that sacrifice.

She covered her face with her hands. Her chest tightened and she found it hard to breathe. It had turned out just like Ma had said it would. Her shame and humiliation stung far more than the bitter wind lashing her ankles and cheeks.

"You'll be able to get a good price for the ring . . ." Edward's voice hardened a fraction. "Enough to start afresh." Essie could tell by his tone that he was still trying to convince himself as much as Essie. He spoke in a clipped voice—as if he were in one of the talking pictures they'd seen on the silver screen, not warm flesh and blood standing in the evening drizzle.

"I'm sorry, Essie," he said again. "I shouldn't have made promises I was in no position to keep. My family's name would be disgraced if this"—he waved at her stomach—"were ever found out. It's for the best that you leave London. To avoid any, er, *confusion* . . ." His neck was flushed above his crisp collar. "It's best to make a proper break."

She was just another one of his jobs that needed finishing off. She blinked away the tears that were starting to form and gulped down the sobs that lodged in her throat like a stone that couldn't be swallowed.

If she spoke, Essie knew, she might vomit all over his shiny new shoes. A part of her wanted to.

Edward glanced back over his shoulder, as if he was in a hurry to leave now. If he saw the bronze sculpture of Eros with an arrow, he chose to ignore it.

When Edward turned back to Essie, he said, "I hope you're not going to make a scene. I've been more than reasonable under the circumstances." His voice was lower, colder. "I've given you a bloody *diamond*, Essie, for Christ's sake."

Once, Essie recalled, he'd cried her name in ecstasy. She thought she might split apart. Her dashing beau had become a cruel stranger.

Unreliable. Unpredictable. Selfish.

Essie could smell the yeasty brew on his breath. It was the drink that made people sour and bitter.

With that smell came the realization of the ugliness that lay ahead if she were to stay in London. She recalled their high teas taken in shadowy corners, the hats lifted in the street as she was hastily ushered past ladies and gentlemen in expensive silk suits and dresses, never introduced. Edward would never be proud to be seen with Essie. And who could blame him? Essie's own cheeks burned with shame on the rare occasion she walked with her disheveled mother to school, or the greengrocer, or to church.

It was time for Essie to end this pattern of shame.

Edward started to talk. "When you get to Boston, you can sell the ring—"

"Stop." Essie held up her palm. She didn't want to hear his instructions. She was finished with following everyone else's rules.

All her life she'd imagined that, if only she kept to the rules, one day there would be a space for her. A warm bath, buttercup curtains. A clean, happy home filled with enough food for a loving family. Gertie would finish school and it would be the proudest moment of Essie's life.

But Ma had been right all along. A lifetime of factory work, ragged clothes, and dealing with the self-serving likes of Father McGuire and Mr. Morton lay ahead. Essie's life would be no different from the life her mother had.

Essie wanted to keep her baby, but how? The child growing inside her deserved more. She didn't want to bring this baby into her world of despair, decay, and death.

She wouldn't.

Essie turned on her heel and started to walk away.

"Essie! Wait!" cried an indignant Edward as he grabbed her by the wrist. "I just gave you a diamond ring. You could at least say goodbye."

"You're hurting me."

"*Essie!*" She swore she could hear her name being called as if from a distance, but it was probably just the drizzle and hiss of the wind. She was imagining it, just like she'd imagined the little faces of the twins . . .

Several people eyed the pair with curiosity as they scurried past in the rain, but they pursed their lips as they saw Essie's muddy skirt and old boots. Who cared what business this handsome man had with the bedraggled girl? She didn't warrant stopping and making a fuss.

"Let go!"

Edward dragged her into the shadows around the corner, away from prying eyes. "Essie, you need to understand how sorry I am. It's not my fault!"

She refused to meet the coward's eyes.

He grasped her chin, trying to force her to look up at him. "I need to hear you say you understand."

"I understand all right—you're a coward," she hissed through gritted teeth as she tried to wrest herself from his grip. "Now let go of me."

"Calm down. You're making a scene."

Essie's chin started to throb, and she winced.

Hooves thudded on cobblestones, a motorcar honked as a dray skidded into the gutter. Her chest thumped as the horse whinnied and tossed its head as it was yanked sideways by the out-of-control tilting dray.

"She said to let go!" All at once Gertie flew out of the mist with wild eyes and lunged at Edward, pushing him away from her sister with both hands.

Edward toppled backward on one foot, left leg flying and arms flapping as he tried to regain his balance. Gertie grabbed Essie by the elbow and whispered, "Quickly," as they ran toward the pale-faced Mr. and Mrs. Yarwood who stood by a nearby lamppost.

For the rest of her life, Essie would never forget the horror on her neighbors' faces, the crack of bone on cobblestones, and the splatter as the metal wheel of the dray made contact.

Chapter 25

KATE

LONDON, PRESENT DAY

The Serpentine Gallery stood neat and proud in the heart of Kensington Gardens. Manicured lawns stretched in every direction, and the classical lines still felt more teahouse than art gallery. Crowds milled about, turning their faces to the morning sun like sunflowers.

Bella greeted her in the foyer. "London's going all out, isn't she?"

"And I thought Bostonians were obsessed with the weather!"

Bella laughed and slipped her arm through Kate's as they entered the gallery. "It was only when Mum went through all the stuff in the attic that she found out Gertrude had been painting and sketching for years. Plus there were her diaries from when she was a girl."

They'd wandered along the corridor to the final, well-lit room. As they stepped through the doorway, Kate stopped, arrested by the sight of a huge canvas of a female nude with her back to the viewer. The woman was painted the deep cornflower blue of a sapphire.

Kate glanced at the painting as her phone pinged. She pulled it from her pocket to check the message.

Sorry I haven't been able to catch you to chat. Hope you enjoyed Paris. Shows insane. Will try tonight. Miss you, Marcus xx

The tone was breezy—typical Marcus—but the last few words made her shiver. *Miss you.*

Bella gave Kate a quizzical look. "You are somewhere else today . . . Look! That painting is the exact shade of your earrings."

"Blue was always Essie's favorite color. Mine too. I think that's why she gave me these."

"Clearly the sisters shared the same taste. I mean—" Bella waved her arm at the far wall, where the same nude figure lay curled asleep in one picture, and leaped across a river—a lake?—in another. As Kate drew closer, she saw faint lines across the bodies, like facets, as if they were made not of flesh, but gemstones.

"These are remarkable. The figures are so sensual; they seem to have the luster of gemstones."

"I thought these would appeal to you." Bella nodded. "But apparently the only jewels Gertie ever wore were her gold wedding band, a pair of pearl earrings, and this pendant."

They walked along, studying the canvases, until they came to a break on the wall. The museum had placed a series of black decals as quotes, perhaps to give the visitor a moment to pause and reflect as they went through the exhibition.

Sapphires possess a beauty like that of the heavenly throne; they denote . . . those whose lives shine with their good deeds and virtue.
Marbodius of Rennes (11th-century bishop and poet)

Kate thought of Essie raising funds for libraries and public schools, establishing college scholarships, and her endless campaigning for free women's health centers. Back in London, her younger sister Gertrude had been doing the same type of thing: campaigning for women's rights, opening shelters.

Two women, two cities.

Kate looked at the gold button pendant peeping from under Bella's silk shirt. There were no definitive answers about the button. No leads, only speculation. But if Kate could prove Gertrude's button was a Cheapside jewel, it belonged at the museum. Yet it also belonged with Bella.

Not everything in life is black and white.

At their allocated time to examine the diaries, Bella and Kate made their way into a private reading room and were seated at a mahogany table. A prim assistant in a button-down shirt and cardigan entered carrying a stout oak box and placed it on the table. With a flourish, he produced a giant Victorian iron key from a keychain on his belt, unlocked the box, flicked back the gold clasps, and lifted the heavy lid. The release of pressure made it sound like the old oak box was sighing. Bella raised her eyebrows and covered her mouth to stifle a giggle at this theatrical gesture.

"You have one hour—and please use the gloves when handling the documents."

Kate picked up a pair of protective gloves and handed them to Bella, before pulling on the second set. "Of course. Thank you."

The assistant left.

Kate lifted out some letters and diaries, then reached for her eyepiece and spread her sketches from Boston across the table in front of her. Bella leaned toward her as she opened an accounting ledger book and saw the girlish script on the front page: *Gertrude Murphy*.

The letters were cataloged chronologically, the first from Essie dated 1918. Essie told Kate when she was writing her college entrance essay that she'd left London in 1912. Why weren't there any letters from Essie in the years immediately after she left England?

Dearest Gertie,

I've received your monthly letters but I'm sure you'll understand why I thought it not safe to respond until now. I'm both shocked and proud to hear about your work for the war effort and pray that this madness will be over soon and we can arrange to see each other . . .

Kate smiled as she read the descriptions of her grandfather Joseph's first day of elementary school, his refusal to wear his socks pulled up, and his *constant sullied shirts* and *torn collars from the playground* and the *precious dimpled cheeks and lopsided smile that so reminds me of our Freddie . . .*

She flipped through the letters before starting on the diaries and sketches. The archives contained page after page of sketches: chickens; twin girls holding hands and laughing; a trail of flowers down a drainpipe; a corner view of the dome of St. Paul's. Every page was crammed with drawings, and every image was vivid.

Each one told a tale. As she turned the pages, she noticed where some had been torn out and held her own ledger pages up one by one, ragged edge to ragged edge. Each was a match, as true as the line of freckles and dark curls trying to escape from the braids of Flora and Maggie.

The last picture was a sketch of the twins asleep, eyes closed, candles by their heads. There was a stillness to them that filled Kate's eyes with tears.

Bella reached for her hand and squeezed it. "Well," she whispered. "I think we've solved the mystery of who drew the pictures."

"I think so," said Kate as she started flipping through the ledger again, looking for a glimpse of a button—or any other jewel. There was none.

She sighed.

As Kate turned the final page, the light overhead caught the slightest impression on the page. The previous page had been torn out, but a ghost of script remained. Using her eyepiece, she recognized the handwriting that had graced so many of her birthday and Christmas cards for years.

Mrs. Edward Hepplestone

Mr. Edward and Mrs. Esther Rose Hepplestone

That was curious. Who was Edward Hepplestone? Essie quickly jotted the name into her notebook. There was no mobile reception in this room, so she'd have to wait until she was elsewhere to google it.

"Does the name Edward Hepplestone ring any bells with you?" she asked her cousin.

"None," replied Bella.

"I've been asking the wrong questions and looking in the wrong places. I wanted to link Essie with the Cheapside collection based on a few fairy tales . . . but really it's Essie's story I need to uncover. There's so much about her early life I know nothing about. Gertrude and Essie wrote frequently, judging by this stack of letters."

"Yes. It's lovely. Standard letters and clippings, news of the family, christenings, occasional rages against Thatcher, a picture of Gertie in her academic gown flanked by two elderly people in their Sunday best."

Kate flipped the picture over and saw written in Gertrude's hand: *Graduation, St. Hilda's. Mr. and Mrs. Yarwood.* Mr. and Mrs. Yarwood . . . *Who were they?* she wondered.

She looked from Bella to the stack of letters and the inky shadows of the sleeping twins in the ledger book.

"For the life of me I can't work out why Essie never returned to London," she said. "She could afford it. She met her sister in Hawaii every year, and Gertie came to Boston a dozen times. But why did Essie never come here? I mean, it's London. And it's family. Why stay away forever?"

"Well . . ." Bella tapped her chin thoughtfully, "from my experience in family court, people leave their families behind for any number of reasons. I've seen mothers leave their children because they felt it was for the best; they felt that the child would be better provided for by the father or another family member. Or they knew that they simply did not have the capacity to care for the child. They were severely traumatized, suffered crippling postnatal depression—or they were drug addicted."

A tear ran down Kate's cheek. "I just can't imagine leaving behind someone so precious. A baby—or a beloved little sister." She traced one of the twin's sunken cheeks with her gloved finger.

"I can't begin to imagine your pain, Kate," Bella said softly. "Losing your baby . . . Jonathan."

Kate nodded, wishing she could dive into the blue expanse of one of Gertrude's paintings and ease the pain and grief laced around her heart. "Do you think Essie left London because she thought her family was better off without her?" she asked.

"I don't know. But I met Essie that summer when we visited the US on our family-tree tour. Remember? She was really something . . . She offered me my first sip of champagne out in your back courtyard, you know. She lived every moment." Bella recalled the Marbodius quote they'd seen out in the exhibition: "Essie had a life that shone *with good deeds and virtue.*"

"I get that, but—" Kate stopped, remembering the haunted look in Essie's eyes that day in her study on Kate's eighteenth birthday. Essie had said she'd made a terrible mistake . . . *and I live with that guilt each and every day.* Kate had assumed Essie's mistake, her regret, was not returning to London. But what if it was the mistake that had forced Essie to flee her home in the first place?

"There are no answers here," Kate said as she placed the ledger and letters back in the box and closed the lid, deflated.

Bella put her hand on Kate's forearm. "Kate, if there are any dark secrets in Essie's past—or Gertrude's—isn't it better to leave them be? When someone leaves a loved one behind, in my experience it is *never* because they don't care. It is perhaps the single most torturous decision they will make in their whole life.

In court—and in counseling—it is almost always referred to as a breaking point."

"But—"

Bella held up her hand. "No buts, Kate. Every single time, the woman feels she had no choice but to walk away. Stay and she might be killed by a partner who beats her. Stay and she might overdose. Stay and she might find herself unable to cope with the demands of a child. A woman very rarely leaves her loved ones in danger."

"You're saying that Essie left Gertrude behind not to start a new life for herself, but so that her sister would have a better life?"

"Both can be true. See those blurred lines?" Bella pointed at Kate's scraps of paper spread across the table. "Life's full of messy edges."

Following the morning at the Serpentine, Bella had rushed back to court and Kate to her hotel room at the Mandarin Oriental.

She'd fallen behind on the Cheapside essay, and the magazine's deadline was next week.

A cold cup of Earl Grey sat on her desk, and chocolate licorice bullets lay in a small pile by her computer—she'd decided to reward herself with a bullet per paragraph. So far the candy pile was barely diminished.

Taking a moment to procrastinate, she googled *Edward Hepplestone 1912*, and a small notice from *The Times* appeared on her screen. As she read, she tugged at a curl and made yet another futile attempt to tuck it behind her ear.

26 NOVEMBER 1912

MAN KILLED BY HORSE TRAP AT PICCADILLY CIRCUS

Mr Edward Hepplestone, son of Mr George and Mrs Audrey Hepplestone of Mayfair, was knocked down and killed by a horse and cart at Piccadilly Circus yesterday evening. Police are looking for witnesses and the family have offered a £1,000 reward to any persons who come forward with information.

Two women of small build and dark hair were spotted running from the scene, but as yet have not been identified. The investigation is ongoing and police expect charges to be laid.

Chapter 26

KATE

BOSTON, PRESENT DAY

On her first day back in Boston, Kate met Molly and Emma for a bowl of deconstructed lobster bisque at a new bistro overlooking the Charles River. Rowers glided past in neat pairs, battling the fine misty rain and sharp wind sending ripples across the river.

The sisters first caught up on Molly's news; she was coming up for partnership in the fall, and she and Jessica had plans for their new kitchen. Jess wanted pale blue, Molly wanted charcoal and stainless steel.

"Why doesn't that surprise me?" Kate asked with a chuckle.

As the wine was poured, Kate produced the envelopes of Essie's—Gertrude's—sketches. She pulled the sketch of the button to the top and described how similar it was to Bella's button, then showed her the photos of the buttons at the Museum of London.

"Well, the button in the sketch looks the same as the ones in the photos, but this evidence is circumstantial at best. It'd never stack up in court. Have you told Bella?"

"A little. I showed her the images from the museum, of course."

"And?"

"And nothing! But if we had concrete evidence . . ."

"You'd suggest she donate it to the museum? I know you. But no one can identify who the original owners are, Kate. What's the point?"

"I'm not sure. But I want to find out."

Kate was interrupted by a poke to her thigh.

"I went to a Dora party," said Emma.

Molly laughed. "It's a thing!" She reached for her wineglass. "God help us. How are we into themed parties when they can't even—"

"Mommy! I'm talking to Aunty Kate." Emma turned back to Kate and began to recount in great detail the party she had attended. "There was a Dora birthday cake, and a whole backpack full of candy!"

"I thought candy was only allowed at *my* house," Kate said.

"Shh," Emma said. "Mommy doesn't know . . ."

Her niece smelled of milk and soap, and Kate couldn't stop stroking her flyaway wisps of blond hair. The little girl was heaven. It had only been a few weeks, but Emma looked older already. Her cheekbones were a little more defined, and her words were clearer.

"So how many cities did you go to this time, Aunty Kate?"

"Four."

Emma counted out four on her fingers and held her hand up for approval. "Are you staying here now?" Emma's chin jutted out, and she wrinkled her nose. Her niece looked a little like the twins in Gertrude's notebook. Kate leaned over and gave her a hug.

"Yes. For a bit."

Molly reached across the white tablecloth and squeezed Kate's hand. "You look different."

"It's the tan. My delicate Irish skin is not used to the rays."

"I don't mean the tan. I mean something's changed. Your posture, your . . ." Her eyes narrowed as she sat back in her chair. "Did you get laid?"

"Mol—" Kate looked at Emma, who was now occupied with *The Very Hungry Caterpillar*, which Molly had brought along as a distraction.

"I knew it! It was that spunky Aussie photographer that you were working with on the Cheapside job, wasn't it? Marcus. I met him when I was your date to the Tiffany thing in New York, remember?"

"Honestly . . ."

"What? That's great. He's gorgeous." She raised her eyebrows as she took a sip of her Chablis. "So when are you seeing him again?"

"I don't know."

"Don't know *when* you're seeing him, or *if* you're seeing him?"

"Both, I guess," said Kate as the waiter placed bowls piled with steaming lobster and scallions on the table. Emma was given a small bowl of pasta and some fries, so naturally Kate and Molly each stole some.

"Hey," said Emma, trying to swat away their hands. "Mine."

"Yours!" the sisters said at the same time, and burst into laughter.

Outside, a sculler was heaving the oars in a steady rhythm. His arms were lean and powerful, and Kate remembered Marcus's arms tight around her in her Sri Lankan hotel room, then again at the stifling Colombo airport when he'd hugged her goodbye.

"Did you get that postdoc application in?" Molly asked.

"Not yet. I've been thinking it's not for me at the moment. But I *did* send my divorce papers back to the lawyer."

"Cheers to that!" Molly clinked her glass against Kate's. "You okay?"

"I'm good." And for the first time in years, she actually meant it. Marcus still hadn't sent the champlevé ring images, and she didn't know when, or if, she would see him again. But she felt steady and strong—as if she'd just stepped outside onto fresh wet grass after a storm had passed overhead.

Her phone beeped, and she pulled it out of her pocket to turn it off, but saw Marcus's name. Was the man a mind reader?

"Sorry! Text."

"No phones at the table," said Emma as she waved a fry at her aunt.

"It's him, isn't it?" Molly exclaimed. "Look how red you are!"

"I'm not . . ." Kate tapped on the text to open it.

Madness here. Sorry I keep missing you. Here are the best details of the ring. Take a look at the last one. Miss you. xx

THE CHAMPLEVÉ RING

Aurelia was startled by the knock at the door.

Mother and daughter were busy in the kitchen, preparing traditional treats for the feast of St. Nicholas, but their guests—the neighbors and her lovely Jacob—were not expected until dusk. It was unlikely to be a customer for the shop, since Papa's clients were aware that he had embarked on his journeyman Wanderjahr *to Amsterdam and Paris. Occasionally a nobleman or merchant— swathed in silk, gold thread, and his own importance—would stop by regardless, only to have Aurelia explain that they would have to come back when Papa returned in spring. "No, milord, I don't know where Papa stores his stock," she'd reply—though she always crossed her fingers behind her back as she said it.*

As the knocking grew louder, she said aloud to her mother, "I suppose I'll have to see who it is."

She hurried down the narrow passageway and threw open the door to find Dirk Jenk, her father's apprentice, on the doorstep.

"Mr. Jenk! I thought you were still in Amsterdam with Papa?"

"Aurelia. I'm sorry to intrude . . ."

His ruddy face paled when Aurelia's mother bustled down the passage toward them, her belly straining against the apron.

"What's all this fuss and—Mr. Jenk! What are you . . . ? Oh!" Mama swayed on her feet. Aurelia and Mr. Jenk both leaped forward to steady her. Together they guided her into the parlor and helped her into a chair.

No one spoke for several seconds.

In Mr. Jenk's tight lips and averted eyes Aurelia read the news he couldn't bear to utter.

"When?" Mama's voice was hoarse.

"A little over a fortnight ago," Mr. Jenk replied softly. "He contracted a fever. It was very sudden." He gestured to a chair. "May I?"

"Of course," said Aurelia, though she was barely aware of saying it—her mind had gone suddenly and completely blank.

"I'm sorry," the apprentice said, his voice cracking. "He talked of you constantly. He was so looking forward to seeing the new babe when it was born." He shook his head, as if he couldn't quite believe his employer was dead.

"I brought you this." He unbuckled his satchel, pulled out a scroll and a letter, and handed them to Aurelia's mother.

Mama unrolled the scroll. The document was in Dutch, Aurelia saw, but she recognized the official seal of the Amsterdam Goldsmiths Gilde and her father's name.

The accompanying letter had been written in English by Master Goldsmith de Jong. It was a recommendation that the guild admit Papa—now Master Goldsmith—into the Ordinances of the Goldsmiths' Company.

As her mama covered her mouth with a hand to stifle a sob, Aurelia felt a fleeting elation. At last, her father—the best goldsmith and jeweler in London—would be recognized as a master. But the feeling vanished and her chest tightened as she realized it meant nothing.

Papa was dead. His magnificent work—the gold chains, the rings—would never be granted his assay and touch. His pieces buried downstairs in the cellar would remain unmarked.

As her mother covered her face with her hands and wept, Mr. Jenk shifted his gaze to Aurelia. "He asked that I give this to you." Reaching into his satchel once more, he withdrew a small leather pouch.

With a heavy heart, Aurelia took it and loosened the string. Then she tipped the contents into her palm.

It was a champlevé ring set with the finest of table-cut diamonds.

"He said it was for your marriage," Mr. Jenk said somberly. "This is his masterpiece."

Chapter 27

ESSIE

LONDON, 1912

"Was there anything else?" Mr. Lawrence frowned, as if trying to make a decision.

Essie and Gertie stood before the desk in his shop, shivering, wet, and frightened. They'd presented the antiquarian with the jeweled button Freddie had gifted Gertie all those months before.

Essie swallowed, then reached into her pocket for the black-and-white diamond ring Edward had given her.

Mr. Lawrence's face lit up as he picked the ring up between his thumb and forefinger. The gemstone glinted in the light, and he used his eyepiece to study the diamond.

"Remarkable! Very clear. Must be almost four carats."

Gertie and Essie exchanged a hopeful look.

Mr. Lawrence continued, "The faceting is exquisite. See these corners here? They've been chipped with a scorper."

The girls must have looked confused, because he explained, "A scorper is a tiny chisel. They use it when the stone is set, to give it that extra sparkle. This one in particular has a slight angle. See?"

He held a pencil up and pointed to each side of the diamond, where there was indeed an extra facet. "But this is rather beautiful." Now he was examining the black-painted enamel flowers and florets on the hoop. "Champlevé. See the pansies and forget-me-nots dancing around the base? Love and death. Was this originally made for a mourning ring, or a betrothal, I wonder?"

The ring was suspended in a shaft of light coming in through the shop window. As he swiveled it to examine the ring from every angle, the black flowers looked fluid, like ink dropped into water.

Essie felt dizzy and nauseated. She swallowed and remained expressionless. This ring was a transaction. It meant nothing to her. Yet she was mesmerized by the patterns. The diamond. She'd not permitted herself to slide it onto her finger. Not once.

"I take it you wish to sell?"

Essie nodded, not trusting herself to speak.

"And it's from the same place?"

"I . . . don't know." As she said these words, she realized this ring had never been intended for her. This exquisite ring was intended for another woman's hand. Edward had not chosen this for her, nor had it made with love. There was no care behind it at all. He'd picked it up out of the dirt and passed it on. Silly of her to place faith in something plucked from the rubbish, even for a moment.

Essie looked across at Gertie, patted the steamer ticket in her pocket, and knew exactly what she had to do. They'd both be leaving London tonight.

Mr. Lawrence placed the ring back on the desktop and pushed his chair out from the desk. He left the room via a small door set into the bookshelf and could be heard moving around in the next room.

Gertie raised an eyebrow and took herself across to the shelf to study the new additions. A leather sandal, a bronze dagger that had seen better days, and some cut-glass vases.

When the antiquarian returned, he held a thick cream envelope in his hand. The ring and the button sat glistening on the desk in front of him.

"Here is your payment. I trust you feel this is a fair price."

Gertie gasped when she read the huge amount written on the envelope, and Essie's hand involuntarily moved to her stomach.

Mr. Lawrence narrowed his eyes a fraction, but said nothing.

"Thank you, sir," they said in unison as he handed Essie the envelope. She felt the smoothness of the paper before she slipped it into her pocket. It seemed awkward to count the notes in front of him. She'd do it as soon as they stepped outside.

Mr. Lawrence said gently, "I believe our business here is done, ladies. Thank you most kindly for thinking of me. I trust you'll mention it to any of your friends, should they find anything of interest." He tapped the side of his nose and winked.

Essie nodded. "Goodbye, Mr. Lawrence. Thank you."

The antiquarian must have caught the note of finality in Essie's voice, and he held her gaze—and hand—for a beat too long. His eyes moved from her reddening cheeks to her swelling bosom and thickening waist.

A jolt of recognition, though not pity. He knew. He understood.

Mr. Lawrence released Essie's hand and stepped back. He reached for the button on the desk and handed it back to Gertie. "You may not wear it in your neckpiece ruff like Queen Elizabeth and her consorts, or on a velvet gown to a ball, but I hope it brings you luck. Every artist needs a talisman, no?"

"Sir! Mr. Lawrence, we can't accept—" Essie stepped forward to protest.

"Nonsense!" He gave a slight wave as he coughed. "Quite the clump of clay your boys found."

Gertie accepted the button, held it up to the light and watched the rainbow hit a sliver of uncovered wall. "Thank you, Mr. Lawrence," she said as if in a trance.

Tears filled Essie's eyes, and she tried to swallow. She was too scared to speak, lest a torrent of sadness, gratitude, and heartbreak spill from her. If she let it out, she might never be able to contain it.

"I . . . we . . . can't . . ." Unable to finish the sentence, she shook her head.

"The button is yours," the antiquarian said to Gertie. "I insist. My mother once told me that every lass should have a little something sewn into the hem of her skirts."

"Thank you, sir," said Gertie.

"Goodbye, Mr. Lawrence," Essie repeated and she ushered her sister toward the door.

She and Gertie stepped out onto the street, but instead of retracing their steps along West Hill, Essie directed Gertie to the nearest underground station. If Essie's plan was going to work, they had to leave London.

THE GREAT FIRE

THE CHEAPE SIDE, LONDON, 1666

Outside, the fire that had blazed across London for days continued to burn, but in the cellar the air was damp and cool as Aurelia began to dig. She'd promised Papa she would look after her mother and brother, but for that she would need his stock.

A gust of wind slammed the cellar door, sealing her in silky darkness. And still she kept on digging.

She didn't notice that, above her, the house had started to burn until it was too late. A flaming joist fell and pinned her to the floor. Her back cracked loudly as she landed. Red and blue flames danced a duet along the wooden beam and licked her skirts.

Aurelia watched the flames merge and twirl, reminding her of the life and fire in the treasures buried in the dirt below.

She'd wanted to make Papa proud—to keep her promise to look after Mama and Samuel.

Her stockings were ablaze, and the thick air turned musky and bitter. She screamed as the fire reached her skirts, but she was helpless, trapped beneath the joist. Soon her throat constricted and she couldn't swallow. Her breathing grew ragged as her lungs filled with smoke.

The girl's head lolled back, and she closed her eyes. Searing heat smothered her body.

Aurelia counted the faces of those she loved.

Mama.

Samuel.

David.

George.

Jacob.

Papa . . .

She prayed for the Lord to take her to her father and brothers before the flames swallowed her face. For how would they recognize her otherwise?

Aurelia recalled her mother's smile, little Samuel clasping her finger in his fat fist . . . Jacob's first sweet kiss, tasting of plums. Her last image before the world turned dark and still was of the pretty black-and-white ring her father had made for her betrothal.

His masterpiece.

Chapter 28

KATE

BOSTON, PRESENT DAY

Kate plugged her laptop into the second big screen she kept on her desk. She was in a bit of a funk. She hadn't finished the article for Jane. She was no closer to knowing who had buried the Cheapside jewels, and why.

This academic low-pressure system came so often after trawling through books and archives, checking dates and studying details of jewels. After she'd pushed herself but failed to come up with something new. There was a hell of a lot of luck involved in historical research. Nobody liked to admit it, but "right time, right place" and all that certainly came into it. But the words of Madame Parsons spurred her on: *If you look closely, the ring will reveal itself. The black and white will overlap . . . will penetrate one another, if you like? With champlevé, you have to let time take its course . . .*

Marcus's oversize images of the champlevé ring appeared on the screen, and she clicked to enlarge them to get a closer look.

It was evening, and the velvet curtains were drawn and a heater blasted at her feet.

The diamond shimmered at various angles, the gold bezel was slightly uneven at each of the corners. Part of the enamel had been chipped, or worn away—definitely stained with what looked like soil. She blew the pictures up further, and now she could see what Madame Parsons had been trying to explain. The white enamel looked almost translucent, and the black did bleed slightly into the white. What appeared so perfect to the naked eye was actually pretty blurry up close.

She smiled, thinking of Bella's words at the Serpentine. *Life's full of messy edges.*

So it was.

An email came up on the screen from Marcus, and she clicked on it immediately. He'd gone straight to Colombia after the New York shows to do a job in a mine there.

He'd sent images of men hauling trolleys of shale by hand, crouched over rocks, hands black as charcoal on a cutaway mountainside that tumbled away to a lush green valley with a river that flowed to the horizon. Men in waders and polo shirts stood knee-deep in mud, shoveling. The final image was of a hand holding up a chunk of rock, pieces of luminous emerald poking out at all angles. And all of sudden Kate got it. Among the grime and toil and darkness, that handful of translucent green made the heart beat a little faster. It really was magic. No wonder the native Colombians hid their emeralds for years from the Spanish conquistadors. Emeralds were indeed sacred.

Marcus had sent the email—clearly written after a few beers. *Check these out! Not far from our watch.*

Just had dinner of rice, beans, shredded chicken, and chorizo with Jesus, my fixer. Call me when you get this!

Kate dialed his number immediately.

"Hello!" he exclaimed. "I've made a slight change to my travel plans. You home in Boston now?"

"Sure am. Back to grilled cheese and pasta." Kate sipped her chardonnay.

"Thought I might come visit next week, if that's okay. I'm the keynote speaker at the Boston Photographic Society's annual lunch next week. The guy they booked can't make it as he injured himself skiing, so they asked me. Good excuse to visit! I'll be there Wednesday. I'll be heading to Sydney a couple of days afterward. I promised Jules and Liv I'd be there for the valedictory dinner. Can't believe my baby is almost done with school."

"I imagine it feels . . . strange," said Kate.

"Strange. Exciting. Proud . . . all the things," said Marcus. "I've made so many mistakes, but Liv's—" His voice cracked.

"Liv's amazing! She's a credit to you . . . and to Julia," Kate said as her chest tightened.

"Thanks." Marcus's voice steadied. "So, is next week okay with you? To stay, I mean?"

Kate hesitated.

She was anxious about her growing feelings for Marcus. He was more than just a shiny distraction for her, and Kate worried about being hurt. She wasn't sure she had the strength for it.

"Kate?" His voice was softer now.

She took a deep breath. "Yes, please come. I'll be here." She was giddy with the thought of seeing him—touching him again.

"Fantastic!"

When she hung up, she realized she hadn't thanked Marcus for sending the images of the ring. She zoomed in on the diamond ring yet again . . .

Then she gasped, peering at it. Was she seeing things, or was there a faint script engraved into the inside of the gold band?

She'd missed it at the museum; the curatorial staff too; the human eye could pick up only so much with a handheld loupe. Even now, with the ring magnified a hundred times, it looked like the merest scratch. It was so delicate; the engraver would have had to have worked with a diamond tip and beat a tiny hammer into the curve of soft gold.

I GEVE ZOU VIS IN LUIF AURELIAE

Kate read the words aloud and they echoed around her study. *"I give you this in love, Aurelia."*

And just like that, she felt the words start to flow. She started to type the final section of her article:

The Champléve Ring
There is no greater symbol of love—of commitment—than the finger ring. It was the Greeks who developed these tokens of love, and the Romans quickly added their own charm, with secret inscriptions inspired by Ovid quickly becoming the norm . . .

Kate's fingers flew over the keyboard, describing the forget-me-nots and pansies, quoting Madame Parsons and detailing the craftsmanship and risk it took to produce a black-and-white enamel ring that would fit on a small finger. She wrote about London's talented goldsmiths in the seventeenth century, and the trail of trauma—war, plague, and fire—that soured the history books. Stories of grief, betrayal, and death that brought London and her subjects to their knees time and time again.

This Golconda diamond ring had endured it all.

Kate gulped the last of her white wine and banged out her final line.

This ring was made for a woman named Aurelia, and she was loved.

Chapter 29

ESSIE

LONDON, 1912

Essie stood at the ticket counter at Paddington Station, Gertie pressed close beside her.

They were surrounded by noise and movement: whistling locomotives, guards yelling for tickets, the hiss of steam. Excited children circled their parents, tired workers looked for a place to rest their feet. The clatter and chaos of London's streets was condensed, echoing under the wrought-iron fretwork that arched over the platforms.

"Two second-class tickets to Cheltenham Spa, please."

Essie counted out the coins carefully as Gertie watched, wide-eyed.

These tickets would be the last of the extravagances. She had two boiled eggs and a thick slice of bread wrapped in a handkerchief in her apron pocket for the five-hour train trip. Miss Barnes had written that their destination was a twenty-minute walk from the Cheltenham Spa station.

"A spa!" Gertie whispered as the stationmaster handed over their tickets. "Are we leaving London? No wonder you made me wear my Sunday dress."

Did Gertie think they were going on a holiday to the seaside? There would be time enough to explain once they were on the train. Mrs. Yarwood had brought *The Times* over that morning to show Essie, her face downcast. "I'm so sorry, love. They'll be looking for you. Maybe it's for the best that you leave London . . ." She'd sobbed as she clasped Essie to her bosom. "I just worry about you traveling alone," she leaned in close so only Essie could hear, "what with your condition . . ."

Essie had had to stop herself crying with gratitude as she clasped both Mrs. Yarwood's hands between her rough palms. Ma had seemed to think it was only proper that Essie sail for Boston—to save her the embarrassment of explaining her daughter's condition to Father McGuire.

Essie hadn't breathed a word about her plans to Gertie. Only Miss Barnes and the Yarwoods knew. She hadn't been sure she'd be able to see her plan through until they had seen Mr. Lawrence. It would have been cruel to get her sister's hopes up only to have them dashed if Essie couldn't come up with the money.

The huge clock on the station wall chimed, and Essie grabbed Gertie's hand and started to run toward the platform.

"Hurry, Gertie."

Gertie ran beside her, notebook clutched to her chest. They mustn't miss this train. It would ruin—

A man in a bowler clipped Gertie's shoulder and sent her sprawling across the platform. The notebook flew open, and stray sheets of paper she'd torn out because the sketches hadn't lived up to her intentions fell out and fluttered across the platform like autumn leaves.

Gertie managed to sit up and retrieve her book, while Essie tried to retrieve all the random pieces of paper just as she always had when Gertie had the urge to throw away a less-than-perfect sketch. Essie would never stand for it when they were at home, and she wasn't having it now.

Snatching up the first page, Essie recognized the lined paper from Mr. Yarwood's accounting ledger, and she thought her heart might break for all the kindness their neighbors had shown them through the years. They nursed their own sorrows but opened their hearts to Essie and the girls. The sketch was such a perfect likeness of the twins laughing that Essie found it difficult to breathe. The next sketch was of Gertie's button, another of the scoundrel cockerel that scratched up every bit of green in the backyard. Surely that bit of gristle didn't warrant his own page? But the cockerel looked dignified, his eyes knowing and his comb standing proudly. Gertie managed to make these simple line drawings feel alive . . .

A businessman carrying a leather satchel stepped on a piece of paper and bent to retrieve it from under his shoe.

"Thank you, sir," said Essie as she grabbed it from his hand and tried to wipe away the muddy footprint with her sleeve before hastily gathering the other drawings.

When she'd collected the last of them, she slipped the pages into her apron pocket, then grabbed Gertie's hand and yanked her sister onto the train as the guard blew his whistle. They were no sooner aboard than the doors were slammed shut and locked.

In the years to come, Essie would remember that afternoon in Paddington Station when she sank into her seat beside Gertie and decided not to fish the drawings from her apron pocket. Nor did she notice Gertie's trembling hand slip a small envelope inside her other apron pocket.

Once seated beside the window, Gertie flipped open her notebook and started to sketch the crisscross pattern the huge spans of iron made across the roof. The child was lost in another world full of light and shadows and had already forgotten the kerfuffle on the platform.

Essie needed to soak up the essence of this girl. This moment. Before her family, and her heart, splintered forever.

Nobody had ever told Essie that doing the right thing could be the most painful act of all.

Chapter 30

KATE

BOSTON, PRESENT DAY

Kate stood in her study, sipping her hot chocolate and watching the golden leaves outside her window glow in the afternoon light. Marcus stood at her office door, swinging it back and forth to check the hinge, after just having spent the afternoon rehanging it to stop the squeak.

"I had been meaning to get it fixed."

"Sure." Marcus gave her a warm smile. "Just like the dripping tap in the upstairs shower."

Kate opened her mouth to protest, then stopped. She *had* been meaning to have these things fixed, but she'd never been home long enough to arrange a contractor, or she'd been too busy to care. But the restlessness that had seemed to accompany her everywhere had stilled. Instead, this last week Kate had taken comfort in weeding Essie's herb beds between finishing off her Cheapside piece and planting seeds she was sure she would be here to see bloom.

Marcus had delivered his lecture to the Boston Photographic Society, then taken over her great-grandfather's offices on the first floor of the Louisburg house. His return to Australia for Olivia's valedictory dinner was looming. He was planning to stay in Sydney for a few weeks to renovate his flat. Liv had promised to help—negotiating half a fare to Europe in exchange for a few weeks of painting and tiling. Marcus had grinned as he told Kate about it. "It'll be fun. Although I'm not sure about the colors she's chosen . . . I was thinking Scandinavian-style cool grays and white, while she's thinking Sardinian summer by the looks of it. It'll feel like living in a fruit salad!"

Kate studied Marcus in his green work shirt, and imagined his sandy hair spattered with bright yellow and blue paint. She smiled and blew him a kiss.

Neither had broached the subject of when, or if, they would next meet up. But now that Marcus was here—quietly making small repairs and cooking her two-course dinners each night—she was regretting that they both had to fly out in another couple of days: Marcus off home to Sydney, Kate briefly to a museum in Amsterdam.

She'd mentioned when Marcus arrived that she wouldn't be starting her postdoctoral fellowship at Harvard; instead, she wanted to putter around at home a bit, do some writing, take Emma out for piles of forbidden pancakes and loaded milkshakes.

"If you're going to be home more than a week, all these squeaks, drips, and slamming shutters will drive you nuts. Let me help."

And so she did let him, while working in her office, putting the final touches to her article, then emailing it off to an elated Jane last week.

Jane rang her with some feedback—and to engage in some friendly teasing, it seemed. "Best yet, Dr. Kirby. And the pics from Marcus . . . the folks upstairs haven't stopped raving." Her voice dropped conspiratorially. "You two make quite the duo."

Kate didn't respond, surprised at her editor's candor.

"Kate?"

"Yes, I'm listening. Thank you."

"I mean it."

"Goodbye, Jane." She hung up the phone, rattled. When had she become so transparent?

Marcus wandered over to the desk where she sat sorting life admin into piles, ignoring bills and trying to put off her monthly invoicing. His shoulder nudged a picture frame on the wall, and immediately he set to straightening it, giving it a dust with his sleeve as he went.

It was the bill of sale for her great-grandparents' first ship, SS *Esther Rose*, adorned with the Massachusetts seal, then signed and dated at the bottom with a florid signature.

Marcus said, "Huh!" as if something made no sense.

"What?"

He tapped at the date on the certificate: 1915. "Just seems odd. It must have been hard to find a steamer to lease. There was a war raging in Europe. Didn't you say your great-grandmother Essie was poor, and Niall was a sailor? So how could your great-grandfather have afforded to lease a ship on his merchant sailor's wage just a couple of years after arriving in Boston?"

"I have no idea. I know the company made money quickly, doing naval yard supply runs . . . I guess the navy contract was secure in those first years. But this has always been here—even though they ended up with an entire shipping line. This first certificate is the only one they kept at home, even though the *Esther Rose* was decommissioned before the next war."

"Can we look it up?" He craned his neck toward the bookshelf. "Where's the rest of their stuff?"

"The family donated all the records—logbooks, ledgers, shipping charts, and maps—to the Bostonian Society at the Old State House. I did one of my first research projects there, actually."

Kate moved from behind her desk to stand beside Marcus and peered at the certificate. It was as familiar to her as the wrinkles on her great-grandmother's face and the tiles on her front stoop. It had always hung in this spot—though judging by Marcus's sleeve it had been a while since anyone had bothered to give it a clean. Kate resolved to take more care.

The paper had yellowed, the ink faded. The frame also seemed dimmed, the knots of the wood less obvious. She ran her fingers around the edge and then wiped more dust on her jeans. As she stepped to the side and the afternoon light clipped the edge of the frame, she saw a faint outline of something behind the backing.

A shadow line ran along the bottom corner.

"Look." She pointed the shadow out to Marcus.

"There's something in there," he replied as he slipped the frame from the hook and carried it across to her desk. He placed the frame facedown on the desk, then stepped back to make room for Kate.

Kate reached into her top drawer for her white archival gloves and slipped them on. The back of the frame was sealed with tacks, and she used a scalpel to pry them from the wood. She worked slowly, careful not to tear away any of the wood as she lifted the back of the frame and placed it on the carpet beside the desk.

Sitting behind the bill of sale was a crinkled handwritten note.

Receipt

December 1912

Marcus read the receipt aloud: "*One thousand dollars for the sapphires, rubies, and one diamond, two carat.*"

"A thousand dollars!" Kate placed the receipt gently on her felt mat and turned the frame over so the bill of sale was visible.

"It's the same amount," Marcus noted.

They looked at each other, and Kate bit her bottom lip. But before she could say anything, Marcus stepped closer and pointed to a tiny corner of paper protruding from the walnut frame.

"It looks like there's something else. See? Hidden behind the frame."

Kate used tweezers to remove another sheaf of paper folded as tightly as a Chinese fan and wedged tightly into the frame. Someone had intended to keep this hidden.

She unfolded the brittle paper slowly, so as not to tear it.

To her surprise, it had nothing to do with shipping or receipts. It was a letter, dated "26 November 1912."

Kate swiveled her light to read the cursive ink, written with a neat, youthful hand—vowels rounded. Full of vigor and hope.

Marcus started to read: *"Dearest Essie, I was sitting at the top of the stairs and heard everything . . ."*

As she listened to the gentle timbre of Marcus's voice reading words from long ago, Kate sank into the sofa and let the words drift around her. They were like a shawl fashioned from gossamer threads that enveloped her, warmed her. Comforted, she thought of the strength and generosity of the Murphy women—despite the sadness that haunted their days—the gold button with missing gemstones on a chain around Bella's neck, Essie's sapphire earrings, the sepia photo of a young woman standing with a mix of pride and sadness outside St. Hilda's, Oxford, a young woman crossing an ocean with a baby in her belly . . . and then, inevitably, her own lost baby with the translucent skin and crimson lips.

Somehow, all these things were connected.

Grief and hope threaded through the letter and mingled with Kate's own so she wasn't sure where one person's story ended and the other began. But she sat upright as Marcus finished reading the sign-off. *"Your loving sister, Gertie."*

Chapter 31

ESSIE

TILBURY DOCKS, 1912

Tilbury Docks was as busy as Paddington Station. Mothers herded toddlers as though they were flocks of ducklings while porters in waistcoats strained to push barrows loaded with trunks. Barrels stood in neat rows, waiting to be rolled up the gangplank by spritely sailors.

Everyone was dressed in their Sunday best: coats, hats, and gloves. A woman smelling of fresh gardenias and wearing a fox pelt pushed past Essie, soft fur brushing against her cheek. It made a nice change to the scratchy wool and linen she'd been pressed against on the train.

The imposing RMS *Laconda* rocked against the jetty, lashed to the dock with thick ropes.

It was hard to believe that just a few hours from now, when the tide was at its peak, those ropes would be unfurled and cast aside, and with them, Essie's old life.

She swallowed and stole a glance at Freddie from under the brim of her hat. Her brother looked so forlorn, so repentant. Overly eager to help.

They each grieved for the twins—for their broken family—in their own way. She clutched her small suitcase against her legs and refused to let Freddie help her to carry it.

It was not the going away she'd always imagined. Rather, she wore a dress identical to the one she wore to work in the Rubens' factory, with a coat she'd fashioned from an old blanket.

A sailor with pink cheeks and sharp creases in his pants approached.

"Can I help you, miss?" He gave Essie a warm smile, and she found herself returning it despite herself.

"My sister is looking for—"

"Thank you, Freddie." Essie quickly cut her brother off and gently touched his arm. She had not had a man speak for her in the past, and she wasn't going to be starting now.

She shifted her body weight and composed herself. Gertie would be proud. "I'm looking for . . ." She held her ticket out and pointed.

The young man squinted and leaned over to read the ticket, before straightening.

"Right you are then. You'll be downstairs. Up the front." He paused, and began to say something before stopping and starting again. "Are you the only one traveling today, miss?"

Essie lifted her chin and looked the sailor directly in the eyes as she imagined Gertie might do. "Yes, just me, thank you." She felt a flutter in her stomach, as if the little one had heard her and kicked in protest.

He nodded. "Very well. They're all shared cabins down in third."

Third class. It was like a final kick in the shins. The bastard could not even stump up for a second-class ticket. Still, all she had to do was get on that ship. When she disembarked in Boston, Esther Murphy would be free to be whoever she wanted.

The breeze caught her skirt, and it billowed a little at her ankles. Another sailor had come over and smiled apologetically.

"Officer Kirby, sorry to interrupt"—he nodded at Essie and Freddie—"but the captain wants to see you, on the foredeck."

"Thank you, Smith. I'll be there just as soon as I've finished showing this lady to her cabin." He turned to Freddie and said, "I'll escort her to her quarters."

Essie put down her bag and embraced her brother. She could feel his ribs and bony shoulders through his thin shirt. He smelled of smoke and hair cream.

"Goodbye, Freddie," she said, her voice cracking. She drank in his smell, and his lean frame. Her brother had always seemed younger than her, almost like one of the twins.

"Goodbye, Es. Take care."

She released her brother and took a step backward. "Make sure you write to Gertie and Ma when you move into your new lodgings. And call in on Mr. and Mrs. Yarwood from time to time, won't you?"

"Here, let me carry your bag," said Officer Kirby. "Just up the gangway, at least." He looked concerned. "There's a bit of wind about, and I'd hate for you to slip and the bag to end up in the drink."

This young officer was simply doing his duty and offering to help. Edward had always been similarly thoughtful—right up until his cowardly betrayal. Essie was furious with herself for seeing Officer Kirby as anything other than dutiful. Despite Ma's warnings when Essie bid her final farewell, Essie still refused to believe every man she met had a sinister agenda. She could feel her ears burning as she mumbled her thanks.

"Righto. Best be boarding." And Officer Kirby gestured to indicate Essie should precede him.

She grabbed the cold rails and felt the dappled sun on her face. She took a couple of steps before turning back to see that Freddie had grabbed the officer's shoulder and was speaking to him urgently.

The sailor was nodding slowly, and Essie caught the last words on the wind.

"If you could just look out for her . . ."

The officer glanced her way and caught Essie's eye for a brief moment before nodding at Freddie. "Aye. Of course. I'll keep an eye out for the lass. Though I must say—if you'll beg my pardon—she has the look of someone who is well able to take care of herself."

"That she is." But Freddie's chuckle was heavy with sadness.

"Still, a young woman, traveling alone downstairs . . ." The officer shook his head, and Essie turned away quickly, not wanting the men to know she'd been eavesdropping.

Her brother was only trying to do the right thing. He blamed himself for not being able to save the twins. And for Edward.

Her stomach heaved as she recalled the sound of a head cracking on a cobblestone, the squelching of a wheel and a whinnying horse.

Edward had been a coward, but he hadn't deserved to die under the wheel of a cart. His death was a dreadful accident—one she'd regret for the rest of her life.

Essie tried to still the guilt and loss and longing churning in her belly. She would not let it feed into the little one. She was not going to allow *him*—a mistake—to define her or her baby. She needed to find a way to live with her own regret and guilt but give this baby the clean slate it deserved. With that she strode up the gangplank and stepped onto the steamer, ready to depart for her new life.

When she turned back, Freddie had been pushed into the shadows by a sea of dark coats elbowing each other out of the way. She could barely make out her brother's pale features.

The wind stung her face—her cheeks were wet with tears—and she took the sharp sea air deep into her lungs. A lone seagull swooped and shrieked overhead, piercing the low hum of family farewells and whispered words.

Essie couldn't know, of course, what lay ahead on the Atlantic or in her new country. But she gripped the handrail and surprised herself by praying to the shuddering steamer, the captain, and the calm officer with the kind eyes to deliver her safely to land—to her new life.

Chapter 32

Essie hadn't planned on falling in love during the voyage, but that was what happened.

The first officer—Mr. Niall Kirby—managed to secure a "spare" cabin and saw her safely ensconced on the top deck. When he left her alone in the gleaming cabin with its plush carpet and feather pillows, she tucked her tattered suitcase under a table, collapsed onto the huge bed, and slept for eight hours. When she awoke to a dark cabin with her boots and coat still on, she tugged them off and went back to sleep again until morning.

Essie hadn't realized the toll that caring for her mother and the girls had taken. All her energy had been expended on protecting and nurturing them. Her desperation for Gertie to finish school and to keep Ma from the workhouse had drained her. Edward had offered her an idyll: a brief, shining moment of happiness and attention; a glimpse at an alternative life.

But his love had been no more hers to keep than the ring he gave her and the jewels Freddie found over on Cheapside.

First Officer Kirby, however, quickly proved that his primary concern was for her comfort and safety.

It was easy to love Niall. He took time to make life aboard the RMS *Laconda* a little better for everyone. Whether it be arranging a walking stick and a firm arm for the unstable Mr. Henry as he took his evening constitutional, moving a family from third class to another spare cabin in first class so their ailing child could recover with the aid of the ship's doctor, or the little jug of Guinness and dry crackers he arranged for the cook to leave in Essie's cabin when he noticed she couldn't stomach her dinner of sausages and mash in the dining room.

"You need to keep your strength up. For you . . . and the little one."

Shocked, Essie looked up and met his gaze.

"How did you . . ." Essie spluttered.

The first officer shrugged and gracefully steered around the topic. "Big fat red cheeks, my sister's lad has . . ." The officer's cheeks turned a deep pink that spread all the way to his ears. She would later recognize it as an endearing family trait.

"It'll be worth it, trust me," Niall said softly.

And just like that, she did.

Essie trusted Niall's kindness, his steady goodness and sincerity.

And Niall trusted Essie enough not to dig up the muck and mistakes of her past.

And so, in a mid-Atlantic swell, they agreed to draw a line under the past and step over it together. They were married by the captain on the bridge on a bright Friday afternoon with a handful of curious well-wishers as witnesses. Niall had offered to wait and book a church when they were ashore in Boston, but Essie declined.

First Officer Niall Kirby declared one evening as they walked around the top deck that his ambition was to start a shipping line of his very own.

"I mean *our* own," he corrected himself. "Because I can't . . . I won't . . ." He paused. "What I mean to say is that this is my dream, but if it isn't yours, or you want to be trying something else, then we can follow a different path."

Essie didn't doubt Niall for a moment. Instead, she pictured herself swinging a bottle of champagne to launch their first ship, just like she'd seen in the moving pictures.

"I can do the bookkeeping for your—our—ships." Essie smiled. "My neighbor Mr. Yarwood was an accountant, and he showed me how to keep a ledger." She grabbed her new husband's warm hand, thinking of Mr. and Mrs. Yarwood sitting at the table in their yellow kitchen, helping the girls with their homework and coaxing Essie through columns of red and black.

Soon, she was going to have her own clean, neat kitchen with a husband and child to make it a home. That was her dream; anything more than that was a bonus.

Niall had been supportive until the day he died, bless his soul.

But on that first day aboard the RMS *Laconda* as the ship steamed away from Tilbury Docks—before she fell into a deep sleep—Essie had sat on the bed, little suitcase beside her, and reached into her apron pocket for her handkerchief to wipe away her tears.

Only then did she remember the sketches of the twins she'd rescued from the train platform. And in the other pocket was a small envelope containing a letter from Gertie.

Who would have thought that this letter would launch a hundred ships?

Chapter 33

KATE

BOSTON, PRESENT DAY

Kate and Marcus wound their way up the grand spiral staircase toward the Old State House library.

The volunteer archivist, wearing a tartan skirt, sensible shoes, and a warm smile, clapped her hands together. "Dr. Kirby! I'm Verity Doyle. This is exciting. I have to ask, are you curious about Niall Kirby's logbooks for family research, or are you here in a professional capacity? I couldn't help but look you up . . . I always love to know what people's research specialties are. Curiosity keeps our world spinning, doesn't it?"

"Indeed! It's a bit of both, personal *and* professional. I'm not sure where one begins and the other ends, to be honest."

"Well, *no one* has touched these for years, I'm sorry to say. It's quite a story: a merchant seaman who goes on to own a ship and then a whole fleet. Those Kirbys sure did create something special; they were good people! While your great-grandparents grew up, so did Boston."

"Thank you. It's kind of you to say."

"They left quite the legacy," said Marcus as he stepped across to the bookshelf. "Not just here, but the women's clinics, the schools . . ."

"They sure did," said Kate. She sighed faintly, remembering the archive at the Serpentine, with the newspaper clippings detailing Gertrude's achievements and the huge pile of letters the two women had exchanged, the photos, birthday cards, Joseph's obituary, and Bella's christening snaps. The ledger books brimming with images of trauma and loss and sadness. Two little girls at peace. Two candles. There was also undeniable joy, energy, and exuberance squeezed in on the same page, refusing to be snuffed out.

Gertrude and Essie had been given a chance at another life, and they had each seized the opportunity with both hands.

Kate studied Marcus as he surveyed the room. The line of his shoulders and chest just visible under his old V-neck T-shirt made her tummy tingle. But it was his easy manner that stilled her. He was thoughtful and kind, and had taken the time to coax her out of darkness. He'd shown her how he'd learned from his past and forgiven himself. He tried his best. That was enough.

The sturdy archivist pulled out a sheet that itemized everything in the collection. "We have bills of sale, logbooks, charts, a couple of private diaries." She gestured to the shelf on which the leather-bound logbooks were stored and a cardboard archive box on the table. Then she looked at her watch and said, "I'm afraid I have a meeting, then some catalogs to finish. But please make yourself at home. All the material donated by your family is here."

"Thanks again for allowing us access at short notice," said Kate as she walked Miss Doyle to the door.

Marcus was already at the bookshelf, scanning the spines of the logbooks. "November 1912 you say?" When he came to one labeled RMS *Laconda* he pulled it from the shelf and passed it to her.

Kate looked down at the faded cursive script. Most texts she read in museums had the translations attached at the front with a summary for academics. But as she opened the pages, she saw the annotations and sketches and realized this was a sailor's personal logbook—a diary of sorts.

She ran her finger down the margin, marveling at Niall Kirby's sketches. There were mackerel and black sea bass anatomically labeled and whale tails poking up above a wave. An entire page was devoted to a landscape featuring an island and rocky outcrop.

She leaned in to smell salt water and ink. The scent of her history.

Marcus began to read the columns: "*Latitude, Longitude, Distance, Run . . .*"

He turned a page and read what was before him, then sucked in his breath.

"Listen to this: *Today I met the woman I'd like to marry. Esther Murphy, but she prefers Essie. Irish by birth, she has a smile I'd juggle forever to keep.*"

He turned over some more pages. "Shipping info, a list of supplies . . . Oh, wait, we're into mid-December 1912 in this section. That's, what, two weeks later?"

He put the diary on the desk. On the left-hand page was a drawing of gulls swooping into waves. On the right-hand side was this entry:

In the two weeks I've taken to having the cook leave a pitcher of Guinness and some dry crackers in her cabin every night after our walk around the length of the deck.

E. thinks I haven't noticed the dry-retching, the clammy hands and sweat at her temples. My mother and sister were both the same when they were with child . . .

"What? Essie was pregnant already? But they'd only just met."

E. thinks I haven't noticed . . .

But Essie had noticed. The story of how Essie agreed to marry Niall Kirby during the Atlantic crossing had become family folklore. It had been during the beginning of a storm, when the boat was lurching and heaving across the top of the swell. Essie was on deck clinging to the rails, wobbly with seasickness. Niall coaxed her back to the cabin, then went to fetch Guinness and dry crackers.

Kindness and hope, Katherine—that's what you should look for in a man. Your great-grandfather Niall spent the entire Atlantic crossing tending to the ill, instructing the newer sailors on the ship on their ropes and seamanship, helping them practice navigation, fixing ropes . . . I never heard him raise his voice or utter a sharp word.

It was the same when Joseph was learning to sail the little dinghy or ride a bike. Or—heaven help me—learning to drive his first automobile. Niall was always there right by Joseph's side, like a true father should be. Essie had smiled dreamily.

Kate's great-grandfather may have showered Essie with gifts over the lifetime of their marriage, but whenever Essie spoke of Niall, it was with the easy tenderness of one who loved deeply and knew she was cared for in return. In Essie's stories, it wasn't the jewels that sparkled—it was Niall. Gestures were far more important to her than gemstones.

Niall had brought her a cup of Irish breakfast tea in bed every morning until the day he died. Set the table for their breakfast before he went to bed each night—always with a little vase of roses, or forget-me-nots he'd picked specially from the garden. He'd planted roses outside her window for summer, and bulbs for winter.

Kate's breath started to shorten as her eyes ran over and over the same lines:

> . . . *the dry-retching, the clammy hands and sweat at her temples. My mother and sister were both the same when they were with child . . .*

Kate too had experienced all of these symptoms when she was with child.

She placed both hands on her stomach and closed her eyes for a beat—wanting the pain to pass, but clinging to the memory of those first flutters. Loss and hope knotted in her stomach.

Chapter 34

ESSIE

LOUISBURG SQUARE, BOSTON, 1994

Essie lowered herself into the swinging chair on her stoop. In her hand was a glass of fresh lemonade brought to her on a tray by her dear friend and housekeeper, Mrs. Mackay.

It was a humid Sunday afternoon—the kind that promised a late afternoon squall off the Atlantic. But for now the sun was high and fuzzy, and Essie was grateful Mrs. Mackay's lemonade was not too far off from sucking a lemon. She shook the glass to get the last drops, then fished out a few ice cubes and wrapped them in her handkerchief, before pressing them against her neck as she watched her great-granddaughters Molly and Katherine play soccer across the road. The relief was immediate. How those girls could keep running around the park in this steamy summer heat was beyond her.

Her son and grandson were in the backyard with their glamorous wives—no doubt burning expensive steak and laying out an elaborate lunch table with potato salad and corn with peppery lime butter. Once the dessert was cleared they were all going to *have a little chat* about the Sunny Banks Retirement Village being constructed in Cambridge. Glossy brochures had been left with her *to have a think about* two weeks ago after a similar lunch culminating in a far-too-sweet sticky date pudding.

Aside from the fact there was no "sunny bank" anywhere within a hundred-mile radius of Boston, Essie was not leaving her home. Her son and his offspring would never understand, of course. They just wanted her to be safe. Cared for. But how could Essie explain to her family—with their privilege, comfortable houses, and education—that this house was as much a part of her as her arm? It represented everything she'd longed for as a child in London. Shelter, books, food. Family.

Someday soon this house would be passed to the next generation. She hoped they'd fill it to the brim with children, laughter, and godawful plastic toys.

She loved it when these two energetic great-granddaughters visited and shrieked up and down the staircase, trailing sticky fingers down the wallpaper and carelessly spreading books and Legos across the floor for everyone else to trip over.

Molly had the ball, but Katherine was making a determined tilt for it. Long skittish limbs flew in all directions. Their skin glowed with summer tans, and their hair fell in loose ponytails at their shoulders. Katherine sliced a goal past her older sister, and they slapped hands and danced around with their hands in the air, shaking their skinny butts. Gloriously gleeful and cocky.

She thought about the sheep guts the boys had used in the back alleys of Southwark and how they too shook their fists when they scored. She recalled the wistful way Flora and Maggie had watched them, desperate to hoist up their skirts and join in.

Essie's breath caught, and she thought of the twins with their bandy legs. It had been over eighty years, and still the grief made her bones ache. Gertie's recent passing compounded her sadness, though it gave Essie some comfort that her sister had slipped away quietly in her sleep instead of enduring illness or pain.

Nobody told you that, as you got older, grief and joy ebbed and flowed like the tides.

This afternoon, these filthy girls running about in denim cutoffs and bare feet were perfect.

As the girls leaned their freckled faces in together to share a secret, Essie caught a glimpse of her sisters, and it filled her heart to know that Gertie, Flora, and Maggie's blood—their spirit—ran through the veins of these glorious, healthy young girls. Molly and Katherine would finish school. Likely go to college. Choose their own paths.

Katherine—now bored with soccer—was climbing Christopher Columbus. She clutched at his rather bulbous nose and hauled a leg over his shoulder. *What would become of them?* Essie wondered. Molly was the more outspoken: precocious and articulate. Perhaps she'd become an attorney, like her great-great-aunt in London. Her younger sister, Katherine—now sitting on Columbus's shoulders, lost in her own thoughts—was quieter, more thoughtful. She liked to sneak away to the library, burying her head in Essie's books. Last week she'd caught a pink-faced Katherine reading Jackie Collins when she'd insisted she needed to go upstairs and read *Little Dorrit*.

She was curious, too. Katherine loved nothing more than to sit at Essie's dressing table, going through her jewelry box and asking her about each piece.

Just that morning, Katherine had sat beside Essie on the sofa, smelling of apples, sweat, and cut grass, and touched Essie's sapphire earrings.

"What are these called?"

"Sapphires."

"Are they from Grandpa Niall too?"

"Why, yes . . . he had the stones made into earrings."

"I love the blue. They match your eyes. Blue is my lucky color."

Essie's breath had caught in her throat. Then she said, "Mine too."

Essie pressed her hands to her eyes to suppress the tears that threatened. She had no right to cry. No claim to this grief since she'd left London all those years ago. She and Gertie—along with the Yarwoods—had made a pact to never speak of that night in Piccadilly Circus.

"You girls had best be moving on," Mrs. Yarwood had advised in her tiny yellow kitchen. "It won't be long before the police put two and two together. I'd say you could argue self-defense—we saw him raise a fist to you—but if his wealthy family decide to fight it, I'm afraid a judge would be more likely to side with them. You'll be in jail before you know it, Essie."

"But it was me . . ." sobbed Gertie.

"Shush, Gertie. You did the proper thing to save your sister. But, Essie, you need to get on that ship. There are likely people who would be able to connect you with Mr. Hepplestone."

"I can't! I won't leave."

"You *must*. Stay and you'll go to jail. Try to see this as an opportunity. Make the most of it. Don't be looking back with regret. Gertie can stay with us—she's like our own."

Essie's heart broke all over again. "Thank you. For everything. I'd be very grateful if you could keep an eye on Gertie. Come, let's get you home to bed now, Gertie. Mrs. Yarwood, I'd be grateful if you'd come with me while I settle Gertie, then I'll explain to you and Ma my plan . . ."

Afterward, when Essie bid her neighbor good night, Mrs. Yarwood had clapped her hands and said, "Well, Mr. Yarwood and I would love to assist. Now, I meant what I said. No regrets. Only love."

And oh, how Essie had loved. She'd been married to a good man—a kind man—for over fifty years. She'd been a poor judge of a man's character only once.

And yet . . .

It had been a shock to see yesterday's obituary in newsprint—although the family had telephoned the news through some weeks before. Essie was far too old now to travel to London, so was unable to make it to the funeral.

Reaching into her pocket, she pulled out the newspaper clipping she'd carefully cut from the London *Times*. Her hands were unsteady as she unfolded it. Eventually she flattened the clipping onto her lap.

Ford, Gertrude Mary
1898–1994

Former City of Westminster Chief Magistrate Gertrude Mary Ford passed away quietly in her South Kensington home, aged 96.

Mrs. Ford dedicated much of her legal career to the support of women and children who had experienced extreme poverty, disability, or family violence.

During both the First and Second World Wars, she suspended study to volunteer in schools by day and hospitals by night, and built a fine academic and legal career in between.

Known as a champion of women's rights, she was the first to appoint a female head of chambers and long campaigned for more women to sit the bar exams. "I'll be forever grateful that kind people chose to give me my schooling. I believe everyone needs a second, third, and perhaps a fourth chance."

Lord Tony Rushsmith says Professor Ford leaves an indelible mark on the British legal system. "She will be missed as much for her sharp wit as her sage judgments. Many a disadvantaged minor has Mrs Ford to thank for their rehabilitation. She preferred to address the cause of the crime, rather than simply administer punishment."

Gertrude Mary Ford (née Murphy) was one of seven children born to Irish immigrants Clementine and Conrad Murphy. Ford was the recipient of scholarships to Cheltenham Ladies' College and Oxford.

Not content with a formidable career at the bench, then in academia, Ford held her debut watercolor exhibition, Jewel, *at the Serpentine Gallery last year. Each canvas depicted the female form rendered in gemstones. When interviewing Ford for* The Sunday Times, *art critic Joyce Oxley asked about the consistent use of a particular blue, to which Ford insisted the correct term be used: sapphire. In her opening speech, Ford dedicated this exhibition to her sisters, "who were true treasures."*

In 1937, Gertrude Murphy married Hubert Ford, a military surgeon who was killed in Normandy during World War II. She lost her daughter to cancer twenty years ago and is survived by granddaughter Mary Scott of Suffolk and great-granddaughter Bella Scott.

Essie sat on her front stoop and studied the photo of Gertie in her academic gown and mortarboard, the university insignia embroidered at the chest. Mr. and Mrs. Yarwood stood proudly on either side.

Gertie's letter was tucked safely in a wooden frame in her study. It seemed only natural to keep the essential papers together. One day—when Essie was gone—perhaps one of these sparky girls might read them.

By then the sediment would have settled, and they wouldn't be dragged into the muck. Although she was tempted to pull Gertie's letter from its hiding place just to press it against her cheek—to have proof that her sister lived—she knew she wouldn't. Besides, she'd read it so often until it almost tore along the fold lines.

Essie knew every word by heart.

Her memories were interrupted by shouts from Kate and Molly, who had spotted Essie on the steps. She poured them each a glass of lemonade from the jug and watched them gulp it down and put their hands out for another.

"Tell us a story, Granny Essie," said Molly.

"Ple-ease!" added Kate. "Tell us the one about the jewels. That's my favorite."

Essie looked at the disheveled girls sitting at her feet.

"All right, but we'll have to be quick. Mrs. Mackay will be out soon enough to fetch us for lunch. Your father will have turned the steak to cinders by now. I'll have to take my teeth out to eat it!"

Molly exploded with giggles. Kate looked between her sister and great-grandmother, as if gauging how much she should laugh.

"All righty. Do you believe in buried treasure? A long, long time ago, in London's Cheapside, buckets and chests of jewels were pulled from a pile of rubble. The men who found it were so shocked, one of them tripped over backward and fell into a hole."

More giggles from Molly.

"What was in the bucket?" asked Kate, always one for detail.

"I'm getting to that bit. Rubies and an emerald as big as your fist, strings of pearls, bags of diamonds. Brooches, fine necklaces that looked like daisy chains. When they held up a clump of dirt as big as your soccer ball it dripped with gold, sapphires, rings, and buttons. I swear, you never did see so much sparkle in your life."

Molly gasped. "What did they do with the treas—"

"Did you touch it?" interrupted Kate.

Essie paused, taken aback.

"Who's telling this story? No questions until the end, please. Now, where was I? Nobody was allowed to touch the jewels. But there was a man, with eyes as green as emeralds. He cast a spell on me." She tickled Kate's tummy.

"Was he the handsome prince?" said Molly in disgust. "Why does every fairy tale have to have a prince?" She frowned.

This one was definitely going to be an attorney. Heaven help the person who crossed Molly.

Essie chuckled. "Well, if you let me get to the end of the story, Little Miss Impatient, I think you'll find—"

But before Essie could continue, Mrs. Mackay appeared at the front door. "Time for lunch," she said. "You girls help your great-grandmother, now."

The girls jumped up and raced to be the first to assist Essie, each yanking her arm a little too exuberantly. She wished the girls were here every lunchtime to bicker and tug her arms all the way to the lunch table. She missed this energy, this human touch.

As Essie walked down the hallway between the girls to where the rest of her family waited in the backyard, her heart swelled.

Sunny Banks be damned; she belonged here in Louisburg Square with her family. This old house needed to be filled with laughter, children, and food. They'd have to carry her out of here in a box.

The smell of grilled corn and sweet star jasmine wafted inside.

She leaned in close. "The point of the story is this, girls: don't be dazzled by the sparkle—green eyes, diamonds, or emeralds. The real treasure is right here." She squeezed their shoulders tight and clasped them to her chest.

"Where?" said Molly, eyeing Essie's sapphire earrings—still looking for actual treasure.

But Kate squeezed back, as if to say, *I know exactly what you mean.*

Essie smiled at her youngest great-granddaughter and whispered in her ear, "And may you never forget it, my love."

Chapter 35

26 November 1912

Dearest Essie,

I was sitting at the top of the stairs and heard everything.

It was all I could do to stop myself from tearing downstairs. It broke my heart to hear you promise Ma and Mrs. Yarwood that you would leave London.

But if I came downstairs and fled with you, I'd have only been a burden. I understand.

You've spent all your years raising us, loving us as much as any parent. Now you need to parent your own little one.

I'll be forever grateful that you arranged for me to go to school. I'll honor your promise and work hard. I will make you so proud.

My kind Essie, I enclose a parting gift for you. After we visited Mr. Lawrence for the last time and he gave me back the button, I prized the stones from it for you, me, and Ma.

But now I understand that you have given mostly everything to us, and left nothing for yourself.

Check your hems. It seems only fitting to give you precious stones, some of them the color of the sea.

I shall think of you every day on the other side of the ocean. My love for you could fill the Atlantic.

Your loving sister,
Gertie xxx

Essie was shocked to find that Gertie had stitched gemstones into the hem of her skirt.

She'd told Niall about the gemstones on their wedding night, as they lay with his strong body curled protectively around hers, stroking her protruding belly. Their legs were intertwined, skin sticky and warm from a long night of shy, tender lovemaking.

Essie told him that very first night that if Niall was serious about leasing a ship, she would sell the gemstones to use as the deposit.

He'd nuzzled his face into her curls and hugged her tighter. "They are yours to do with as you wish. I already have my treasure, *Mo stóirín.*" He'd held her close until the waves rocked them both back to sleep.

As it happened, a gemologist from Tiffany & Co. who was returning from a purchasing trip to London had the cabin next to theirs in first class. He acted as a buyer for collectors in the United States, in particular a prominent New York–based banker, J. P. Morgan.

His eyes had widened at the sapphires, and again as he examined them under his looking glass. "Superb," he breathed. "You say you got these in London?" Essie nodded and swallowed. No more questions were asked as the merchant took in her worn shoes and Sunday dress with a brisk nod.

"One day, I promise I shall buy you some more, Essie," Niall had whispered when they were back in their cabin, check tucked away in the captain's safe. "Sapphires—to match your eyes. And our sea."

"I don't—" Essie started to protest, but he'd lifted her hand to his lips and kissed it before slowly removing her dress and undergarments and kissing his way down to her belly, and all her words melted away.

Epilogue

KATE

BOSTON, PRESENT DAY

Kate sat curled up on her peacock sofa, laptop perched on her gigantic belly. Two cups of hot chocolate steamed on the coffee table on top of an embossed save-the-date notice for a special evening at the Museum of London in six months' time. The cardboard was so thick Kate had taken to using it as a coaster.

It had been Lucia who had insisted on pushing back the gala until Kate and Marcus might be in a position to travel. She'd even written a note on the back:

Looking forward to seeing you. Might I suggest this would be the perfect location for your next project's launch?

Over the past eight months Kate's breath had caught at times, when she and Marcus started to make plans for their future, but Marcus always held her gaze and wrapped his arms around her belly until her breathing steadied. He never tried to brush away her hurt. He cradled her fear, along with her ballooning belly.

"I understand. I'm here." He'd whispered it over and over until her fear was replaced with something new, something . . . calmer.

The baby grew, along with her excitement—though the dread never dissipated entirely. How could it?

It was Essie who'd shown Kate how to carry a heart full of sorrow and joy.

And just like Essie, Kate started to rearrange her life around those she loved. She'd relished a recent road trip from Los Angeles to Salt Lake City with Liv and Marcus, stopping at the Grand Canyon, where father and daughter rode partway down on mules while Kate had a much-needed massage and mud body scrub. Liv had flown home afterward, with promises to come back and stay for a month when her new sibling was born. "Trust me, I'm the baby whisperer," she'd said wryly. "Just look how calm my brothers are!" She'd giggled, and Kate couldn't resist reaching out to give her a grateful hug. She couldn't wait to be tripping over Liv's backpack and a corridor full of fermenting travel clothes again soon.

After the baby was born and settled, she and Marcus planned a trip to London to see Bella donate her button pendant back to the museum, then an autumn spent squirreling around in Louisburg Square with Emma, Jessica, and Molly, with their bundled-up newborn strapped and snuggled into Marcus's chest. In the new year Kate would start up a board position with the Old State House and a mentorship program for young historians.

She wiggled her feet and poked Marcus in the thigh with her big toe. "I think I've just finished the last chapter. Your friend

Natalya from J.P. Morgan was super helpful. She tracked down Essie's receipt and emailed it through. Confirmed J.P. Morgan did indeed buy the gemstones that launched a hundred ships." She twisted her sapphires in her ears, relieved that the receipt from J.P. Morgan proved that *these* earrings were indeed just a gift from a doting husband to his beloved wife.

"Great." Marcus looked over the top of his own laptop and smiled. "So can I read the last chapter?"

"Sure." She jumped up, took his laptop, and placed it gently on the table, replacing it with her own before snuggling in beside him.

"You're seriously going to stare over my shoulder while I read?"

"Maybe!"

The Cheapside Jewels
A memoir of jewels and family

"I'll sit right here and let you read while I drink my hot chocolate." She leaned her head against his shoulder as he started to read.

My work as a jewelry historian has taken me deep into tragedies of the past.

But sometimes tracing the stories and the line of a jewel—the light bouncing off a diamond, the hue of an emerald, the floral detail set into champlevé enamel, solder marks on the back of gold buttons—has shown me that, just like jewels, people can be transferred to a new setting and have a different kind of life . . .

My great-grandmother Essie Kirby wasn't from wealthy stock. She was an Irish lass who sailed from England to Boston with one suitcase and arrived in America with a clean tunic, a starched apron, a spare petticoat, a new husband, and a baby in her belly.

We knew the provenance of the baby, my grandfather Joseph— or so we thought.

My great-grandfather Niall Kirby was a merchant seaman who made his money in shipping out of Boston. The custom-made sapphire earrings were his gift to Essie on their fiftieth wedding anniversary.

He died quietly in his sleep not long afterward, with a smile on his face and traces of smoke and his favorite Caribbean rum on his breath. So my family never heard the story of where the sapphires came from—but I suspected from their velvety blue that they were picked up for a song in Sri Lanka back when the Brits called it Ceylon.

My father, Joseph Jr., was a scrap of a child neatly tucked into shirts and long pants at his grandparents' anniversary dinner. But for as long as I can remember, he loved to spin the tale of how his grandpapa's eyes sparkled as he handed the earrings to his beloved Essie Rose—the old man's smooth Irish lilt whispering: "Mo stóirín."

My treasure. My love . . .

"So?" Kate studied Marcus's face, the cup warming both hands as she clenched it a little too tight.

"So . . . it's wonderful. It's the story of you, Essie, and Bella. Who'd have thought a buried bucket of jewels would unearth your own family tale of heartbreak, loss, and—"

"Murder?" Kate winced. "Too much?"

Marcus chuckled and tickled her belly. "I was actually going to say love. Unconditional and crazy bighearted love." He kissed her nose, then her lips. He tasted of chocolate, cinnamon, and hope.

"Wait! I just have one more bit to add before I email it off to my publisher."

Kate put down her cup, elbowed herself upright, and grabbed her laptop. She found the title page and typed her dedication:

For Essie, who showed me what to look for.

And Marcus, who helped me find it.

About the author

About the book

Insights,
Interviews
& More . . .

Read on

Meet Kirsty Manning

JK Henshaw

KIRSTY MANNING grew up in northern New South Wales. A country girl with wanderlust, her travels and studies have taken her through most of Europe, the east and west coasts of the United States, and pockets of Asia. Kirsty's first novel was the enchanting *The Midsummer Garden*, published in 2017. Her second book, the bestselling *The Song of the Jade Lily*, was published in 2018. Kirsty is a partner in the award-winning Melbourne wine bar Bellota and the Prince Wine Store in Sydney and Melbourne. She lives with her husband and three children amid an old chestnut grove in the Macedon Ranges, Victoria. ᴄᴖ

Author's Note

The Lost Jewels is a work of fiction inspired by the true story of the Cheapside Hoard, dug up in a Cheapside cellar in 1912, which now forms a significant collection at the Museum of London, and also at the British Museum and the Victoria & Albert Museum.

While the Cheapside Hoard is one of the most famous caches of jewels in the world, it is also the most mysterious. How could someone neglect to retrieve five hundred precious pieces of jewelry and gemstones? Why did nobody claim it in the subsequent years? Who were the workmen who actually discovered the jewels in 1912?

These questions remain unanswered.

The Lost Jewels is my imagined tale woven between the facts. Timelines have been massaged and altered to fit the plot. My Museum of London is a fictional version, as are the jewels I describe.

The Cartier workshop is also fictional, based on the workshop displayed at the *Cartier* exhibition at the National Gallery of Australia, Canberra, in 2018.

I love bringing to life forgotten pockets of history—in particular, women's voices that have long been overlooked or dismissed. For me, a novel begins in the gaps of history. I build my world on the bits we don't ▶

Author's Note *(continued)*

know. This gives me the opportunity to explore the dark, difficult, and joyful parts of human nature.

In the 1600s, Cheapside was the hub for gold, silver, and precious gems that had threaded their way around the world to London. However, this century was also filled with fire, plague, revolution, and an expanding empire . . . Seventeenth-century London was a city equal parts thriving and in turmoil. There were a million reasons why someone might not return for their precious jewels.

London was in turmoil again in 1912: on the brink of war, and with women marching in the street demanding the vote. Both these eras seemed ripe for fictionalizing, placing strong, interesting women at the forefront of each story.

As for Kate, my main contemporary character—I'm in awe of historians, curators, and conservators around the world. They tenderly dive into our past to give us stories for our future. To teach us lessons, to give comfort and warning where needed. This is my love letter to your important work in libraries, museums, and galleries around the world.

People can dismiss jewels—diamond rings, necklaces, gold buttons—as frivolous and superficial. But the story of a jewel tells a bigger story of trade and globalization, design trends, economics, and politics. Also, a story about care and craftsmanship.

Lastly, the story of a jewel is always about power, love, and loyalty. The perfect starting point for a novel, right?

A special mention to all the artisan jewelers creating beautiful work. When you buy a bespoke piece of jewelry, it really has been made with the utmost consideration and care. My friend Emma Goodsir, jeweler and owner of Melbourne gallery e.g.etal, was very patient as she explained just what character traits it took to be someone who crafts jewels for a living. She even let me tag along with her to the *Cartier* exhibition in Canberra and took time to step me through the tools and processes of gem cutting, stone setting, design, and the role of the goldsmith and enameler.

All my characters are fictional depictions, but I explore the

About the book

4

mystery surrounding two real people in *The Lost Jewels*. Antiquarian and local character George Fabian Lawrence, "Stony Jack," allegedly set about acquiring the Cheapside collection from navvies on street corners and pubs. In the course of my research, this pawnbroker/antiquarian seemed generous in spirit and an enthusiastic amateur historian, so I couldn't resist fictionalizing a little snippet of him in *The Lost Jewels*. For a firsthand account of the man, see journalist H. V. Morton's classic memoir *In Search of London*.

The second character, Gerhard Polman, the Dutch merchant, is also my imagined version. For more thorough depictions see Kris Lane's *Color of Paradise: The Emerald in the Age of Gunpowder Empires*; and, reproduced on pp. 169 and 170, original transcripts recorded and translated in *A Calendar of Court Minutes, etc. of the East India Company 1635–1639*, Ethel Bruce Sainsbury (ed.) (Oxford, Clarendon Press, 1907, pp. 261–62).

The account of diamond mines, markets, and life is inspired by *Travels in India* by Jean-Baptiste Tavernier, written in 1676. Special thanks to the librarians at The Goldsmiths' Company, London, for allowing me to visit their incredible building and access a wealth of archival material about the Cheapside Hoard, and various other historical documents and images documenting the work of goldsmiths.

In all cases, any mistakes are my very own.

In the Further Reading section, I've included a list of these books as well as sources for those interested in learning about the history and facts of the Cheapside Hoard. Also, there is a list of links where you can see information about the real jewels. Please don't ask to see the jewels in a secure basement should you happen to visit the Museum of London. According to their website, the Cheapside Hoard is not currently on display.

You may be able to see a handful of items allegedly from the Cheapside Hoard at the British Museum and at the Victoria & Albert Museum as part of their breathtaking permanent jewelry collections. ▶

Author's Note *(continued)*

My eldest son, Henry, accompanied me to London to research *The Lost Jewels*. He proved to be a thoughtful, wise, and funny traveling companion who soaked up the history. There wasn't a historical walking tour, museum, or gallery he wasn't up for—as long as the food kept coming! I look forward to many more adventures together.

Jane and Maurice Cronly kindly gave us an entire floor in their magnificent London home, directed us to significant places, explained the bus network, recommended restaurants and history contacts. It was lovely to sit in your sunny conservatory overlooking the garden with a glass of wine at the end of each day, and mull over where this story might lead. I hope you enjoy *The Lost Jewels*.

Thanks to the team at the British Museum who opened up a special room just for me (and Henry!) to spend time with some of the pieces allegedly from the Cheapside Hoard. To sit quietly and imagine where those gems started their life, to wonder whose hands have passed over the roughs across trade routes and oceans before they were fashioned into necklaces and buttons, blew my mind.

Thanks to my Bellota ladies—a group of talented Melbourne writers who fill my soul. Special mention to Sally Hepworth, Lisa Ireland, and Jane Cockram for making this writing gig a whole lot funnier than it has any right to be.

Hurrah to my intrepid team of early readers: Sara James Butcher, Kate Daniel, Kate O'Donnell, and Sue Peacock. Seriously, you guys have the knack of filling me with hope while dishing out some hard truths! To my team of editors and publishers: Christa Munns and Annette Barlow at Allen & Unwin, Australia, and Tessa Woodward at William Morrow in the US—what would I do without your considered feedback and kind words? You are the real diamonds.

I'll be forever indebted to my agent Clare Forster of Curtis Brown, along with the UK Curtis Brown crew and Stacy Testa at Writers House New York for giving my writing wings.

Finally, love and gratitude to my family: Alex, Henry, Jemima, and Charlie—I'd cross every ocean for you.

This is a work of fiction, and I am very respectful of all those people whose lives have been touched by the periods, politics, loss, and circumstances I write about. My thoughts are always with those people and their families.

If you need to reach out and talk to someone after reading this novel, please call the National Suicide Prevention Lifeline at 1-800-273-8255.

Reading Group Guide

1. Before reading *The Lost Jewels*, were you aware of the real Cheapside Hoard? What intrigued you most about this story?

2. The story of a jewel tells a bigger tale of trade and globalization, design trends, economics, and politics. It is also a story about care and craftsmanship. And lastly, it is a story about power, love, and loyalty. Do you have a special piece of jewelry? Was it a gift from a loved one, or was it an inherited piece? What does it mean to you?

3. In chapter 10, Kate observes, "Sometimes tracing the line of a jewel, the light bouncing off a diamond, [shows you] that, just like jewels, people can be reset and have a different kind of life." Do you believe people can reset and change their future?

4. There is much written about the leaders of the suffragette movement and the fancy times in Edwardian London, but very little written about the poorer classes. One of the joys of being a novelist is bringing those overlooked female voices to the page. Do you enjoy reading fiction with strong female characters and voices? Does it make you rethink history, or give you a different perspective?

5. The mystery of Kate's great-grandmother Essie provides the story's driving search. Did the answer surprise you? How did Kate learn and change during this search?

6. Woven in between the dual timelines of Essie's and Kate's vivid lives is another story: the four-hundred-year narrative journey of a champlevé ring with diamonds from a mysterious Indian mine to the Museum of London. Did you enjoy tracing the journey of the imagined origin story of this champlevé ring?

7. Themes of loyalty and devotion to family run deep in *The Lost Jewels*. Is the bond between sisters (and cousins) as important as that between lovers?

8. Essie is forced to leave London quickly, with very little money. What would you take with you if you had to move to a new country quickly?

9. Essie left London to save her sister Gertrude and guarantee a strong future for her sister by allowing her to get an education. But leaving London came with considerable sacrifice. Would you make the same decision?

10. In chapter 3 we get a hint of Essie's story: "The jewels were discovered the same day Essie Murphy fell in love. She had her brother to thank for both, of course—though in the years to come she'd often wonder which one came first. A buried bucket of jewels. A man with emerald eyes. The tale would become as much a part of her Irish folklore as Midir and Étaín. Cut and polished over the years with the roughs tossed out with the sorrow, betrayal, and loss. No one would know it was equal parts tragedy and romance." It's common to cut and polish parts of our own stories when we retell our past to family and friends. Is there a story you've embellished—or diminished—as you've retold it to cast your past in a different light? Or has someone close to you done this? ∾

Further Reading

The complete list of sources consulted in the writing of *The Lost Jewels* is too long to detail here. Below is a list of essential resources.

WALKING TOURS

Westminster
Great Fire of London and Plague Tour
Dickensian London
Southwark
Edwardian London
Borough Markets
Suffragettes Tour with historian and
    author Ian Porter

MUSEUMS

The Museum of London (*Suffragette: Votes For Women* exhibition, 2018)
The British Museum, London
The Victoria & Albert Museum, London
The Natural History Museum, London
The Goldsmiths' Company (Library), London
Royal Observatory, Greenwich
National Gallery of Australia, Canberra (*Cartier* exhibition, 2018)

BOOKS

JEWELS

The Cheapside Hoard: London's Lost Jewels, Hazel Forsyth (London, Philip Wilson Publishers, 2013); *Silversmiths in Elizabethan and Stuart London: Their Lives and Their Marks*, David M. Mitchell (Woodbridge, The Boydell Press, 2017); *Jewels and Jewelry*, Clare Phillips (London, V&A Publishing, 2008); *Treasures and Trinkets: Jewelry in London from Pre-Roman Times to the 1930s*, Tessa Murdoch (London, The Museum of London, 1991); *Rings: Jewelry of Power, Love and Loyalty*, Diana Scarisbrick (London, Thames and Hudson, 2017); *The Crown Jewels: The Official Illustrated History*, Anna Keay (London, Thames and Hudson, 2017); *The Color of Paradise: The Emerald in the Age of Gunpowder Empires*, Kris Lane (London, Yale University Press, 2010); *Diamonds and Precious Stones*, Partick Voillot (London, Thames and Hudson, 2010); *Cartier: The Exhibition*, Margaret Young-Sánchez (Canberra, National Gallery of Australia, 2018); *Jewel: A Celebration of Earth's Treasures*, Judith Miller (London, Dorling Kindersley, 2016).

LIFE IN LONDON

Lost Voices of the Edwardians, Max Arthur (London, HarperCollins Publishers, 2006); *The Edwardian Guide to Life*, Cornelia Dobbs (West Sussex, Summersdale Publishers, 2011); *Butcher, Baker, Candlestick Maker: Surviving the Great Fire of London*, Hazel Forsyth (London, I.B. Tauris & Co Ltd, 2016); *1666: Plague, War and Hellfire*, Rebecca Rideal (London, John Murray, 2016); *Victorian and Edwardian London from Old Photographs*, John Betjeman (London, B.T. Batsford Ltd, 1969); *Dynamite, Treason and Plot: Terrorism in Victorian and Edwardian London*, Simon Webb (Gloustershire, The History Press, 2012); *Pepys London: Everyday Life in London 1650–1703*, ▶

Further Reading *(continued)*

Stephen Porter (Gloustershire, Amberley Publishing, 2012); *Diamond Street: The Hidden World of Hatton Garden*, Rachel Lichtenstein (London, Penguin Books, 2012); *Samuel Pepys: Fire, Plague and Revolution*, Margarette Lincoln (ed.) (London, Thames and Hudson, 2015); *The A–Z of Edwardian London*, Anne Saunders (ed.) (London, London Topographical Society, 2007); *Women in England 1500–1760: A Social History*, Anne Laurence (London, Phoenix Press, 2002); *Suffragette: Autumn Women's Spring*, Ian Porter (Leicestershire, Matador, 2014); *In Search of London*, H. V. Morton (London, Methuen, 1951); *London's Triumph: Merchant Adventurers and the Tudor City*, Stephen Alford (London, Penguin Books, 2017); *Edwardians: London Life and Letters 1901–1914*, John Patterson (Chicago, Ivan R. Dee, 1996); *Booth's Maps of London Poverty: East and West 1889*, Charles Booth (London, Oldhouse Books, 2013); *Edwardian England: A Guide to Everyday Life, 1900–1914*, Evangeline Holland (London, Plum Bun Publishing, 2014).

For video footage and documentaries featuring the Cheapside Hoard, see:

www.gia.edu/gems-gemology/fa13-cheapside-hoard-weldon
www.thejewelleryeditor.com/jewellery/article/discover-more
-about-the-cheapside-hoard-in-our-exclusive-video/
www.bbc.co.uk/programmes/b03d6b1j

FOOD

The Land That Thyme Forgot, William Black (London, Bantam Press, 2005); *The Modern Herbal Dispensary: A Medicine Making Guide*, Thomas Easley and Steven Horne (Berkeley CA, North Atlantic Books, 2016); *Culpeper's Complete Herbal: Over 400 Herbs and Their Uses*, Nicholas Culpeper (London, Arcturus Publishing Limited, 2018); *A Modern Herbal: The Medicinal, Culinary, Cosmetic and Economic Properties, Cultivation and Folk-Lore of Herbs, Grasses, Fungi, Shrubs & Trees with Their*

Modern Scientific Uses, Mrs. M. Grieve (USA, Stone Basin Books, 1931); *The National Trust Farmhouse Cookbook*, Laura Mason (London, National Trust Books, 2009); *London Eats Out: 500 Years of Capital Dining*, Grossman, Ehrman et al. (London, Philip Wilson Publishers, 1999). ᶜᵚ